Rachel's Song

Lois Jean Thomas

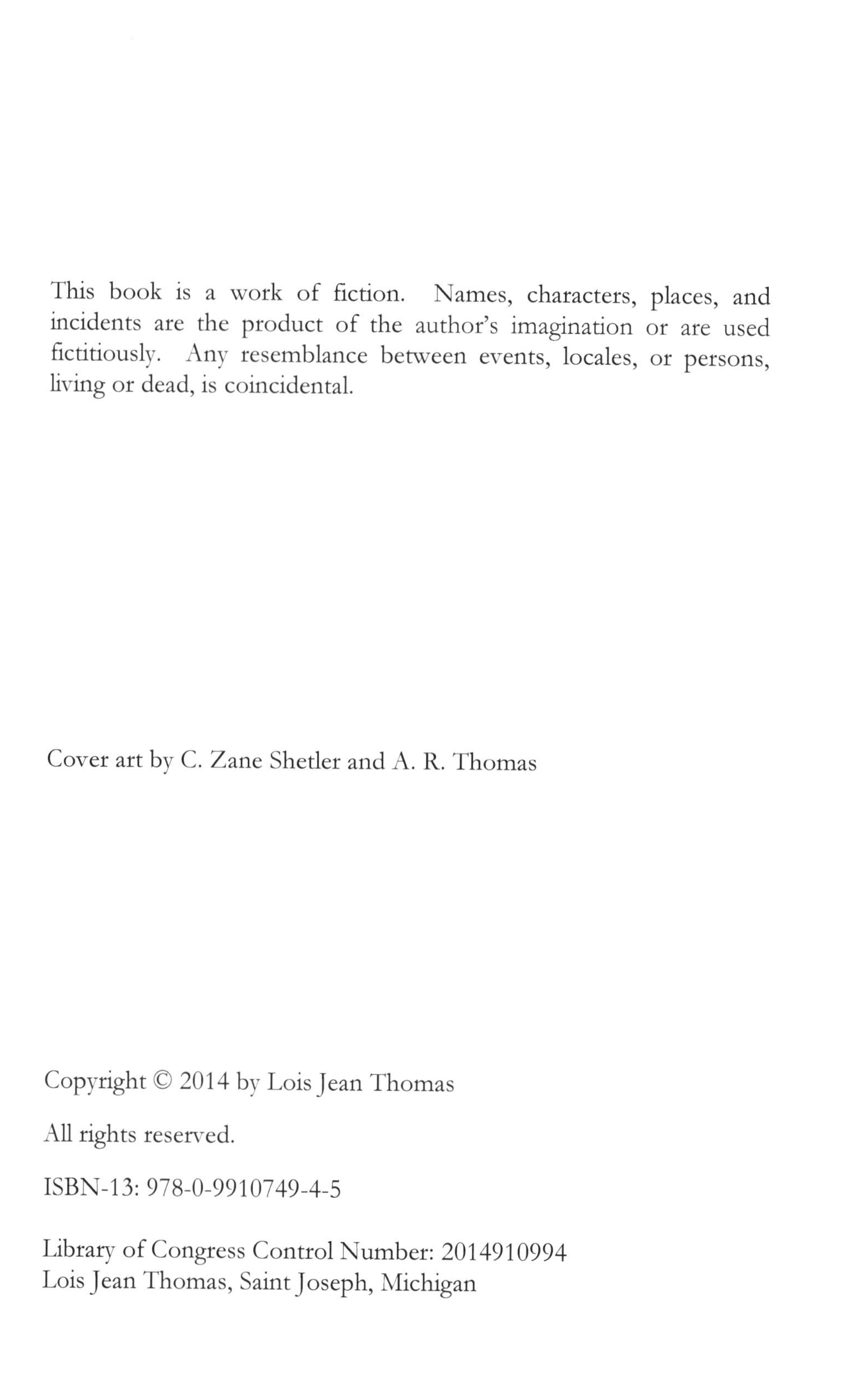

This book is a work of fiction. Names, characters, places, and incidents are the product of the author's imagination or are used fictitiously. Any resemblance between events, locales, or persons, living or dead, is coincidental.

Cover art by C. Zane Shetler and A. R. Thomas

ISBN-13: 978-0-9910749-4-5

Library of Congress Control Number: 2014910994
Lois Jean Thomas, Saint Joseph, Michigan

For Judy, Earth Mother
Thanks for all you've shared with me.

CONTENTS

ACKNOWLEDGMENTS

I can't begin to express how much I appreciate my husband Allen's help in formatting this manuscript. I couldn't have done it without you, Allen. You've been steadfastly supportive and infinitely patient.

Thank you to my son C. Zane Shetler for creating the cover art. I'm so grateful I can count on you, Zane.

The members of my writers group, Marnie, Sue, Judy, Richard, Ann, Isabel, Elaine, and Ron, deserve credit for their help in making this a better story.

Most of all, thank you to the muse who inhabits my dream life. May you continue to offer inspiration.

Rachel's Song

Chapter 1

We were sitting on the deck overlooking the river when Jake first told me about Rachel.

It was a warm Sunday evening in early May, and Jake had just come home from an art show, one of the early ones of the season. I stepped out the patio door and stood on the deck, watching him unload supplies and inventory from his van.

"Sell anything?" I called.

He slammed the van door shut. "I did alright."

Then he ambled toward the deck, eyes on the ground, hands shoved into the pockets of his faded jeans. "Lee, I need to talk to you," he said.

"Okay, Jake." I stretched out on one of the cedar deck chairs he'd built, sipping my glass of sun tea, staring at my dusty bare feet, wiggling my toes. Looking dead tired, Jake climbed the steps and lowered his muscular body into the chair next to mine.

I sensed what was coming. At that point, I was strangely calm, although I didn't relish the thought of what Jake was about to tell me. I listened obligingly to his awkward, guilty buildup, to the moment when he revealed his budding relationship with another woman.

Suddenly, his sheepish voice took on a tone of authority. "You don't have any reason to be upset," he said. "You know you and I haven't been . . ."

I interrupted him. "Jake, I know we're through as lovers."

"Lee, I've been faithful to you for seven years."

"I know." I'd never doubted that fact. "To be honest with you, Jake, I was gearing up to tell you something. I'm planning on leaving. I'll be out of your way in a couple of months."

"I'm not saying you need to go, Lee. I'm not trying to boot you out of your home."

"What?" I laughed bitterly. "Are you crazy, Jake? You really think I want to stick around for this?"

Jake leaned forward with his arms resting on his knees, looking down at his clasped hands. I waited for a response.

When none was forthcoming, I said, "Just give me a little time to make other arrangements. Give Thor and me until the end of the school year, and then we'll move on."

Jake's face looked pained. He opened his mouth to say something, but closed it when our red-haired six-year-old son bounded around the corner of the house and scampered up the steps to the deck.

"Look what I found!" he exclaimed. He extended his arm to show us the caterpillar creeping on his open palm.

"Isn't that pretty, Thor!" I said. "Now you need to put it back where you found it. Be careful, now. Don't squish it."

Thor shot me an indignant look. "Mom, I know better than to hurt it." He held his hand up close to his face and addressed the caterpillar in a silly voice. "Don't worry, Mr. Fuzzy Wuzzy, I won't hurt you." With that, he scampered down the steps and disappeared around the corner of the house.

"Are you sure you want to uproot Thor?" Jake asked. "He's happy here."

"Well, Jake," I huffed, "why didn't you think of that before bringing this woman into our lives?"

"I couldn't help it," he responded. "Rachel was just there. I wasn't looking for anyone. She just showed up, right there in front of me."

I found myself sympathizing a little bit with Jake's sense of destiny. "You're bringing her here, then?"

Jake nodded, looking nervous.

"Wait at least a month, until the school year is over. Then Thor and I will go to my mom's for the summer."

"I can't do that. Rachel's coming next weekend."

I jumped out of my chair. "What the hell, Jake?"

"She's got to leave where she's staying. She doesn't have anywhere else to go."

I glared down at him, shaking my head in disbelief. He dropped his head, absent-mindedly running his calloused fingers along the boards of the deck he'd so expertly crafted.

"Well, this is a fine mess!" I hissed. Then I sat down again, burying my face in my hands, trying to think.

We sat in silence, neither of us wanting to look at the other. Finally I said, "Just be discrete, then. For Thor's sake, be discrete."

Suddenly, Jake laughed, dispelling the tension hanging in the air between us. "River Leah Jorgensen, my bohemian friend! Since when have you become the champion of mainstream values?"

"You know what I mean," I snapped, trying not to laugh myself. "Thor doesn't need to be confused."

"Don't worry, I'll be careful. Thor's a kid. He's not going to pick up on anything."

It seemed to me Jake was far too comfortable with his proposed arrangement, and it made me uneasy. "You think you'd be okay with two women in your house, Jake? Your new girlfriend and your ex?" I shuddered. "That sounds terrible."

"Sounds okay to me." Jake grinned, and I knew he was joking.

Then his face took on an earnest expression. "I feel kind of bad about this, Lee. Even though we're not together anymore, I still care about you. You'll always be the love of my life."

I knew his last statement was a lie. "That's a pretty lame thing to say when you're bringing another woman on the scene," I said. "Jake, in seven years, you've never told me you loved me. If you really loved me, you wouldn't feel the need for Rachel."

He shrugged. "Well, I guess you fill one spot in my life, and Rachel fills another. She does something to me. I can't explain it. But I know I need to be with her."

"Do what you need to do, then," I said. "But let me make this crystal clear, Jacob Potter. A month from now, I'm gone. Thor and I will be gone."

I stood up and walked through the patio door into the kitchen, trying to feign an anger I didn't quite feel. I wasn't in love with Jake, and I had no claim on his heart.

Several weeks earlier, I'd told my mother I thought I was ready for a new chapter in my life. She'd nodded wisely and said, "I had a feeling this was coming, River. Just trust your path. Let the stream of life carry you where you need to go."

I didn't begrudge Jake his new lover. I was just irritated that he'd beaten me to the punch. I wanted to start my new chapter on my terms, not his.

Chapter 2

I suppose I'm a member of rare breed in this country, a person who's never rebelled against her parents. But you can't push the limits if no one establishes a boundary for you to kick against.

My parents, Melody James and Larry Jorgensen, gave me the best of each of their worlds. A flower-child of the sixties, my mother taught me to follow my heart and to honor the world of the Spirit. My father, a physics professor, made sure I had access to a good mainstream education.

My mother and father never married, and they lived together for only the first year of my life. But their separation never diminished their affection or respect for each other. My mother refused to apply the term "broken up" to their relationship. She's always said their parting of ways was not because of conflict; it was just a matter of needing to pursue individual interests. Of course, my mother has never seen herself in conflict with any aspect of life.

Both of my parents were followers of Ram Das in their youth. They met at one of his events in Chicago, connecting with each other while chanting, "Hare Krishna, Hare Rama." The Spirit was moving, my mother said, and evidently it moved my parents into a rapturous embrace, because I was conceived later that night. My mother was convinced that a conception after such a sacred occasion was auspicious, that I was a special child. She's never worried about me, as she's confident that all the forces in the universe are aligned to ensure my protection.

When my parents met, my father had dropped out of college and was living in an ashram. He was twenty-five then, a tall, thin man with a bushy beard and a long blonde braid hanging down his back. After he and my mother parted ways, he returned to a more conservative lifestyle. He cut his hair, trimmed his beard, and went back to school, eventually earning a Ph.D. in physics and a teaching position at the University of Chicago.

During my childhood, I'd happily spend a week with my father in his suburban Chicago home, but I could never tolerate long stretches of time with him. We'd go to the museums, the zoo, or a Cubs game. I loved my father, and he was kind and generous, but he was introverted and not very engaging. After the entertainment was over, I'd mope around his rather colorless home, missing my mother.

A creature of habit, my father lived a quiet, orderly lifestyle. His typical attire was a white cotton shirt tucked into khaki trousers. He moved around his house so silently, I'd often be surprised to discover he was in the same room with me. I'd have no idea where he'd come from or how he'd gotten there, and I'd amuse myself by pretending that this pale, gaunt man in his light-colored clothing was actually a phantom who could pass through walls.

As I've grown older, I've sensed my father is deeply spiritual, a quiet mystic, but he rarely reveals his inner world to anyone. He's not demonstrative, and the only times I've see his eyes light up with passion are when he's gazing at my mother, his beloved Melody.

I'm almost certain my father never had another lover after he and my mother parted ways. I'd like to think he was content to be single all the years they were apart, just biding his time until the day when he could be with her again.

My father developed Parkinson's disease when he was in his early fifties, which brought a premature halt to his teaching career. Without thinking twice, my mother decided it was time for them to resume their relationship. She convinced him to sell his Chicago home and move in with her, and now she happily devotes her life to tending to his health.

"Larry and I are soul mates," she often says, "even though we weren't meant to be together all of our lives. We each had our own paths to explore."

But she considers it to be her destiny to care for my father in his later years. She pours out love for him on a daily basis, and his limited reciprocation doesn't dampen her spirits. He spends his days reading in his chair by the window, and when the weather is nice, he sits in the back yard. My father asks for little, but my mother offers him abundance. No doubt, the daily energy treatments she gives him, balancing his chakras and cleansing his aura, have kept him alive and stable long past a Parkinson's patient's life expectancy.

My mother was twenty-one when I was conceived, a young beauty with a voluptuous figure, curly auburn hair, and sparkling brown eyes. Although she never attended college, she began studying energy healing in her teen years. Her interest in healing was sparked by her close relationship with her Native American grandmother, who'd possessed a boundless reservoir of spiritual wisdom. My mother felt a deep affinity for her grandmother's tradition, and when she entered her thirties, she began training to become a shaman, a role she embraced as her soul's highest purpose in this lifetime.

In contrast to my time with my reticent father, every minute spent with my mother was filled with warmth, color, and affection. Nurturing me was never an effort for her, as she simply exuded love. Caring for me required no sacrifice of time or activities, as she included me in almost everything she did.

My mother didn't hide things from me, and I faced some interesting facts of life at a young age. Others criticized her for not protecting my childish innocence. But she'd say I had a gift for understanding things beyond my age level. She believed that to treat me as less than that would be condescending.

We lived in a modest ranch house on the outskirts of Mishawka, Indiana, but the traditional structure of our home belied the magic my mother created within. She was an artist, and our home was graced with her creativity: sculptures, oil paintings, and fabric art in warm, sensuous colors.

My mother was a work of art herself, arrayed in her colorful skirts, caftans and shawls, handmade or imported from other countries. Her long, curling locks framed her lovely face and cascaded down her back. Strings of colorful wooden and crystal beads surrounded her neck and wrists, and tinkling ankle bracelets adorned her pretty feet. Eight months of the year found her barefooted, as she insisted she could feel the vibration of Mother Earth better without shoes.

We had a bit of wooded acreage surrounding our home, and my mother created a retreat setting with flower gardens, a water fountain in a small pond, and benches for contemplation. She enjoyed arranging little shrines with statues and other spiritual artifacts.

I can't say my mother ever disciplined me. I felt so close to her, I had no desire to displease her, and she allowed me a great deal of freedom to learn my own lessons from life. When I showed an aptitude for art, she was enormously pleased, and provided what I needed to pursue my passion.

In contrast to my father, my mother had lovers, as she was far too sensual a woman to remain celibate. None of her lovers ever lived with us, and I never expected any of them to be a permanent fixture in my life. She instilled in me the belief that relationships come and go. "Most people are in our lives for only a season," she told me. "Just long enough to teach us what we need to learn from them."

When she'd part ways with yet another lover, any sadness was short-lived. "I enjoyed my time with him," she'd say. "I'm just grateful for what he offered me."

My mother converted one of our three bedrooms into a treatment room. Her income from her energy healing was rather sporadic, but she never doubted that the universe would provide everything we needed. And indeed it did, primarily in the form of generous child support checks from my father. My mother never considered this to be his legal obligation. Rather, she viewed each check as a bit of grace, a gift from the divine.

Traveling was part of my mother's work, as she frequently attended healing seminars, and unless I was staying with my father, I'd go with her. I'd listen quietly, soaking up the knowledge that over time would form an integral part of my consciousness. I'd be treated graciously by the other participants, who never objected to the presence of a child at these events.

My mother's traveling schedule, coupled with her propensity to include me in her spontaneous adventures, pushed the bounds of the public school attendance requirements. After an incident when my school principal chastised her for keeping me home to watch the birth of a litter of kittens, my mother decided it was time to home-school me. That way, she could whisk me off to a Native American powwow any day of the week, or take me out star gazing in the middle of the night. I was a good student and never fell behind, and I was more than prepared when I returned to public schooling my freshman year of high school.

My full name, River Leah Jorgensen, is the result of my mother's desire to give me options. River, of course, is symbolic of her devotion to nature, which she instilled in me. Leah was the name of her grandmother. My mother always taught me to be true to myself, but she never dictated what that self should be. I could go by River Jorgensen or Leah Jorgensen, two very different personas. I could have made up a completely different name, and she wouldn't have objected.

I never met my Native American great-grandmother, but my mother said she and I both inherited her spirit. The thought pleased me, although I wished I'd also inherited her jet-black hair and angular features. But several generations had watered down the gene pool, and I ended up bearing a strong resemblance to my father's Scandinavian lineage.

Once while in high school, I attempted to demonstrate my loyalty to my Native American heritage by dying my hair black, but the color looked ghastly with my pale skin and made me appear unwell. I decided the look didn't suit me, and my mother agreed. So I accepted the life of a blue-eyed blonde with soft features and a buxom body.

I've discovered that, in some circles, the name River generates more odd looks and questions than I care to deal with. In those situations, I present myself as Lee Jorgensen. My mother calls me River, but Jake always called me Lee. Rachel was one of the few people who ever called me Leah.

Like my mother, I've always been a peace-keeper, a seeker of harmony. No doubt, this trait is in my DNA, and it was certainly in my childhood environment. But looking back, I can see that my mother's beautiful example became a big part of my undoing.

Chapter 3

During my last two years of high school, my father came out of the shadows of my life and took on a more directive role. As my free-spirited mother had no inclination to discuss higher education with me, he shouldered that responsibility, pointing me in the direction of college and graduate school.

Thus, my mid-twenties found me straddling the worlds of both my parents. I had earned a master's degree in fine arts, and was conforming to the confines of lesson plans in my career as an elementary school art teacher. But on my own time, I indulged in the art I really loved, the type of expression I'd begun in childhood: painting fantasy scenes in acrylics and water colors. On my canvasses, wild animals roamed through exotic jungles; tiny fairies and gnomes perched on magnificent flowers or peered out from under tree roots; mermaids and brilliantly colored sea-creatures frolicked in frothy waves; celestial beings danced among the stars and planets.

I'd moved out of my mother's home by then, and was renting an apartment in Mishawaka. I'd accumulated quite an inventory of paintings, and during the summer of my twenty-sixth year, I decided to begin entering art shows.

I first met Jake in June of that year, at a festival in Elkhart, Indiana. It was early on a Sunday morning before the crowds arrived, and I was busy arranging my merchandize. Suddenly, I sensed someone was watching me, and I turned around to see a man standing in the entry to my booth. He looked to be in his mid-thirties, tall and broad shouldered, sturdily built but lean. His hair, an unusual shade of dark red with streaks of white at the temples, flowed down his back in a long tail. His broad, rugged face was deeply etched and sunburned. He wore jeans and a light blue cotton shirt with the sleeves rolled up, and I noticed the freckles and pale blonde hairs on his muscular forearms. His hands looked thick, strong, and work-worn.

He stepped into my booth and rifled through a rack of my prints, then looked at me with penetrating dark brown eyes. "I like your work," he said. "How were your sales yesterday?"

"Thanks," I replied. "I sold a few things, enough to make it worthwhile being here."

He studied the paintings displayed on the walls of my booth. "Your work is heavenly . . . and it's earthly . . . and something else. I don't know what it is, but I like it."

"Thank you," I said. "That's a nice compliment."

He turned away from my paintings and directed his gaze at my face. "And you look like Mother Earth."

I glanced down at my leather sandals, my colorful cotton skirt, and the beaded bracelet on my wrist, then shrugged and smiled at him.

"No, maybe more like an angel, with that gorgeous blonde hair."

I felt myself blushing. "Thanks."

"I've got a booth two rows over, toward the other end." He nodded in that direction. "Come check it out when you get a chance."

"Okay," I said. "What do you do?"

"I've got woodworking with me this time," he said. "But I also do ceramics, in keeping with my name."

"And your name is . . . ?"

"Potter. Jacob Potter."

I laughed. "Oh, I get it. Potter. Someone who does pottery."

"And you are . . ." He squinted to look at the signature on one of my paintings. "Lee Jorgensen."

I found myself offering this stranger more information than I intended to give. "Actually, my full name is River Leah Jorgensen. I use Lee Jorgensen as my artistic name. It's easier."

Jacob grinned. "River. You must've had hippie parents to give you a name like that."

I chuckled. "I guess so."

"I go by Jake. Well, I've gotta get going. Come see my booth when you feel like taking a break."

A friend of mine arrived later that morning to help me tend my booth, freeing me to take a stroll along the rows of displays. I spotted Jake's booth, and saw that he had wooden deck chairs and tables for sale, along with decorative shelving and beautifully crafted wooden boxes. He was busy with customers, but gave me a nod and a slight smile.

Three weeks later, at an art fair in Saint Joseph, Michigan, I looked up to see Jacob Potter standing in the entry to my booth again.

"So we meet again," he said. "I was hoping I'd see you here. How many shows are you doing this summer?"

"Half a dozen," I replied. "How about you?"

"Almost every weekend."

He stepped closer to me and picked up a lock of my curly hair. I felt a shiver of electricity as his hand brushed my shoulder.

"I can't get over this hair," he said. "It's gorgeous." Then, with a "see you later," he turned and walked away.

Early the next day, he stopped by my booth again. "What are you doing after five this evening?" he asked.

"Packing up to go home, I guess."

"Wanna have dinner with me?" The man who'd seemed so at ease with himself suddenly looked shy and uncomfortable.

"That sounds like a nice idea," I said.

At some point in the day, Jacob Potter must have made dinner reservations at a downtown restaurant, because at 6:00 PM, we were ushered to a prime table overlooking Lake Michigan. I gasped when I saw the view.

"Oh my God, Jake, this is gorgeous."

"Yes, isn't it? I thought you'd like it."

We gazed silently out the window, watching the boats drifting across the vast expanse of water. Then Jake said, "Did you know that if you sailed straight across the lake from here, you'd end up in Wisconsin?"

"Interesting," I murmured.

But then the silence between us grew too long, making me uneasy. My efforts at small talk fell flat, and I regretted having accepted this date. I was exhausted and sticky from the heat of the day, and I told myself I'd rather be at home taking a cool shower than staring across the table at this taciturn man.

But by the time our food arrived, our conversation began to flow, albeit slowly. Jake informed me he lived in the country near Niles, Michigan, on the banks of the Saint Joseph River.

"The house wasn't much of anything when I bought it," he said. "So I got it pretty cheap. But I've done a lot of work on it since then." He told me that, five years earlier, he'd been in a relationship with a woman who had three children. At that point, he'd built on several bedrooms and an extra bathroom.

"So they're gone now?" I asked. "Your girlfriend and her children?"

"Yup, they are."

"Do you have any children of your own?"

"Nope. None."

"Me either. Ever been married?"

"Nope. How about you?"

"No."

Jake looked at me intently. "Are you seeing anyone right now?"

"Not at the moment."

"I'm not either." He stared out the window for a few minutes. When he turned his attention back to me, he changed the subject and began talking about his art. He told me he used one of his empty bedrooms for his ceramics studio, but that he did his woodworking projects in an outbuilding on his property.

The conversation rolled around to our families, and Jake gently poked fun at my unorthodox upbringing. He informed me he was raised in a Mennonite family, on a dairy farm near Goshen, Indiana. He had four older brothers who'd followed their father's footsteps into farming.

"I'm the odd duck of the family, getting into the arts," he said. "Nothing like the rest of them. Although you could say I take after my old man with the woodworking. He's pretty handy at carpentry."

He talked about his church-going brothers who'd married old-fashioned wives and raised large broods of children. "Again, I'm nothing like them." He chuckled, and then added, "I tend to go after the off-beat, artsy women."

I felt my face getting hot. "Like the ones you find at art fairs?"

"Yup, that's where I find them."

Jake's revelation triggered an inexplicably dark feeling in me, which I didn't understand until much later. But I shrugged it off and commented on the serenity of the scene outside our window, the brilliant sunset over the lake.

"Saint Joseph," Jake said. "Supposedly the most romantic city in Michigan."

I wondered if he was trying to lead into something, but when I looked into his dark brown eyes, they held no seduction, no hint of any self-serving intention. They just seemed to be asking, "Are you interested in pursuing anything with me?" I hoped my own eyes were saying, "Yes."

The evening ended on a low-key note. Jake handed me his business card, and I saw that he called his business *Potter's Woods*. He told me to give him a call sometime if I wanted to get together. I gave him my card in return, and let him know I'd welcome a call from him as well.

I didn't know at the time whether anything would come of this new acquaintance I'd made. I had no idea whether I'd see Jacob Potter again, or whether I'd tuck his memory into my voluminous file of one-time dates.

Chapter 4

A month passed, and I didn't hear from Jake, nor did I see him at the next art show I attended. I finally decided to take his invitation seriously, and I gave him a call.

He seemed genuinely glad to hear from me. "Lee Jorgensen. I was hoping you'd call." After a brief chat, he invited me to his home.

So on a late July evening, I drove from Mishawaka across the north border of Indiana into Niles, Michigan. With Jake's directions in hand, I ventured down country roads, until a sign bearing Jake's business logo and the words *Potter's Woods* alerted me to the long dirt lane leading to his home.

I chuckled at his cleverness in using the term *woods* to describe both his handiwork and the setting in which he lived. The lane wound a quarter of a mile through trees and brush, until it opened into a small clearing where his odd-looking residence stood.

The original part of the house, a small bungalow, was sided with old clapboards covered with peeling mint-green paint. The newer section consisted of rooms added on like train cars, giving the residence an elongated look. That part of the house was actually quite attractive, as it was sided with cedar shingles weathered to a silvery gray. I imagined Jake had planned on re-siding the older section of the house as well, but hadn't gotten around to it yet.

He must have heard me drive up, because he came around from behind the house. "Good to see you, Lee," he said, lifting a hand in greeting.

"It looks like you have a comfortable place here, Jake," I observed. "It reminds me of where I grew up, surrounded by woods."

He smiled. "Should I give you a tour, then? We'll start out back."

He led me around the house, and I gasped with delight at the sight of the river running at the edge of his property. It was wide at that point, flowing in a mighty rush, with lush green trees overhanging the banks.

"My God, Jake!" I exclaimed. "You're so lucky to be here!"

"I suppose I am." He gazed at the river, a faraway look in his eyes. "This is my own little corner of the planet. I'd never want to be anywhere else. The view is always changing. In the spring, the redbuds and dogwood are in full bloom. In the fall, the color is spectacular, with the red and gold of the oaks and maples. The landscape is even magnificent in the winter, when the heavy snow covers the branches." He turned to look at me. "I can't imagine ever leaving here."

As I stood there beside him, it struck me that this solitary man was as much a part of the indigenous landscape as the river and the trees. I couldn't imagine him anywhere else, either.

Then Jake led me to a large outbuilding sided with the same graying cedar shingles as on the house. "This is my woodworking shop," he announced as he ushered me through the door. "I built it myself."

I glanced around the large room as Jake proudly pointed out his workbench, his table-saw, his band-saw, his sanders, and a lathe. Hammers and chisels lay in trays on a shelf, and several tools lay on his workbench, as if he'd just put them down when he heard me drive up. Large projects in various stages of construction sat on the concrete floor.

I ran my hand over the smooth maple of a finely crafted Shaker-style kitchen cabinet. "Beautiful," I murmured.

"I build custom cabinets," Jake explained. "That's actually the bulk of my business. The art shows, they're more for fun."

A wood-burning stove stood at the far end of the room to my right, with scraps of wood piled up to one side. "The stove keeps this place pretty cozy when I work out here in the winter," he said. "I burn my scrap wood."

He placed his hand on the small of my back and guided me to the left, where we entered a second room. "My finishing room," he announced. Buckets of paint, varnish, shellac, and stain lined several shelves, and beautifully stained and varnished cabinets stood drying on a large table.

"Wow!" I said as I inspected his work. "I'm impressed. You're quite the craftsman."

Jake looked at me for a long moment, his dark eyes smiling, his hands clasped behind his back. Then he said, "Ready to see the house?"

We left the workshop, and he led me to the side door at the end of the new section of the house. It opened into a long hallway that gave access to the rooms.

Gesturing for me to pass through the first door off the hallway, he said, "This is the biggest room. I use it as my ceramics studio."

I glanced around, taking in the potter's wheel, the kiln, the utility sink, and the shelving loaded with ceramic pieces. The room was slightly messy, but reasonably organized. It seemed as if Jake was on top of what he was doing, but didn't waste time keeping his surroundings spotless. I felt at home in his workspace.

My curiosity was aroused by the narrow bed pushed up against the wall in one corner of the room, with an old patchwork quilt thrown haphazardly across it. Jake must have noticed me staring at it.

"I end up sleeping in here some of the time," he said. "Actually, most of the time. I don't share a room with anybody. I have a thing about my personal space." I wondered if he was laying the groundwork for any future developments between us.

We left the studio and proceeded down the hallway, and Jake invited me to poke my head into each room we passed. The second room was Jake's actual bedroom, containing a full-sized bed and an old dresser. It appeared the bed hadn't been slept in for some time, as it was laden with large ceramic pieces. Boxes of inventory were stacked against one wall.

The third room was a combination bathroom and laundry room, with stark white walls, a simple shower stall, and plain white fixtures. The washer and dryer looked fairly new.

"I figured we needed the second bath when Lisa and her kids were here," Jake said. "I don't suppose I need it now, but who knows."

The fourth room was unfurnished, and appeared to be used for general storage.

The hallway then opened into the kitchen in the original part of the house. A large oak table stood in the center of the room, and Jake informed me he'd built it. In contrast to the beauty of the table, the stove and refrigerator looked ancient. A few dishes were stacked in the chipped porcelain sink. The battered cupboards, painted an ugly shade of dark green, appeared to be original to the house. One of the doors on the lower cabinets was missing, revealing shelves lined with old, garishly patterned contact paper.

I couldn't help but compare the sorry state of Jake's kitchen with the top-of-the-line furnishings he produced in his workshop. It was as though he heard my thought, as he said, "This kitchen's in pretty sad shape, isn't it? Someday, I'll get it fixed up with new cupboards and everything. Seems like there's never an end to things that need to be done around here."

He pointed out the newly installed patio door on the back kitchen wall, leading to the deck outside. "I built this deck just a couple of years ago. I use it all the time. I'll be an old geezer some day, still sitting out there staring at the river."

He then led me through the original kitchen doorway into a sparsely furnished living room, which looked dusty and unused. A small pile of logs was stacked next to a wood-burning stove, apparently left from the previous winter.

The two original bedrooms at the far end of the house, with a small bathroom between them, were devoid of furniture or any other signs of previous occupancy. Dust bunnies scurried around the hardwood floors as we stepped in. All the unused space made the house seem forlorn.

"Do you get lonely in this house?" I asked as we stood in one of the empty bedrooms.

"Not really," he said. "I'm not the kind of person to get lonely. Not that I don't like being around people, but I'm okay by myself."

He gestured toward the bare walls. "As you can see, I don't use this part of the house much anymore, except for the kitchen."

Now that our tour was finished, I suddenly felt ill at ease. I wondered whether Jake had anything else planned for the evening, or whether he was expecting me to leave.

"Do you . . . uh . . . do you know how to work with a potter's wheel?" he stammered, sounding as nervous as I felt.

"I did a little bit when I was in art school," I said. "But that's been a few years back."

"Wanna give it a try?"

I smiled. "Sure, why not?"

Jake led the way back down the hallway to his studio at the other end of the house. He placed a lump of clay on the potter's wheel and gestured for me to take a seat.

Self-consciously, I began to knead the clay, and Jake showed me how to operate the foot pedal. But I immediately began to fumble, and the bowl I was attempting to form was soon misshapen.

Exasperated, I looked up at Jake. "Need some help?" he asked, his eyes twinkling with humor. He pulled up a stool behind me, and straddling my body with his legs, he reached around me with his muscular arms to hold my hands in proper form.

The intimacy of the position both excited and unnerved me. I took a deep breath, allowing myself to take in the secure feeling of Jake's strong arms around me, his clean masculine scent, his sensual earthy energy. I closed my eyes, basking in the experience, before reminding myself to return my focus to the lump of clay in my hands.

When Jake was satisfied that I knew what I was doing, he scooted away and watched in silence while I completed my project.

"Not bad," he said when I was finished. "I'll fire it for you next time I run the kiln."

I got up to wash my clay-covered hands in the utility sink. "I guess I'd better get going."

"Okay, then." Jake walked me the few steps to the side door.

We stood under the outside light, moths fluttering around the naked bulb. "The stars are awesome, aren't they?" I said, gazing up at the summer night sky.

When my observation failed to elicit a response, I wondered whether Jake was impatient for me to leave, whether I'd overstayed my welcome. But as I fished around in my handbag for my car keys, he suddenly said, "I like you, Lee. I like having you around. You can come over any time."

"I might do that," I said coyly, "if I get an invitation."

Jake chuckled. "I guess that's the way women prefer it, the man taking the lead."

"I'm pretty liberated," I said, "but I'm generally not forward with men."

Jake scrutinized my face in the dim light, tenderness in his dark eyes. "Come here, Lee," he said, holding out his arms.

Without thinking, I walked into them, and he kissed me so sweetly, so sensuously, I thought I was going to swoon like a girl in an old-fashioned movie. I stood there feeling dreamy, my face up-tilted, my eyes closed, hungry for more.

But Jake released his embrace and stepped back. "I'll call you soon, Lee," he said. "You can count on it."

True to his word, Jake called me four days later. "This is your invitation, Lee," he said, humor in his voice. Late that afternoon, I drove to his house for the second time.

The August evening was clear and pleasantly cool. We spent an hour sitting on his deck overlooking the river, engaging in languid conversation. By that point, I'd accepted the fact that my new friend was not a talkative man. I told myself I liked his quiet nature.

Suddenly, Jake reached across the space separating our two chairs and took my hand. "I like you, Lee. You're a pretty cool gal."

His overture both surprised and pleased me. "I like you, too, Jake," I said. "I like being with you."

I immediately wondered whether I'd been too forward with my feelings, but Jake smiled and squeezed my hand. "Do you want . . . do you want to get closer?"

I wasn't sure what he meant, but decided my answer to all possible interpretations of his question was going to be affirmative. "I'd like that," I said.

He promptly stood up, helped me to my feet, and then led me through the patio door, into the kitchen, and down the hallway to his bedroom. I saw that he'd removed the clutter from the bed, and I wondered if he'd done this in anticipation of intimacy with me.

To my delight, I discovered Jake was much more expressive in love-making than in conversation. The combination of his robust masculinity and his surprising tenderness suited me perfectly, and I found the experience to be enormously satisfying. Afterwards, I lay relaxed and satiated in his arms.

He gently brushed the hair from my face. "So are we officially seeing each other, Lee?"

"Of course," I murmured.

"Good." He gave me a quick kiss, then rolled over and got out of bed.

I felt disoriented by the abrupt transition from intimacy to separation, but knew it would be wrong to interpret Jake's actions as rejection. I lingered in bed watching him dress, admiring his broad muscular back as he pulled on his blue jeans.

I can't indulge in hurt feelings, I told myself. *If I'm going to pursue a relationship with this man, I need to adjust to his idiosyncrasies.*

And so began my love affair with Jacob Potter. Once a week, I'd make the thirty-minute drive to his house. We'd share simple meals, take walks along the river, or hike in the woods. I started bringing along my art supplies, and Jake cleared a space in his ceramics studio so I could set up my easel. We'd work together for hours on our individual projects, barely speaking to each other.

Outside the bedroom, no one would have spotted us as lovers. Jake was not physically demonstrative, and he rarely touched me unless there was a purpose to it. Once, I laid an affectionate hand on his shoulder when I passed by where he was sitting. He looked up at me, puzzled, as if he didn't understand the gesture. I quickly learned not to cling.

Jake was never seductive, never teased me with innuendos. Our relationship was virtually platonic, until we entered the bedroom. There, it felt like I was on a rendezvous with a secret lover, a being from another realm, who tenderly ravished me and then vanished after we indulged in our sensual pleasure. The experience was mystical, yet earthy. We didn't soar to the stars; rather, it seemed like we traveled to some enchanted forest or visited a magical kingdom in the bowels of the planet.

There wasn't much cuddling at the end of lovemaking, just the gentle separation of solitary travelers whose paths had momentarily converged.

Sometimes when I'd watch Jake at work in his woodshop or stretched out on one of his deck chairs, he'd look so ordinary, like the farm boy he was. And I'd be unable to fathom the mystery of what we created together.

I never spent the night with Jake. After our shared intimacy, I always went home to my own apartment. But invariably, the night after making love with him, I'd be visited with strange, surreal dreams. They weren't frightening, just lovely explorations in sensory delights.

The next day, I'd feel drawn to my painting, and I'd soon recognize the images from my dreams showing up in my work. I began to see Jake not only as my lover, but also as a spirit who sparked something in my spirit. I almost became addicted to him as a source of inspiration for my creativity.

Apparently, Jake was enjoying a similar experience. When I arrived at his house one evening in late September, he hurried out the door to greet me, a wide smile on his face. Grabbing my hand in an uncharacteristic gesture, he said, "Come with me to the workshop, Lee. I want to show you something." I'd never seen him that excited.

"I think you're having a good effect on me," he said as he led me into his finishing room. "Look at this." He picked up an object from his table and placed it in my hands. It was a jewelry box, exquisitely crafted in a delicate, ornate design.

I was astounded. "Jake, did you make this?"

He nodded, still grinning from ear to ear. "Yup, I did."

"It's incredible!"

"I'm glad you like it. I've never made anything this fancy before. But the design just came to me, out of nowhere. It was weird. I think having you around inspires me."

In that instant, my mind told me that Jake and I were the perfect couple, lovers who delighted each other with sensual pleasures, artists who sparked in each other infinite creative possibilities. I thought my heart would burst with my overflowing emotion. At that moment, Jacob Potter was everything I wanted.

"It's the most beautiful thing I've ever seen," I said. "Jake, you're amazing."

Because of the way Jake had delighted in placing the jewelry box in my hands, I had assumed it was a gift for me, his heart-felt creation for his new lover, a token of his growing affection. I continued to gush over the wonders of the box, the little drawers and tiny compartments. Just as I was ready to utter an expression of profound gratitude, he took the box from my hands and placed it back on the table.

"Well, I'm glad to know this will be a hit with women," he said. "I'm going to take it to the show this weekend. Think it will sell?"

At no other time in my life has my heart soared to such ecstatic heights, only to hit the floor with a terrible thud a moment later. Making a valiant effort to pull my shattered emotions together, I said, "I'm sure it'll sell, Jake. It's a fantastic piece of work."

He looked at me, puzzled. "You all right, Lee? You look like you're not feeling well."

"I'm not," I said, speaking the truth then twisting it into a lie. "I might be coming down with something. I probably should've stayed home."

I sat on the deck with Jake for awhile, not saying much, declining the food he offered me. I played up the theme of not feeling well, and left early to avoid our usual encounter in the bedroom.

Lying awake that night, I examined my relationship with Jake, tearfully admitting to myself that even though I served as an inspiration for his work, I still hadn't found my way into his heart. *Is this going anywhere?* I wondered. *Should I back off?*

In the morning, I felt better. I laughed at my previous night's hurt feelings, telling myself I'd been acting like a silly child. *You barely know this guy,* the reasonable part of me said. *Don't let your emotions get ahead of you.*

I had to acknowledge that the probability of Jake and me having a future together was pretty slim. But I knew full well I wasn't done with him yet.

Chapter 5

Only a week later, as I stared in disbelief at the results of a home pregnancy test, I realized that my destiny with Jacob Potter was being shaped in an unexpected way. Eight years of faithfully taking birth control pills had, up to that point, provided me with perfect protection. I couldn't fathom how I could possibly be carrying Jake's child.

An appointment with an obstetrician confirmed my pregnancy. I left her office with my head reeling and my stomach churning, and drove through a chilly October rain to my mother's house.

"What's going on, River?" she asked when she saw me standing on her doorstep, drenched and shivering from the cold. "You look a bit off-kilter."

"I need to talk to you," I said, shaking so hard my teeth chattered.

My mother ushered me into her living room, fussing over me as she removed my wet jacket. I sank down on her sofa, and she tucked a warm afghan around me.

"How about a cup of chamomile tea, dear?" she offered. "It'll settle your nerves."

I shook my head. "That doesn't sound good. I'm feeling nauseated."

She shot me a curious look. "I'll fix you peppermint. That's good for an upset stomach." She disappeared into her kitchen, and then emerged a few minutes later with a fragrant, steaming mug of tea.

"What's on your mind, River?" she asked as she set the mug on the coffee table in front of me.

I slowly stirred my tea, afraid that speaking my news aloud would make it undeniably true. "Well . . . I've been dating someone."

"A new lover?" My mother's voice was cheerful. "That's wonderful! You've been without one for so long. What's his name?"

"It's Jake. Jacob Potter."

"Are you having a problem with Jake?"

"Not exactly."

She furrowed her brow. "Then what is it, dear?"

"I can't believe this, Mom. I'm pregnant."

She didn't look the least bit shocked. "I see. How do you feel about this? How does Jake feel?"

"Well, I'm surprised, I guess. Pretty shook up, to tell you the truth. I certainly didn't plan this. I've never missed a day of taking my pills. I don't understand how this could've happened. And I don't know how Jake feels about it, because I haven't told him yet."

My mother sat with her eyes lowered, as she always did when listening for words of truth. Then she looked up at me and smiled. "Sometimes souls are meant to incarnate on this earth at certain times, in certain places. And if it's meant to be, nothing will stop them from coming. There's nothing to worry about, River. This is part of your life plan. You're meant to have this baby."

"But I just started seeing Jake," I protested. "I barely know him. I don't know how he'll take it. He doesn't have any children, and I don't think he wants any."

The smile remained undisturbed on my mother's face. "Don't question this, River. Just accept this pregnancy for the gift that it is. Everything will fall into place."

She leaned over and patted my knee. "Now, dear, you need to tell your lover he's going to be a father."

I couldn't bear the anxiety of keeping the secret from Jake, so as soon as I arrived home, I picked up the phone and dialed his number. "Jake," I said when he answered. "I've got news for you, and I don't know how you'll take it."

"I'm listening." He sounded unperturbed.

"I'm pregnant, Jake. I'm so sorry to spring this on you. I didn't mean for this to happen." I clutched the phone, white-knuckled, waiting for his response.

"Oh," he finally said. Then after another long pause, he asked, "What are you planning to do?"

"All I know is that I'm going to have the baby," I said. "The rest, I haven't figured out yet."

"I hope you know, Lee, that I'll do whatever I can to help."

"Thanks, Jake." I felt so relieved, so touched by his kindness that tears pooled in my eyes.

"Give me a little time to think things through, then I'll get back with you," he said.

I hung up the phone and collapsed into a chair, contemplating my impending motherhood, trying to sort out the associated complications. I was two months into my fall semester of teaching, and I wondered how administration would respond to an unmarried teacher showing up pregnant. Would they grant me a maternity leave? Would they ask me to resign? In spite of my mother's calm reassurance, fear clutched my heart, fear for myself and my unborn child.

The ringing of the telephone interrupted my anxious thoughts, and I jumped out of my chair to answer it. It was Jake.

"I've been thinking, Lee," he said. "How about moving here with me? That way, you can take a break from teaching, however long you need to, and you won't have to worry about supporting yourself."

I didn't need to think twice about accepting Jake's offer. I knew this was the plan my mother had spoken of, unfolding as it should.

I ended up teaching until the end of the semester in mid-January, hiding my growing abdomen under loose clothing. Then I tendered my resignation, and informed my landlord I was moving out of my apartment.

The day I brought my first load of belongings to Jake's house, I found him moving things out of his former bedroom. "This will be your room now," he said. "I'm putting my stuff in the studio. Sometimes, I work late into the night. This way, I can crash when I feel like it, without bothering you."

I was momentarily taken aback by his expectation that I would sleep alone. *But aren't we a couple now?* I protested inwardly. Then I remembered my first visit to his house, when he informed me of his need for personal space. I had to laugh. *This man told you exactly where he stands. Why would you expect anything different?*

In the process of moving in, I asked Jake if he minded me doing a little decorating in the house. He shrugged and said, "Go ahead. This place could use a woman's touch."

So I had him help me rearrange furniture to make room for my loveseat in the living room. Then I hung some of my paintings, put a few of his ceramic pieces on shelves, and tossed an afghan and decorative pillows on the sofa. The living room now seemed cozy and inviting, no longer forlorn.

In the kitchen, I sorted through Jake's battered pots and mismatched dishes, throwing out items that were no longer usable. Then I replenished the cupboards with my cookware and brightly colored stoneware. I despaired of making the shabby kitchen look appealing, but consoled myself with the thought that Jake would remodel it someday.

Life at Jake's house was pleasant and tranquil. After years of apartment living, I loved being close to nature again. As I grew large with my pregnancy, I spent many leisurely hours in the living room, reading near the warmth of the wood-burning stove or gazing out the window at the late winter snowfall.

Jake was unfailingly kind, but never hovered over me. My presence in the house didn't disrupt his routine, and he went about his usual business in his workshop and ceramics studio. Several times a day, he'd come into the living room to deposit a load of wood next to the stove.

"How're you doing, Lee?" he'd ask. I sensed he was pleased to have me there.

But sometimes, a wave of sadness washed over me when I acknowledged the fact that the emotional bond between Jake and me didn't seem to be growing. Our love life had dwindled to almost nothing, and I wondered whether we were both too independent to create an enduring intimacy.

Jake paid little attention to my enlarging abdomen. Occasionally, I'd place his hand on my belly so he could feel the baby moving. He'd smile at me, and the moment would be so tender, I'd almost believe I was in love.

The last few months of my pregnancy, he began driving me to my obstetric appointments, waiting patiently in his truck until I was finished. Once, I invited him to come in with me, but he declined. "I'm not comfortable with that," he said.

My face must have registered my disappointment, because he said, "Sorry, Lee. You know how I am."

When an ultrasound revealed that our child was a boy, I couldn't wait to tell Jake the news. Rushing out of the doctor's office to his waiting truck, I exclaimed, "Guess what! We're having a son!"

I detected a flicker of interest in his eyes. He nodded and said, "Hmm. That's good to know."

"Are you excited about this baby, Jake?" I blurted out one day when he stepped into the living room to deposit a load of firewood. "Are you looking forward to being a father?"

I desperately wanted to see his face light up. But I'd caught him off guard, and he stood there by the stove staring at me, seemingly frightened by my intrusion into the private world of his emotions. "I don't know about being excited," he finally said. "You know me. I don't get worked up about much of anything. But I'm okay with it."

Suddenly, I was flooded with the awareness that Jake thought of the baby as mine, not ours. It had been my decision to raise the child, not his. He was just being gracious in offering me a place to stay. It was more like he was helping out a friend in need, rather than building a life with the mother of his child.

After he left the room, I burst into tears. I clutched my abdomen as I sobbed, feeling as if this baby and I were all alone in the world. I cried myself all the way to an acceptance of the fact that Jake was rather indifferent about the impending birth of our son.

When my tears subsided, my baby gave me a mighty kick, as if to remind me he was still there, that he was important, that he was someone to be reckoned with. A feeling of elation swept over me. Suddenly, Jake's indifference didn't matter. Even though being in love with him seemed impossible, I felt a powerful, undeniable love for the child he'd given me.

After several months of living with him, I persuaded Jake to meet my mother, and he reluctantly accompanied me on a visit to her home. The event was not dramatic. My mother chattered away in her lighthearted manner, and Jake was his usual taciturn self.

On our way home, he commented, "Your mother's way out there, isn't she?"

I laughed. "Most people think so. Are you okay with that?"

"No problem." He glanced over at me and smiled. "You're a lot like her, and I'm okay with you."

Later that evening, when Jake was out of earshot, I called my mother. "Well? What did you think of Jake?"

"He's a good man," she responded. "A good soul."

I sensed there was more, and I waited for it, hoping to hear her predict a future in which Jake and I and our baby would evolve into a loving family unit.

"River." There was a hint of sadness in my mother's voice. "Jake may be what you need for now, but not for long. Just for a season."

When I was too stunned to respond, she said, "You already know this, River. You'd like it to be different, but you know it won't. But that's okay, dear. It is as it should be."

I hung up the phone with a sinking heart, hoping her prediction was wrong. But as far back as I could remember, my mother had never been wrong in her assessment of any situation.

One day in my late pregnancy, I felt the need to get out of the house, and I asked Jake if I could ride with him to Goshen to pick up a load of lumber. It was a lovely spring day, and on our way back home, Jake drove the truck down the county roads so we could enjoy the scenery.

Suddenly, he asked, "Want to see where my folks live?"

"Sure," I said.

He turned onto another county road, and we passed several dairy farms. "There it is," he said, pointing to a white farmhouse on a tidy piece of property. "That's where I grew up."

A heavy-set woman in her sixties, wearing a long dark dress and a white bonnet, was kneeling over a patch of tilled soil, a flat of petunias by her side.

"That's my mom," Jake said. "She likes working in her flower gardens."

The woman glanced up as we passed, but didn't seem to recognize Jake's truck. Her face looked weary.

I felt an urge to talk to her, to get to know her. "Jake, let's stop and visit."

"No!" His voice was uncharacteristically harsh.

"Why not?"

"Just let it go, Lee."

I turned to face him. "Jake, I don't understand how you could treat your parents like this. I'd never do that to my parents, drive by their house without giving them the time of day."

"Well, Lee, my parents aren't your parents," he said sarcastically. "Want to know the truth? They wouldn't approve of you. Did you really think I'd show up at their house with the woman I knocked up?"

I turned away to stare out the window, feeling terribly hurt.

"Don't make a big deal out of this, Lee," he said, his voice softening. "Isn't it enough that I approve of you?"

I never again broached the subject of meeting Jake's family. I suspected he visited them every now and then. Sometimes, he'd steal away for several hours around holidays or on a Sunday afternoon, never telling me where he went.

It was a long time before his parents even knew that I existed. Of course, they never knew anything about Rachel.

The last few weeks of my pregnancy, I grew so large that I could barely get around. I spent most of my days confined to the sofa. Jake carried to the living room the box of books I'd brought with me, and I sat with my legs propped up on the ottoman, reading volume after volume.

At the bottom of the box, I discovered several books on Scandinavian folklore, given to me by my father when I was a teenager. While my mother had filled my mind with stories about our Native American heritage, my father had told me little about his ethnicity. I suppose the books were his attempt to balance the scale.

In any case, having a child made me more mindful of my lineage, and the books caught my fancy. Up until the point when I experienced my first labor pains, I immersed myself in the world of Odin, Loki, and Thor, the trolls and the giants, the elves, the ghosts and the dragons.

Chapter 6

Our child was born in early June, a ten-pound boy who lingered in my womb two weeks past his due date. Several days prior to his birth, Jake surprised me by asking, "So what do you plan on naming this kid?"

"I'll have to see him first," I responded. "How would I know what to call someone I've never met?" Jake looked at me as if I'd lost my mind.

"Do you have any suggestions?" I asked him, wanting to be fair.

He shook his head. "Nope."

But I knew exactly what to name my red-haired, blue-eyed son when I held him the first time. He was so large and sturdy, with such a powerful bellowing cry, he put me in mind of the mighty Norse god I'd been reading about, and I announced that his name was Thor.

Jake looked bewildered. "Where'd you come up with something like that?"

His reaction brought me to my senses, and I realized my son needed a proper name. Like my mother had done for me, I gave him a name with options: Theodore. That way he could be Ted or Teddy or Theo, if he chose. But to me, he'd always be Thor.

After Jake got used to the idea, he agreed that such a grand name befitted our son. I asked him if he minded me giving Thor my last name, and he didn't object. I decided to give him the middle name of James, my mother's surname. Thus, Theodore James Jorgensen was the name entered on our son's birth certificate.

The closest I ever felt to Jake was right after Thor's birth. One evening when Thor was several weeks old, I was breastfeeding him on our living-room sofa. Jake came in and sat beside me, watching our son suckling efficiently in big, noisy gulps.

"What . . . what would you think . . . about getting married, Lee?" he stammered. "Want to make this family thing official?"

I looked at him and saw fear in his eyes, and I knew he was uncomfortable with what he'd just proposed. So I decided to let him off the hook without ruining the sweetness of the moment. "Let's think about it," I said. But the subject never came up again.

Jake was a good father, in that he took his financial responsibility seriously. But he was never a doting dad, and he kept the same emotional distance from Thor as he did from me. I had envisioned father and son tossing a ball in the back yard or roughhousing on the living-room floor, but that never happened. I'd thought for sure Thor would be his father's shadow in the workshop, and that Jake would delight in teaching him how to use tools, but neither of them showed an inclination toward that kind of bonding.

Clearly, Thor was more mine than Jake's, and I'll admit that I liked not having to share my son's affections. The cradle Jake crafted in his workshop was ensconced in my bedroom, and later, the crib. When Thor was three years old and had outgrown his baby bed, I set him up in the third bedroom in the hallway, on the other side of the bathroom.

The first seven years of living at Jake's house, before Rachel entered our lives, were some of the best of my life: blissful, sweet, and uncomplicated. I stopped fretting about the fact that Jake and I were drifting farther and farther apart. There was no hostility between us, no emotional storms. Although we shared physical intimacy on infrequent occasions, for the most part, we left each other alone to pursue our separate lives.

For the first two years of Thor's life, I accepted Jake's financial support and devoted myself to being a fulltime mother. I no longer missed emotional closeness with Jake, because Thor, my little kindred spirit, filled my entire world. He was a bright, inquisitive, engaging child, and I loved him with a boundless passion.

Jake was no longer necessary for my creative inspiration, as Thor provided all that I needed. I set up an art studio in one of the bedrooms in the original part of the house, and spent hours painting fantasy portraits of my red-haired son: riding on the back of a tiger, cavorting with gnomes and fairies, perched high in a treetop in the nest of an exotic bird.

Thor knew no model of family life other than that of an adoring mother and a distant father who remained on the fringes of family activity. My son didn't seem to desire anything else, and I watched with satisfaction as he thrived in our home and in the world of nature surrounding it.

Of course, my mother doted on Thor as much as I did. She viewed her grandson as the newest arrival in the line of spiritually gifted family members, and she delighted in nurturing him. Thor became deeply attached to his grandmother, and was as comfortable in her home as he was in mine.

When Thor was two, I resumed my career as an art teacher, working part-time at Riverside Elementary School in Niles. I left Thor in the care of my mother on the days that I needed to be at school. My small income provided for my own needs and most of my son's, so I didn't feel like I was a burden to Jake. He never complained about housing me, nor did he ever suggest that I needed to leave.

While I no longer took my paintings to art fairs, I joined an art league, entering contests and occasionally exhibiting my work in local galleries. I became involved with a drumming circle, and several times a year, I honored my maternal ancestry by participating in Native American powwows.

Jake's habits varied little over the years. He occupied himself with his work, and for the most part, his social contacts were limited to his art shows and the people who ordered his custom-built cabinets. We had very few visitors at the house. The few times I entertained friends, I could tell Jake was uncomfortable with the intrusion into his private space, so I created a social life away from home. My mother rarely came to the house, and Jake's parents never came. I suspected they didn't even know where he lived.

But Jake's simple, reclusive lifestyle was disrupted by one delightful variation. On the first Saturday evening of each month, he attended a contra dance, and when Thor was several months old, he invited me to go with him.

The dance was held in a park pavilion just across the state line in Elkhart, Indiana, a thirty-minute drive from our home. I'd never heard of contra dancing, but Jake explained to me that it originated from country dancing in the British Isles, and that the form was several hundred years old.

The first time I attended, I watched the dancing from the sidelines until I felt confident that I could join in. The parallel lines of dancers stepped briskly to the Celtic music of a live band, weaving their way up and down the hall in intricate patterns occasionally punctuated by lively swinging. It was a joyful activity, and I quickly grew to love it.

I soon realized Jake was as devoted to contra dancing as he was to his ceramics and woodworking. In spite of his solid, muscular build, he was a graceful dancer, light on his feet, possessing an impeccable rhythm. All of the women, including myself, adored dancing with him. His swing so was strong and powerful that it nearly lifted us off our feet, yet so smooth that we could have balanced books on our heads.

Jake didn't talk much at the dance, but he was always smiling. His female partners were clearly charmed by his penetrating dark eyes as he gazed intently at them during the swing. I'd watch with amazement as my lackluster housemate lit up like the man of every woman's dreams. The sensuality he exuded would resonate within me, and that night, I'd find my way into his bed.

We always took Thor to the dance with us, and others were eager to watch him while I took my turn at dancing. The contra dance was virtually the only place Jake, Thor, and I appeared in public as a family, and that became one of the reasons I grew to love the dancing as much as Jake did.

As those seven easy years passed, there were admittedly times when I felt bored and restless, when I wondered what else life held for me. But there wasn't enough stress to propel me out of my comfort zone, and I had no inclination to disrupt Thor's happy home life. In spite of occasional urges to leave, I never found a compelling reason to move on.

My mother raised me to understand that nothing lasts forever, and that I must be gracious in accepting change, whether or not it is welcome. So when Jake announced that his new lover was coming to live with him, there was nothing for me to do but step aside in order to make room for Rachel.

Chapter 7

But stepping aside wasn't as easy as I thought it would be. After Jake told me about Rachel that fateful Sunday evening in May, I went straight to the phone to call my mother. When I heard her voice on the other end of the line, my cool composure cracked, and I began to sob.

"River, darling, what's wrong?" my mother asked.

"Nothing's really wrong," I sniffled. "I don't know why I'm crying like this. Would you mind if Thor and I spent the summer with you?"

"Of course I won't mind. You know you're always welcome here. But satisfy my curiosity, dear. Why do you feel the need to come?"

My sobbing renewed with intensity, and I choked out the words, "Jake has another woman, Mom. He's moving her here. I have to leave, of course."

"But you told me you were already thinking about leaving."

"I know. That's why I can't figure out why I'm falling apart like this."

"Every ending must be grieved," my mother said, "even if it's an ending you want. Weep until you no longer need to weep, River. When all the tears are gone from your eyes, you'll be able to see where you're going."

The next day, I focused on preparing Thor for the upcoming changes in his life. "How would you like for you and me to spend the summer at Grandma's house?" I asked him when he came home from school.

His big blue eyes lit up with excitement. "Sure! That would be fun!"

"Good," I said. "We'll go when school's out."

Thor was ready to run off and play, but I said, "Wait a minute, sweetie. There's something else I need to tell you."

"What?" His questioning eyes held only curiosity, no anxiety. He'd had no reason to worry up to that point in his young life. My heart felt heavy, as I knew his carefree world would soon be complicated.

"Somebody else is going to move into our house. She's coming in a few days."

"Why?"

Over the next six years, I often berated myself for how I responded to Thor's simple question. I wished I'd had the courage to tell him the whole earth-shattering truth: that his father and I needed to go our separate ways, that his father loved another woman. Such a response would have sent Thor and me down a completely different path, sparing me years of stagnating in a pool of confusion and frustration.

But at that critical moment, as I gazed into my son's innocent eyes, I couldn't bear to break his heart. Opting to put a happy spin on the situation, I said, "She's coming here because she doesn't have anywhere else to live. We have an extra room, so she can stay with us."

"Oh." Thor nodded wisely. "We're going to share with her. What's her name?"

I looked away so he couldn't see the distress on my face. "Rachel. Her name is Rachel." Then I leaned down and gathered my son in my arms. "You're such a good boy, Thor."

He wrapped his arms around me. "I love you, Mom," he chirped in a silly cartoon-character voice.

I laughed and squeezed him tightly. "I love you, too, Thor. I love you more than anything in the world." He giggled, and then wriggled out of my arms.

"There's one more thing I need to tell you, Thor," I said.

He rolled his eyes in exasperation. "Boy, Mom, you sure are telling me a lot of stuff today."

"You're getting bigger," I said. "I think maybe you're ready to have a bigger room. How would you like to start sleeping in that empty room on the other side of the kitchen?"

"You mean the one next to your studio?"

"Yes. There's some stuff I'll need to move out, then it will be all yours." I ruffled his curly red hair. "You'll have a lot more room for your toys. What do you think?"

"Wow, that would be so cool! When can we put my stuff in there?

"We'll start this evening," I said, "right after dinner."

Thor scampered off to his room, and I could hear him chattering to himself as he sorted through his toys in preparation for the move. I sank onto the living-room sofa, in a dark mood. I hated having to use a lighthearted story to sugar-coat the reasons for the changes in our household. The truth was that I wanted Thor as far away from those hallway bedrooms as possible, to protect him from any evidence that the new friend moving into our home was also his father's lover.

"Jake, you're so selfish," I muttered as I roused myself from the sofa and went to the kitchen to prepare dinner. I pulled a pot from the battered old cupboard, and then slammed the door a little harder than I needed to.

Thor and I moved most of his things that evening. I didn't have to work the next day, and while Thor was in school, I began transferring my own belongings to the bedroom he'd just vacated. The longer I worked, the angrier I became about the circumstances Jake had thrust upon me.

It was close to noon when I realized Jake was standing in the hallway, watching me. He'd come in the side door from his workshop, and was heading toward the kitchen to get something to eat.

"What're you doing, Lee?" he asked. "What's all this moving about?"

"I'm making room for Rachel," I said through gritted teeth.

"She could've moved into the empty bedroom on the other side of the house," he said. "That's what I was planning on."

"I'm trying to get Thor as far away from this mess as possible," I snapped. "And I'm not going to be sleeping between the two of you. It's better if Rachel has the room next to yours."

"I suppose you're right." Jake walked past me into the kitchen. I waited until he was finished before I went to make my own lunch.

Jake and I barely spoke the next few days. Gradually, I began to calm down and accept the new realities of my living situation. I reminded myself that since Jake and I had almost completely disconnected from each other, he had a right to move on with someone else, and I had no right to stand in his way.

I tried to focus my mind on the next change, moving myself and Thor to my mother's house at the end of the school year. I thought about what I would take with me and what I would leave at Jake's house until Thor and I settled into a home of our own.

At times, I found myself in tears as I contemplated leaving my home of seven years, a home to which I'd grown quite attached. But looking ahead at future possibilities comforted me.

Friday evening, as I sat reading in bed, Jake suddenly appeared in the doorway of my new room. "I just wanted to let you know I'm going to pick up Rachel tomorrow morning," he said.

"Okay," I responded. "I figured you would."

Jake didn't move from my doorway. In the dim light, I could see the melancholy expression on his face.

"What do you want, Jake?" I snapped.

Without invitation, he entered my room and sat down on the foot of my bed. "I just wanted to let you know that I'm sorry, Lee." He hung his head, his voice barely above a whisper. "I really didn't want to put you through something like this."

A lump rose in my throat. I set my book aside and reached for a tissue from the box on my nightstand. "Thanks for telling me that."

"I've been thinking all week," he said. "I know I blew it with you. I haven't been the man you needed. I sort of wish I had the chance to do things over."

"What's happened between us is over and done," I said. "There's no use beating ourselves up about it."

Jake sat with downcast eyes, running an index finger along the outline of the floral pattern on my bedspread. I wondered whether he was having reservations about bringing his new lover into our home.

"Jake, are you having second thoughts about Rachel?" I asked.

"Sort of," he said. "In a way, yes."

For a moment, I thought he was expecting me to talk him out of what he'd decided to do. The old fantasy of him, me, and Thor as a close-knit family, the dream I'd laid to rest years ago, popped back into my mind. I wondered if he and I were on the verge of a new start.

"Jake, do you love Rachel?" I wasn't sure why I asked the question, but it seemed necessary.

He smiled for the first time since he'd entered my bedroom. "Yes, I think I do. I feel something for her I've never felt for any other woman, so I guess that means I'm in love with her."

Then he seemed to realize how this revelation sounded to me, and he dropped his head. "Sorry. You know I think the world of you, Lee."

I suddenly felt like a needy teenager begging for reassurance. "Why do you think we've never been able to get close, Jake? What went wrong between the two of us? Why couldn't we be in love?"

He scratched his head. "I don't know, Lee. I just don't know."

By that point, my emotions were churning, and I resented the fact that Jake had destroyed the equanimity I'd worked so hard to achieve over the past few days. I didn't know whether I wanted to burst into tears or pound him with my fists.

Then he did something that shattered my last reserves of self-control. Placing his hand on my blanket-covered thigh, he asked, "Want to make love one more time, Lee? As a way of saying goodbye?"

At that moment, I was glad Thor was sleeping in his room at the other end of the house, because I lost my composure and screamed profanities at Jake. "Are you kidding me, Jake? Are you fucking kidding me? You're bringing another woman here tomorrow, and you want to screw me one last time before she gets here? Hell, no!"

Jake jumped up, backing away from my outburst.

Maybe I should have let the angry interchange be the last note between Jake and me, as a way of making a clean break. Maybe that would have empowered me to do what I needed to do. But when I saw the devastation on his face, my peacemaking DNA asserted itself, and my anger subsided. We'd never been hostile with each other before, and I told myself it would serve no purpose to build animosity between us.

"Jake, wait," I called as he headed toward the door.

"What?" His voice sounded guarded.

"I'm sorry," I said. "Just let me say something." He looked at me warily before sitting down on the foot of my bed again.

I reached out my hand. "Jake, we're ending one thing and starting another. That's the way it needs to be. This can be a new beginning for us, the beginning of a good friendship." I laughed. "I sound just like my mother, don't I?"

Jake chuckled. "You sure do!" He squeezed my hand. "Okay, Lee, we'll be friends." Abruptly, he stood up and left my room, as if he'd had his fill of emotional conversation.

Chapter 8

When I heard Jake's van pull into the driveway late Saturday morning, I couldn't stop myself from snooping. I stationed myself in the living-room at an angle where I could peek out the front window without being detected.

I saw the driver's side door of the van open, and Jake got out. Then the other door opened, and a young woman climbed down from the passenger seat. I tried to catch a glimpse of her face, but she was turned away from me, watching Jake pull two battered duffel bags out of the back of the van. I assumed they were her belongings.

The girl was of medium height and very thin, her hips no wider than those of a ten-year-old boy. Her faded blue jeans were so threadbare that she'd worn white patches on the seat. Her straight, jet-black hair hung midway down her back.

When she turned to walk with Jake to the side entrance of the house, I caught a glimpse of large, scared brown eyes in a thin olive-skinned face. Tiny pointed breasts barely disrupted the flat plane of her red tank top. I glanced down at my own ample bosom and curvaceous hips, and wondered about Jake's choices in women.

Jake continued to carry both of the bulky duffel bags, and the girl made no move to take one of them. His gallantry surprised me. Except at the very end of my pregnancy, Jake had allowed me to be self-sufficient. I'd thought that was what he'd wanted from me.

I sighed deeply. Disoriented by the presence of this intruder on our property, I couldn't think of what to do next. Suddenly, I realized it was nearly noon, and that I needed to fix lunch for Thor. While I was in the kitchen making sandwiches, Jake popped in and grabbed two bottles of water from the refrigerator.

"Rachel's here," he said in an off-handed manner, as if announcing the arrival of the mailman.

"I know," I said. "I saw her. My God, Jake, she's a child. What is she, eighteen?"

Jake's face darkened uncharacteristically. "She's twenty-four.

That's not so young. You were twenty-six when we met."

"That was almost eight years ago, Jake. You were thirty-three. You're forty-one now."

He stood there red-faced, trying to formulate a response. I'd never seen him angry like that, and I knew I'd touched a nerve.

"I'm sorry, Jake," I said. "This really isn't any of my business."

"No, it isn't, Lee." He turned and stalked out of the kitchen.

I rounded up Thor, and we took our sandwiches and fruit out to the deck. "Rachel's here," I told him. "You'll be meeting her soon."

"Okay." He took a big bite from his sandwich, and then licked the jelly off his fingers.

Then I heard the patio door creak, and I turned to see Jake's new lover standing uncertainly on the edge of the deck. She looked frail, as if she could be blown away any minute by the brisk spring breeze.

"Hello," I said. "You must be Rachel."

"Yes." Her large frightened eyes searched my face, as if looking for signs of rejection or approval. I noticed that her features were classically formed. She would have been beautiful, if not for the scared-rabbit look on her face. "Are you Jake's roommate?" she asked.

"Yes I am," I said. "I'm Lee, and this is my son Thor." Inwardly, I congratulated myself on how gracefully I was managing the awkward moment. I gestured toward an empty chair. "You can sit down if you want to."

Rachel seated herself gingerly on the edge of the chair. She stared wordlessly at me for a few moments, and then turned her gaze to Thor. A smile chased the fearful expression off her face. "Thor?" she asked. "Like the god Thor?"

Thor put down his empty plate, jumped off his chair, and strutted around the deck with his arms flexed, pumping his little biceps. "Yeah, I'm a Norse god!" he announced in a sonorous voice.

Rachel giggled and reached out to ruffle his curly hair. "He's a cute kid," she said to me.

"Thank you," I said. "I think so, too." Thor continued to strut and make silly faces, enjoying Rachel's attention.

The patio door opened again, and Jake poked his head out. "Are you hungry, Rachel?" he asked. "Can I fix you something to eat?" He glanced at Thor and me. "I see you've met Lee and Thor."

"Yes, she's met us, Dad," Thor chirped.

A horrified expression crossed Rachel's face. She looked at Jake and then at Thor, and I imagined she was taking in the resemblance of the red-haired father and son. Jake looked uncomfortable, and quickly withdrew into the kitchen. I realized he hadn't told Rachel the entire story about his roommate, that he'd left a mess for me to clean up.

Thor scampered off the deck and ran to play in the front yard. Rachel buried her face in her hands. "I didn't know," she said. "I shouldn't have come here."

I suddenly felt compassion for this scared skinny girl, and I mentally gave Jake a kick in the pants. "Jake didn't tell you we have a son, did he?" I said, trying to sound nonchalant.

"No," she whimpered. "He just told me he had a roommate that was going to be moving out."

"That part's true," I said. "Thor and I will be leaving in a few weeks. I'm a teacher, and we need to wait until the end of the school year."

Rachel's face contorted with pain. "I feel so awful, like I'm chasing you out of your home. Did I . . . did I break you and Jake up?"

I searched my mind for the right spin to put on my ambiguous relationship with Jake. "Oh, no, Jake and I haven't been together in a long time. This is a big house and we sort of . . . live and let live, I guess. We each do our own thing, and we get along fine that way."

"Really?"

"Yes, really. Don't worry. Before you came, I'd already decided to leave."

Rachel exhaled deeply and sat back in her chair. She looked tired.

For some reason, pity for her overcame my resentment, and I extended myself farther than I'd intended to with this girl. "There's no reason why we can't be friends while I'm still here. And I can already tell Thor likes you."

Rachel's eyes welled with tears. "Thank you," she said.

What's this girl's story? I wondered. *How has fate deposited this fragile waif on my doorstep?*

"Rachel, are you in love with Jake?" The words popped out of my mouth before I could think. I scolded myself for once again meddling in something that wasn't my business.

Rachel looked at me as if she'd never considered the question. "I don't know. Maybe. I think it might be too soon to tell. I haven't known him very long."

I smiled. "Of course. But I'm pretty sure he's quite smitten with you."

She hung her head. "I know. But I don't know why."

Perhaps the moment called for a reassuring statement on my part, but I felt I'd done enough for the girl.

Later in the day, I cornered Jake in his studio. "I'm so angry with you, Jake," I hissed. "Why didn't you tell Rachel about us? She was completely caught off guard!"

"I couldn't find a way to do it," Jake mumbled. "I knew she wouldn't come if she knew the whole story."

"So you left it for me to explain."

"You're better at that sort of thing."

I felt like punching him. "Well, I'm not going to clean up any more of your messes, Jake." I turned to leave, and then stopped. "By the way, is Rachel Hispanic? Native American? I just wondered, because she's so dark."

"No," Jake said. "As a matter of fact, she's Jewish. Her last name is Rosenbaum. Rachel Rosenbaum. I guess she just comes from a dark-skinned family."

The intensity of the day was wearing on my nerves. I didn't know what to do with myself with Rachel in the house, and felt a need to get away for awhile. "How about if you and I go to Grandma's for dinner tonight?" I suggested to Thor.

"Will our friend Rachel come?" he asked.

His question unnerved me. "No, it will be just you and me."

He looked concerned. "What will Rachel eat?"

"Your dad will make sure she gets something."

"Okay," he said. "I don't want her to be hungry."

"We have a new friend that came to live with us," Thor announced to his grandmother at the dinner table that evening.

My mother shot me a questioning look. I shrugged.

"Her name is Rachel," Thor continued. "She's got black hair that hangs down like this." He gestured with his hands. "And her skin is kind of brown."

I tried to hide my smile. *Thor is used to the fair-skinned people in his family,* I thought. *Rachel's dark complexion must be a curiosity to him.*

"She's really nice, Grandma," he said. "She likes to laugh."

My mother and I lingered over coffee after Thor left the dinner table.

"It sounds like your son likes his father's new lover," she observed.

"I guess he does," I said. "Of course, he doesn't know they're lovers. I don't want him to know."

My mother gazed at me, her brow furrowed, and I couldn't read the expression on her face.

"I'm still coming, Mom," I said. "Thor and I will be here in a few weeks."

"Whenever you're ready, River," she replied. "Whenever you're ready."

When I awoke the next morning, I didn't remember Rachel was there until I sensed something different about the energy in the house. I'd grown accustomed to Jake's quiet, sturdy earthiness and Thor's joyful exuberance. But that morning, I felt a cloud of desolation hanging over our home, and I resented the intruder who'd brought it.

I had so much to do that day. Due to the disruption caused by moving our bedrooms, I'd fallen behind in grading my students' projects, and it was imperative that I devote several hours to my schoolwork. But I felt sluggish, and my mood was so dark, I didn't want to get out of bed.

Nevertheless, I threw back my covers and forced myself to get up. Wrapping my robe around me, I made my way to the kitchen, where I encountered my pajama-clad son. He'd evidently grown tired of waiting for his mother to supervise his breakfast, and was pouring himself a bowl of cereal.

"Hi, Mom," he said cheerfully.

"Good morning, sweetie."

"Where's Rachel?"

Oh, God, I'm not prepared for this, I thought. *Ever since Rachel came, some new problem smacks me in the face every time I turn around.* Aloud, I said, "I suppose she's still sleeping, Thor. She's probably tired."

"She might be hungry," he said between bites of Cheerios.

"Well, she lives here now, so she'll need to start making her own food. Your dad will show her where everything is."

"Why don't you show her?" Thor's reproachful look told me I was being an ungracious hostess to the newcomer in our home.

I leaned down and kissed the top of his head. "You silly boy, you ask so many questions I can't keep up with you. Mommy has a lot to do today. I need to get my papers graded. When Rachel gets up, how about if you show her where the food and the dishes are?"

"Okay." Thor drained his glass of orange juice and pushed himself away from the table. He headed out of the kitchen toward his bedroom, then turned and poked his head back through the door. "Just let me know when she gets up." His voice sounded grownup and business-like, as if he had some important commitment to keep.

My heart ached as I carried Thor's dishes to the sink. *If it was just me, it would be so much easier. Oh God, how are we going to get through this?*

As I walked back to my room, I glanced down the hallway to see whether Jake or Rachel were up. Not a soul was stirring. On impulse, I tiptoed down to Jake's studio. The door was open, the light was off, the room was empty, and the ragged quilt was neatly draped over his unused bed. I tiptoed back to Rachel's room and put my ear to the door. I could hear whispers and the rustle of bedcovers, and then a muffled giggle.

I knew Jake was in there with Rachel, and that he'd spent the night with her. In over seven years of living together, Jake and I had never slept an entire night in the same bed. I felt a powerful surge of anger, and could barely stop myself from pounding my fists against the closed door.

Telling myself to mind my own business, I tiptoed back to my room. I took out the stacks of papers and drawings I needed to grade, ready to plunge in and get things done. But I couldn't quell my anger enough to concentrate. My mind kept drifting off to the activity in the bedroom down the hallway. I finally gave up on the schoolwork, and decided to cheer myself up by making a special lunch for Thor and me.

When I walked into the kitchen, I was greeted by the sight of Rachel standing in front of the open refrigerator reaching for a bottle of juice. She was wearing Jake's blue denim shirt, which hung like a sack on her thin frame, exposing her long brown legs.

Even when Jake and I were at our closest, I'd never considered doing something as intimate as putting on one of his garments. But there stood Rachel, looking like a post-lovemaking cliché. I was seized by a jealous rage, and also by a fear that at any moment, Thor might walk into the room. *What in the world will he think if he sees our new housemate wearing his father's clothing?*

"Rachel!" I called sharply.

She swung around, juice bottle in hand, looking like she'd been caught in the act of stealing. "I'm sorry. Is this yours? Jake said . . ."

"It's not about the juice," I snapped. "I don't care what you take out of the refrigerator. But you can't walk around here dressed like that. Not while Thor is still here."

Rachel stared at me with the terror of a cornered animal. Then she put the juice back into the refrigerator and rushed past me down the hallway to her room.

Part of me felt I needed to knock on her door and reassure her that everything was okay. But I told myself I'd done nothing wrong, and I simply didn't have the will or the energy to lure her out of hiding.

By mid-afternoon, I'd calmed down, comforted by the knowledge that in a few weeks, I'd no longer have to contend with the awkwardness of sharing a house with Rachel. I stationed myself on the living-room sofa, a stack of my students' papers beside me, ready to get down to business.

But within minutes, my solitude was broken. I looked up from a test I was grading to see Rachel, now wearing her threadbare blue jeans and a dingy gray tee shirt, standing in the doorway. I felt the impulse to scream at her to go away and leave me alone. Instead, I said, "Hi, Rachel."

She smiled, apparently relieved that flames hadn't leaped from my throat when I opened my mouth. Slowly, she walked around the periphery of the room, staring at the items on the walls and shelves. I realized it was the first time she'd entered that part of the house, and that she was trying to orient herself to her new surroundings.

She picked up a ceramic bowl. "Did Jake make this?"

"Yes, he did." I responded without enthusiasm, not wanting to encourage conversation.

"He's really talented, isn't he?"

"Yes, he is, he's good at what he does."

Rachel put the bowl back in its place and moved on to study one of my paintings. After a few moments, she discovered my signature in the corner of the canvas and read the name out loud: "Lee Jorgensen."

She stared at me in amazement. "Did you paint that?"

"Yes, I did."

"It's so beautiful," she gasped. "You and Jake are both artists. Wow!"

I wanted to tell Rachel that in the early months of my relationship with Jake, art had been the bond that held us together. But I decided it would be unkind to share that information, as it would undoubtedly cause her distress.

"So you're a teacher and an artist," she observed.

"Yes, I am. As a matter of fact, I'm an art teacher."

"You must be really smart."

She stopped her tour of the room and plopped herself down on the loveseat, studying her ragged fingernails. In spite of my irritation with her, I once again felt pity for the girl who seemed so out of place in her new home.

"So what do you do, Rachel?" I asked.

"Nothing," she said, picking at a hangnail.

"That's impossible. Everybody does something."

She looked up at me and grinned. "Well, before I came here, I was helping a friend with her art shows. I watched her booth when she had to leave." Then she added proudly, "That's how I met Jake."

Poor thing, I thought. *You have no idea that you're just one in a series of women Jake has picked up at art shows.*

"Where are you from?" I asked.

"Chicago."

"Oh. Where did you live in Chicago?"

Rachel contorted her pretty face into an expression of disdain. "Before I stayed with my friend, I lived with my parents."

"I take it you don't get along with them?" I tried to empathize with her, although the thought of alienation from one's parents was foreign to me.

"No, we don't get along at all. I'm a huge disappointment to Ike and Essie. All my brothers and sisters are professional people and make lots of money. Ike and Essie want me be like them. The last thing they tried to make me do was go to secretarial school." She laughed. "Can you imagine that?"

"Ike and Essie?" I asked. "Are they your parents?"

"Yes, Isaac and Esther Rosenbaum. I don't like to call them Mom and Dad. I don't think they deserve it."

She glanced at me, seemingly wanting my response to her personal revelation, but I could think of nothing to say to her. She looked disappointed and huddled in the corner of the loveseat, withdrawing into herself. I turned my attention back to the papers I was grading.

But then she spoke again. "Lee, I'm sorry for what happened in the kitchen this morning. I hope you won't hold it against me."

"It's no big deal, Rachel," I said. "I don't have any business telling you and Jake how to live your lives. But while Thor and I are still here, I'd like for you to be careful. Thor thinks of you as a new friend. He doesn't understand that you and his father are lovers. I don't want him confused. Okay?"

Rachel's eyes welled with tears. "I'll be careful, I promise. He's such a sweet little boy. I'd never want to hurt him."

I picked up another paper from the stack beside me. Rachel got up and pulled a book off a shelf. Then she sat back down on the loveseat, folding her long thin legs to one side. My frustration turned to amusement. *This girl is determined to be in my presence. I might as well get used to it.*

A few minutes later, Thor came bounding into the room. "Oh, there you are, Rachel!" he exclaimed. "You sure stayed in bed a long time. Are you hungry? Come, let me show you all the food in the kitchen."

He reached for Rachel's hand. Giggling, she stood up and allowed him to lead her out of the room. I could hear their muffled chatter in the kitchen as cupboard doors opened and closed. When I walked into the room ten minutes later, I found the two of them seated at the oak table, drinking milk and eating graham crackers.

Chapter 9

The next two weeks, I found reasons to spend more time at school. I went in extra days and stayed late into the afternoons, trying to distance myself from what was happening at the house. I brought home empty supply boxes from the school office, and each evening, I spent an hour or two packing what I needed to take to my mother's house. Having a goal to work toward kept my spirits up.

As much as I wanted to be oblivious to what Jake's new lover was doing, I couldn't help but notice that Rachel was quickly making herself at home in the kitchen. When I'd come home from work, I'd find her serving Jake and Thor her latest creations: savory casseroles, pasta dishes, fresh vegetable soup, homemade cookies.

One afternoon when I walked into the kitchen, Thor looked up at me with a milk mustache and crumbs on his cheeks, chocolate-chip cookie in hand. "Boy, Mom," he said, "Rachel sure makes good food!"

I knew he was basking in Rachel's attention, and I resented the way she'd taken it upon herself to nurture him. But I suppressed surges of jealousy by reminding myself it was a short-term problem, that soon Thor and I would be gone, leaving Rachel and Jake to their own lives.

Of course, Rachel offered me the same food she prepared for Jake and Thor. I always declined, saying I wasn't hungry, that I was busy, or that I had somewhere to go. Each time, I'd see a hurt look in her eyes.

One evening, she insisted. "You've just got to try this, Lee. Please?"

Grudgingly, I seated myself at the kitchen table, while Rachel served me up a plate of rice and beans. She sat down across from me, chin resting in her hand, her eyes bright with anticipation as she awaited my response.

I didn't want her culinary presentation to be delicious, but it was. The textures were just right, the seasoning was perfect. I chewed a mouthful, and then exclaimed, "Rachel, this is wonderful!"

She smiled broadly. "I'm glad you like it. I made plenty. You can have more if you want."

"What do you call this?" I asked.

"I don't know. I haven't named it yet."

"You mean you made this up? This is your own recipe?"

She nodded. "I just came up with it today."

"Rachel," I said, "you told me you don't do anything. But you cook. That's something."

She sat with her eyes downcast. "Oh, it's no big deal." Suddenly, she stood up. "I want to show you something." She left the room, and returned a minute later carrying a small metal box with a hinged lid.

"These are my recipes," she said, opening the box to show me the cards inside. "I've been collecting them for years, and I take them wherever I go. I write down the recipes I make up so I won't forget them."

She ran her finger along the top of the cards. "This box is getting too full. Jake told me he'd make me a new one, a wooden one with more room. I can't wait till it's finished."

The now-familiar jealousy welled within me, but I pushed it aside to offer Rachel some well-deserved praise. "You know, Rachel, you could do something with your talent. You could have a career in the culinary arts."

"Oh, I don't know," she mumbled. Her face darkened, and she hung her head. I realized I must have sounded like her parents, trying to steer her toward a productive lifestyle.

Because I was so distracted by the changes in the household, I was caught off guard when Thor said, "It's my birthday next week, isn't it?"

"Of course it is, sweetie," I responded, pretending like I hadn't forgotten all about it. Then, like a good mother, I went out shopping for party invitations and decorations.

Ten of Thor's first-grade classmates accepted his last-minute invitation. The party was scheduled for a Friday evening, and Friday morning found me flying around the kitchen baking batches of cupcakes.

"Let me help," Rachel said from the kitchen doorway.

"Okay," I consented. I felt too desperate to decline her offer.

She picked up a cooled cupcake and skillfully smoothed on the chocolate frosting. After finishing a dozen, she said, "I've got an idea." She arranged the cupcakes on a serving platter. "We can decorate them with different kinds of candy and make it look like a big clown face. I know just how to do it. I'll get Jake to take me to the store to get everything we need."

Before I could consent to her idea, Rachel was off on her mission, and I didn't know whether to be offended or grateful. Half an hour later, she was back with bags of candy. Without saying a word, she expertly created a goofy, smiling face.

I laughed out loud when I saw it. "Rachel, that's awesome! Thor will love it."

"I'm glad you like it," she said. "That means a lot to me." Apparently energized by my approval, she busied herself with cleaning up the messy kitchen. Later, she helped me blow up several dozen balloons and drape streamers around the living room.

I convinced Jake that he needed to make an appearance at his son's party, although I knew he didn't want to. Thor was delighted with his clown cupcakes, and if he hadn't previously been a fan of Rachel, her performance that day would have certainly won him over. But just about the time Thor's friends began to arrive, Rachel disappeared.

Thor was the first to notice her absence. "Where's Rachel?" he asked.

I glanced at Jake. He shrugged and shook his head.

Thor looked at me with a glint of anger in his eyes. "Mom, did you tell Rachel she couldn't be at my party?"

"Of course not, honey!" I said, stung by his suspicion. "Rachel should definitely be at your party." To prove my goodwill, I added, "I'll go see if she's in her room."

I walked down the hall and knocked on Rachel's closed door. "Come in," she called in a weak voice. I opened the door, and found her lying in bed, huddled under the covers.

"What are you doing, Rachel?" I asked. "Are you feeling sick?"

"No," she said.

"Then what's wrong?"

"I'm just sad."

"Why? You were having such a good time earlier today."

"I know. But when I see you and Jake and Thor together, I remember that you're a family, and I'm not part of it. I don't belong here."

"Oh, for Heaven's sake, Rachel!" I said. "Thor expects you to be at the party. Now get up and come on out."

Rachel pushed back the covers and slowly sat up, brushing a tear from her cheek with the back of her hand. I looked at her sitting there in her threadbare jeans and sloppy tee shirt, her shoulders slumped, her long hair hanging in her face. Suddenly, I ran out of patience with her pathetic presentation.

"Rachel," I said sternly. "Don't you have something better to wear? I've dressed up a little bit, and even Jake put on a nice shirt."

She surveyed my outfit, a colorful cotton skirt and a bright pink top. "I don't have nice clothes like yours, Lee," she pouted.

"Don't tell me you didn't bring anything besides blue jeans and tee shirts in those duffel bags." I threw open her closet door and rifled through the scant amount of clothing hanging there, and then pulled out a tunic embellished with embroidery and beads. "This is cute," I said. "Put it on. Then go to the bathroom and brush your hair."

I left her room and rejoined the party. "Rachel's coming," I informed Thor. "She wasn't feeling well, and she needed to lie down for a little bit."

Ten minutes later, I saw her standing in the doorway of the living room, wearing the colorful top I'd picked out. Her hair was brushed and tucked behind her ears, and she'd put on a pair of large hoop earrings. I couldn't be certain, but it looked like she was wearing makeup, a touch of eye shadow and some lip gloss.

She looked exotic, like a gypsy princess. I glanced at Jake. He was staring at his lover like he wanted to devour her.

The next evening, Thor and I celebrated his birthday at my mother's house. I was relieved that it was just the three of us, free from the drama surrounding the previous night's party. I loaded several boxes I'd packed into the back seat of my car, thinking I'd get a jump on the moving process.

My mother informed Thor that seven was a number of great spiritual significance, and that his seventh birthday was indeed a very special event. After lighting some sage and sweet-grass, she did some chanting. Then she presented Thor with his first drum, and the three of us drummed together, celebrating the fact that Thor had reached the milestone of living on the planet for seven years.

The vibrations from the drumming began to melt the tension that had accumulated in my body. I felt at peace in the familiar surroundings of my mother's home, with its comforting scents and sounds. I whispered a prayer of gratitude for my good fortune in having a mother who was most certainly my best friend in the entire world.

After the drumming, we continued our celebration with a birthday cake and ice cream. When Thor was finished eating, he couldn't wait to get back to his drum. My mother and I lingered at the table.

"How are things going at Jake's house?" she asked as she poured me a mug of herbal tea.

"It's interesting, for sure," I said. "It's been hard having Rachel around. She takes a lot out of me."

My mother fixed her compassionate gaze on my face. "I can see that. You look like your energy has been drained. Your world has been turned upside down, hasn't it, River?"

She took a sip of tea. "Mine has been shaken as well, honey. I have some news of my own." She smiled, yet I saw tears in her eyes.

Panic welled inside me. "What is it, Mom? I can't tell whether you're happy or sad."

"Both, I'd say. The sad part is that your father's condition is getting worse. He had to resign from teaching."

"Oh, no," I said. "I was afraid that was coming."

"But the happy part," she continued, "is that Larry has sold his house, and he'll be moving here with me so that I can take care of him." Then she filled me in on the plans they'd made over the past several months.

The thought of having my parents back together pleased me. "Mom," I said, "I think it's terrific that Dad's coming here." But then I stopped short when I envisioned by father, Thor, and me all converging on my mother at the same time. "Aren't you afraid it will be too much for you if Thor and I move in? I don't want to overload you."

"Oh, honey," she said, "I didn't mean to suggest that you shouldn't come. Not at all. We have three bedrooms. We'll just have to move things around to make room for everybody. I think it'll be wonderful for Thor to get to know his grandfather better. We don't know how many years Larry has left on the planet."

Even though I agreed to follow through with my moving plans, my mother's news left me feeling uncertain, and I decided to leave my packed boxes in my car. Then on the drive back home, Thor said something that pushed me over the edge of uncertainty and plunged me into a state of turmoil.

"I changed my mind, Mom."

"About what, Thor?"

"About going to Grandma's house this summer. I don't want to."

"Why not?"

"Because I want to be with Rachel. If we go to Grandma's house, Rachel might be gone by the time we come back home, and I won't even get to say goodbye to her."

"I see." My thoughts spun wildly, and it took all my mental strength to keep my focus on driving.

We rode in silence for a few minutes. Then Thor asked, "Are you mad, Mom?"

"Oh, no, sweetie," I said. "I'm just thinking about what we might do this summer if we don't go to Grandma's."

After I tucked Thor into bed that night, I went to my room and sat on my bed, staring forlornly at the packed boxes stacked against my wall, trying to come to grips with the fact that moving to my mother's house was no longer a viable plan.

It seemed I'd reached the end of a road, with nowhere to turn. I knew I couldn't afford to rent a place for Thor and me on a part-time teacher's salary. And even if I could, the idea of leaving Jake's house would be terribly upsetting to Thor.

I desperately wished I could turn back time, that it could be just Jake, Thor, and me again, and that I could have one more chance to work on creating a proper family life.

"What do I do now?" I whispered. "What do I do now?"

And then an idea popped into my mind. I couldn't see the bigger picture yet, but I could see a possible next step. If there was no way to move out of the house, I could at least move to the other side of the house. I could completely vacate the new addition, leaving it to Jake and Rachel, and set up quarters for myself and Thor in the original part of the house. I envisioned myself creating a little apartment for the two of us, as far away from Jake and Rachel as we could get.

Relieved to have a plan, I laughed out loud, then got up and walked down the hall to Jake's studio. He was alone, sitting at his potter's wheel, his attention riveted on the piece he was creating. He glanced up when I entered the room.

"What's up, Lee?"

"Jake," I said. "It isn't going to work out for Thor and me to move to my mother's house right now. Would you mind if we stay awhile longer, until I can come up with another plan?"

Jake stopped what he was doing to give me his full attention. "That's fine, Lee," he said. "I never said you had to move out in the first place. You and Thor can stay as long as you want to."

I exhaled deeply. "Thanks, Jake. I know it's weird for me to stick around here, but I really don't have any other options right now."

"Why does it have to be weird, Lee?" he asked. "There's no reason why we all can't get along together. I think we've done a pretty good job of it these past three weeks."

You don't know how hard I've worked to put up with Rachel, I thought. But then it occurred to me that Jake might have had to work pretty hard himself.

I knew I couldn't settle down and fall asleep until I called my mother to inform her of the change in plans. "I know it's late, Mom," I said when she answered the phone, "but I had to tell you this. Thor and I won't be moving in with you this summer. He isn't ready to leave this house, and with Dad coming, it just doesn't seem like the thing to do."

"I sensed it wasn't quite the right time for you," my mother said. "Come when you're ready, River."

Chapter 10

Rachel hugged me when she heard I wasn't moving out of the house. "I was just getting to know you," she said. "Now I get to spend more time with you."

She helped me carry my things from the hallway bedroom to the room that housed my studio. Her thin arms looked like they were going to break as she lugged heavy boxes from one side of the house to the other.

My new room had been the house's original master bedroom, and it was quite large. I moved my art supplies to one side and set up my bed and furniture on the other side. I sorted out belongings I wasn't using at the time and stored them in the room I'd just vacated.

"Why are you moving again, Mom?" Thor asked in the middle of the project.

"Because I miss you," I said. "I want to be closer to you."

"Mom," he scolded, "I'm not a little baby anymore. I don't need to be watched all the time." He cocked his head and looked at me with questioning eyes. "Why don't you and Dad sleep in the same room? That's what moms and dads usually do."

I suddenly felt weak, and I set down the box I was carrying. *This is your opportunity,* I told myself. *You can tell Thor the whole story. That Mommy and Daddy aren't together any more. That they never really loved each other like they should have. That they stayed together so you would have a nice place to live. And now Daddy loves Rachel, and that's why they sleep on the other side of the house and Mommy's moving over here next to you.*

I opened my mouth to explain, but as I looked at my son's innocent face, I couldn't bring myself to deliver the news that would turn his world upside down. Not that day. So I said, "Well, that's not the way all families do it."

That summer, I devoted myself to the project of redecorating my end of the house. I painted our bedrooms, the bathroom, and the living-room with fresh new colors. I bought new bedspreads, linens and curtains for the bedrooms, and a shower curtain with matching towels for the bathroom. I put up fancy new window treatments in the living-room, and I loaded the shelves with my own books and knickknacks. I spread my own magazines out on the coffee table. Instead of using the side door, I developed the habit of using the front door as my entry and exit point, which enabled me to stay out of Jake and Rachel's wing of the house for days at a time.

I didn't ask Jake's permission to make the changes, as I knew he wouldn't care. He rarely ventured into the original part of the house, other than to eat in the kitchen.

Rachel seemingly became bored when left to her own devices, and that summer, she wandered over to my side of the house several times a day. Whenever I'd start a new project, she'd insist on getting involved, and while she was often helpful, she was perpetually on my last nerve.

I'd made it clear to her that I'd moved to my new room so we all could have more privacy, but she seemed bent on bridging the gap between the two ends of the house. One day, she stood in the doorway of my newly decorated room and said, "Wow, Lee, this looks beautiful! Can we do my room next?"

"Rachel, that's between you and Jake," I said. "Take it up with him."

"Oh." She walked away looking dejected.

The minute I'd curl up on the sofa with a book, I'd hear a childlike voice asking, "Whatcha doin', Lee?" I'd look up to find Rachel standing in the living-room doorway. She'd plop down on the other end of the sofa and attempt to engage me in conversation. When she'd fail to get my full attention, she get down on the floor and play a board game with Thor or help him build something with his Leggos. Thor was delighted to have a new playmate in the house.

"I like spending time in this room," Rachel would often say when we were in the living-room together. "You've got it fixed up so pretty." Much as I wished she'd go away, I had to admit the space was as much hers as it was mine.

The second weekend in June, Jake attended an art show, and he took Rachel with him. I was glad Thor and I could have the house to ourselves, but he moped because he missed Rachel.

"Why does she have to go with Dad?" he asked, angrily folding his arms across his chest.

"Because he needs help with his booth," I said. "It gets busy, and he can use an extra set of hands."

"Why don't you go with him?"

"Because I have things I need to do here, honey."

But the following weekend, Rachel didn't accompany Jake on his travels. I sensed they'd had a spat, as she was sulky. I didn't ask about it, because I was determined to stay out of their relationship problems. I had plans to attend a solstice party with my drumming group Saturday evening, and Thor was going to spend the night with my mother.

"You can leave Thor here with me." Rachel's voice was plaintive. "I'm good at babysitting."

Oh, no you don't, I thought. *I'm not giving you a chance to bond with my son while I'm gone. You've wiggled your way far enough into his life.* Aloud, I said, "But he's looking forward to spending time with his grandmother, and now his grandfather is there, too. They've got special plans for him this evening."

Rachel looked panicky. "Then I'm going to be all alone tonight."

Her immaturity disgusted me. "Rachel, it's no big deal. I've spent many evenings alone here. There's nothing to be afraid of."

"I don't do well alone," she whimpered. I shrugged and walked away. She followed me. "Lee, can I go with you?"

I stopped and turned to face her, searching my mind for a response to her request. I'd been looking forward to this event, to being away from the drama of the house. I wanted to be with friends who knew nothing of Jake and Rachel, who knew me only as the artist River Jorgensen.

"I don't know, Rachel. I don't think you'd be comfortable at a solstice party."

"Please, Lee," she begged. "Please don't leave me alone here."

"All right, then," I said irritably. "I'm going to run Thor over to my mother's late this afternoon. Then I'll come back here to get ready. We need to leave by 7:00 PM. Okay?" I walked away from her, kicking myself for giving in.

That evening, I made special efforts in getting ready for the party. I put on a pair of elegant palazzo pants and a spaghetti strap top that showed a bit of cleavage, accenting the outfit with some of my showiest jewelry. As I styled my hair, I admitted to myself that I was trying for a sexy look that night. I wanted male attention, as years of being ignored by Jake had made me question my feminine allure.

I thought about some of the men who'd previously shown an interest in me: Nate the musician, Pete the writer, Andrew the yoga instructor. Now that I was officially released from the ambiguous arrangement with Jake, I felt free to welcome their advances. For the hundredth time that afternoon, I wished I hadn't taken on the baggage of looking after Rachel.

A few minutes before 7:00 o'clock, I knocked on her bedroom door. "Are you ready to go?" I called.

She opened the door and gasped at the sight of me. "Oh, Lee, you're so beautiful!" She reached out her hand as if she wanted to touch me. I took a step back, feeling uncomfortable.

"I wish I looked like you," she said, still staring at me. Suddenly, she pulled her ratty tee shirt over her head. "Look at this."

Caught off guard by her action, I was momentarily riveted on the sight in front of me. I hadn't realized how thin Rachel actually was. Her ribs were disturbingly prominent, and her belly, revealed by her low-cut jeans, was nearly concave. The only fleshy parts of her torso were her tiny little buds of breasts, which looked like they belonged to an eleven-year-old girl verging on puberty.

"I don't understand," she said, gesturing toward herself. "Why would Jake want this when he could have someone as beautiful as you?"

I glanced away. "Get dressed, Rachel, we've got to go."

She made no move to put her shirt back on. "What should I wear,

Lee?" she asked, standing half-naked in front of her open closet. "Help me find something."

"You can figure that out, Rachel," I said. "Your jeans are fine. Just put on a nice top." I backed out of the room and closed the door, shaking my head in disbelief.

The solstice party was held at the home of a member of the drumming circle. As Rachel and I approached the small cabin perched on a wooded lot, the crackling of a bonfire drew us around to the back yard. A number of people had already gathered, seated on benches arranged around the fire or on blankets spread out on the ground. I'd brought along a tote bag containing two small drums, several rattles and a blanket for us to sit on. I'd also packed a sweater for myself to put on when the night turned chilly. At the last minute, I'd packed one for Rachel, too, knowing she wouldn't think of that detail.

Rachel clutched my arm when she saw the crowd of people. "What are we supposed to do?" she asked, even though I'd tried to prepare her for the event on the drive over.

"There's nothing to worry about," I said. "We'll just find a place to sit. When it's time to start, the leader will begin drumming. He sets the beat, and others join in. It all happens naturally. After a little bit, you'll get into it. It's very relaxing, and it'll put you in a spacey mood."

"Okay," she said. "But promise to stay with me, Lee. Don't leave me alone. I get nervous around lots of people."

She huddled close to me while I greeted friends, and I sensed she was jealous of the attention I was giving them. "Why do they keep calling you River?" she asked.

"That's my real name," I explained. "Some people call me River, some people call me Lee. Here, they know me as River."

"I don't like it," she said. "It doesn't sound right."

We spread our blanket on the ground, and I laid out the instruments so Rachel could take her choice. She picked up a hand drum. "How do I do this?"

"Just tap it with your hand," I said, feeling impatient with her childishness. "Or you can use a drum stick. It doesn't matter. When we start, you'll see that everybody does their own thing."

When everyone was finally seated, the group leader gave a short speech on the significance of the solstice.

"What's he talking about?" Rachel whispered a little too loudly. "I don't understand."

"I'll explain later," I whispered back, embarrassed by her disruption.

The leader then began a loud, steady beat on his drum. Others joined in. Rachel looked at me uncertainly as I began to beat my own drum, then tentatively followed suit.

Within minutes, she seemed to shed her self-consciousness. She threw herself into the rhythm of the drumming, her eyes closed, her body swaying, seemingly lost in another world.

After some time, a group of women got up and began dancing around the fire. Rachel opened her eyes when she heard the commotion. "That looks like fun," she whispered to me. "Let's dance. Will you come with me?"

"No," I said. "I don't feel like dancing right now. I'd rather drum. But go ahead if you want to. Just get up and join in."

Rachel slowly stood up, watching for a few minutes before stepping forward into the circle of dancing women. Once she began to move, her excitement took over. As she danced her way around the fire, her skinny arms and legs flailed wildly. The sight of her chaotic movements embarrassed me, and I wanted to look away. Yet, I felt compelled to keep a watchful eye on her.

But her movement gradually found the rhythm of the drums. Then her feet began to step in double-time to the beat the other dancers were keeping. I was surprised she was able to keep up the frenetic activity. I knew she was attracting attention, and that she stood out as a curiosity.

As she continued to dance, her movements became increasingly fluid. I watched in amazement as the awkward woman-child transformed into a graceful, leaping goddess, the spirit of the solstice itself. Awestruck, I was unable to take my eyes off her, and I sensed everyone else in the circle shared my experience.

I was momentarily distracted when my friend Nate seated himself next to me on my blanket. I turned and smiled at him, thrilled by the close proximity of this attractive man.

"Who's the girl you brought with you, River?" he asked, leaning in close so I could hear him above the beat of the drums. "I've never seen her here before."

"That's Rachel," I said. "It's her first time."

Nate's eyes were riveted on Rachel's dancing figure. "She's awesome. I've never seen anyone dance like that. It's sensual . . . very sensual. It's like she's floating. I could swear her feet aren't even touching the ground."

How is it that skinny, annoying little Rachel casts such a spell over men? I wondered. *How is it that a man who previously found me attractive now looks right past me and sees only Rachel?*

"Where's she from?" Nate asked.

"Chicago." I hesitated, deciding to eliminate some of the awkward details. "She lives in Niles now."

"Will you introduce us?"

"She's with somebody."

"Who?"

I hesitated again. "A friend of mine."

"Guess I'm out of luck, then." Nate stood up. "See you later, River."

The dancers were beginning to tire. One by one, they dropped out of the circle and went back to their seats. Apparently oblivious to the loss of her companions, Rachel kept on dancing until she was the only one left. All eyes were riveted on the slender ethereal form whose graceful movements floated on the waves of sound.

Suddenly, she stopped, coming back into her awkward earthly body. She looked around fearfully, disoriented while the crowd applauded in appreciation of her performance. Then she spotted me and rushed back to our blanket. Collapsing against my side, she laid her head on my shoulder.

After a few minutes, her body grew limp and heavier, and her breathing became slow and deep. I realized she'd fallen asleep.

"Rachel," I whispered, giving her a nudge.

She startled and shifted her position, then lay down on the blanket with her head resting on my thigh. Shivering, she clutched her arms. "I'm c-c-cold."

I pulled a sweater out of my bag and spread it across her shoulders. Within seconds, she was sleeping again. Without thinking, I began stroking her hair, the same way I did with Thor when I tucked him in bed at night.

Chapter 11

The next morning, I awoke feeling saturated with Rachel's energy, like I'd overdosed on spending time with her, and I felt a desperate need for solitude. I was planning to pick up Thor at my mother's house after lunch, but I told myself the morning hours would be mine.

I hadn't painted since Rachel had moved in. I was eager to reconnect with my artist self, to let go of the frustrations of the previous weeks and ground myself in my work again. I set up my easel for an oil painting, keeping my door closed to prevent a certain unwanted guest from wandering in.

As I gazed at my blank canvas, I envisioned a mystical landscape. Then I picked up a brush and began to paint, my mind relaxing and flowing into my work as I outlined the images in my enchanted forest.

But in spite of my open window, the fumes from the paint and turpentine became too strong, and I was forced to open my door for added ventilation.

Within a minute, Rachel strolled into my bedroom. I figured she'd been hovering around my door, waiting for the moment when she could enter. She was in a buoyant mood, and I suspected she was convinced that after our last night's shared experience, we were now best friends.

She sat on my bed watching me paint, and like a three-year-old, she plied me with relentless pesky questions about what I was doing.

"Rachel, I can't concentrate when you keep talking to me," I finally said.

"Sorry," she said, unperturbed. She got up and walked around my room, looking at things on my shelves and dresser top, picking up objects and turning them over in her hands.

I tried to ignore her, but I couldn't, and I ended up speaking more sharply than I intended to. "Rachel, would you please stop that? You're making me nervous. I'm afraid you're going to drop something and break it."

Sighing, she put down the delicate glass unicorn she was holding and strolled over to my open closet, where she seated herself cross-legged on the floor and began rifling through a box of old paintings I'd stored there. She started to ask me another question, but stopped herself. "Whoops, I'm sorry," she giggled.

Suddenly, she called out, "Leah Jorgensen?"

"Huh?" I said as I rendered a delicate stroke on the gnarled tree branch I was painting.

She scrambled up off the floor, holding one of the old canvasses. "It says right here, Leah Jorgensen." She pointed to my signature in the corner. "I thought you signed your name Lee Jorgensen."

"I do," I said. "That's one of my really old paintings. I used to sign my name as Leah. Then I changed to using Lee."

"Is your name really Leah?"

"That's my middle name. My full name is River Leah Jorgensen."

Rachel stared at me, openmouthed.

"What's the big deal?" I snapped.

"I can't believe it. Jacob, Leah, and Rachel. The three of us living together. That's just freaky!"

"Rachel, I don't know what on earth you're talking about," I said, impatient for the conversation to be over.

"Don't you know that story?"

"What story?"

"About Jacob, Leah, and Rachel."

"Never heard of it."

"You mean you don't know it from your Christian Bible?"

"Rachel, I wasn't exactly raised Christian," I said, keeping my eyes on my work. "So there wasn't much Bible reading in my home."

"Wait just a minute," she said. "I'll show you." She ran out of the room, and I wondered what nonsense she was going to bring back. She returned a few minutes later carrying a thick, worn book.

"This is the Tanakh," she said. "It's kind of like a Bible, only it's for Jews."

Given the fact that Rachel was alienated from her parents, I was surprised that she still clung to their religion. "Did you bring that with you?" I asked.

"Yes," she said. "My Tanakh and my recipe box. I take them everywhere I go." She grinned sheepishly. "I know, I know. I'm not a very good Jew, and I don't even like Jewish people that much. But every now and then, I like to take out my Tanakh and read a little bit. I guess it makes me feel secure."

She opened the book, thumbing through the pages until she found the passage she was looking for. Then she began reading aloud, her eyes following her finger as it underlined the words.

Laban said to Jacob, "Just because you are a kinsman, should you serve me for nothing? Tell me, what shall your wages be?" Now Laban had two daughters; the name of the older one was Leah and the name of the younger one was Rachel.

Rachel looked up at me. "That's like us. You're the older one, I'm the younger one."

I shrugged and continued to paint. Rachel resumed her reading.

Leah had weak eyes.

She looked up again, grinning at me. "Do you have weak eyes, Leah?"

"My eyes are just fine," I said, irritated. "I have twenty-twenty vision."

Rachel was shapely and beautiful. Jacob loved Rachel; so he answered, "I will serve you seven years for your younger daughter Rachel." Laban said, "Better that I give her to you than that I should give her to an outsider. Stay with me." So Jacob served seven years for Rachel, and they seemed but a few days because of his love for her.

In spite of my intention to feign indifference, I found myself intrigued by Rachel's story. I put down my brush and listened with full attention.

Then Jacob said to Laban, "Give me my wife, for my time is fulfilled, that I may cohabit with her." And Laban gathered all the people of the place and made a feast. When evening came, he took his daughter Leah and brought her to him; and he cohabited with her. When morning came, there was Leah! So he said to Laban, "What is this you have done to me? I was in your service for Rachel! Why did you deceive me?" Laban said, "It is not the practice in our place to marry off the younger before the older. Wait until the bridal week of this one is over and we will give you that one too, provided you will serve me another seven years." Jacob did so; he waited out the bridal week of the one, and then he gave him his daughter Rachel as wife. And Jacob cohabited with Rachel also; indeed he loved Rachel more than Leah.

When Rachel looked up from her reading, it was the first time I'd ever seen a smug smile on her face. This girl, who seemingly envied me in every way, had discovered a way to feel superior. "I don't think this is true about us," she said, her words belying her facial expression. "I'm sure Jake loved you as much as he does me, maybe even more."

"Jake and I were never in love," I said.

"Oh," she said, smirking. "Then I guess it is kind of true." She turned a page of the Tanakh. "There's more."

I interrupted her before she could resume her reading. "Rachel, I don't want to hear any more." Her story revolted me, and for a moment, I thought I might need to run to the bathroom to vomit.

"I'm sorry," Rachel said, still grinning. "Did I upset you?"

"No," I lied, "but the whole thing is creepy, and I don't want to talk about it anymore."

"Okay." She closed the Tanakh and set it aside. "But I'm going to start calling you Leah."

"Why on earth would you do that?" I asked, anger in my voice. My great-grandmother's name, which I'd once cherished, now seemed tarnished.

"Because it sounds Jewish," Rachel said. "It makes me feel closer to you, like we're sisters." But I knew full well it was her way of reminding me that I was playing out the role of the pitiful, weak-eyed, unloved first wife of Jacob.

"You need to leave now, Rachel," I said through gritted teeth. "I need some peace and quiet."

Rachel insisted that Thor and I join her and Jake around the oak table for dinner that evening. I desperately didn't want to eat with them, but I knew if I declined, Thor would be upset.

"Leah, would you please pass the bread?" she asked in a voice dripping with contrived sweetness.

"Why did you call her that?" Thor asked. "Grandma calls her River and Daddy calls her Lee. Nobody calls her Leah."

"Because I like the name." Rachel hesitated, and then looked at Jake. "Today I read Leah the story from the Tanakh about Jacob, Leah, and Rachel."

How dare you, Rachel, I thought, seething with anger. *You invited me to the dinner table just to humiliate me?*

I sat with my head lowered, toying with my food, but glanced at Jake from the corner of my eye. His face looked like a thundercloud, and I knew his Christian upbringing had rendered him well aware of the story.

"Please don't call me Leah," I said.

"You heard her," Jake said to Rachel, his voice low and firm. "Don't call her that. She goes by Lee."

But neither Jake nor I ever succeeded in breaking her of the habit.

As the first Saturday in July approached, I realized that, with the distraction of Rachel's arrival in our household, Jake and I had completely forgotten about the June contra dance. I caught him alone in his workshop and broached the subject of the July dance.

"There's something we haven't talked about, Jake," I said. "Who gets the contra dance, you or me?"

He looked up from the cabinet he was varnishing. "What do you mean, who gets it?"

"Well," I said, "I think it might be a little awkward if both of us go when we're not together anymore."

"I don't know, Lee," he said, turning back to his work. "I don't have time to think about that right now. If you want to go Saturday, go ahead."

So that Saturday evening, I put on my dancing shoes and a full prairie skirt that flared beautifully when I twirled, and Thor and I drove to the park pavilion in Elkhart.

"Why isn't Dad coming?" Thor asked on the way over.

"He's busy tonight," I responded. "He has lots of orders he needs to build for customers."

"Then we should've brought Rachel."

"I don't think she knows how to dance," I said, grasping at a feeble excuse for the behavior that appeared so ungracious in my son's eyes.

"We could teach her. It's not that hard."

I could think of nothing else to say. Thor turned away from me and stared out the car window.

When are you going to stop lying to him? I asked myself. *When are you going to tell your son the truth about the new arrangement in our household?* But I couldn't envision a way out of the hole I'd dug for myself.

Thor had been around contra dancing all his life, and was skillful enough to participate in the easier dances. He and I partnered up for the first dance, giggling as we held hands and galloped up and down the set. I felt lighthearted and free, happy that I didn't have the burden of Rachel tagging along with me.

Then Thor ran off to play with several other children. I hooked up with other partners and danced with joyous abandon, relishing the freedom of being single, of not having to restrain myself for the sake of loyalty to Jake.

The fourth dance was another easy one, and Thor came back to join me. "Oh, good!" he said as we were lining up in the set. "Dad and Rachel came after all."

"What?" I exclaimed a little too sharply.

Thor pointed to the top of the set, where Jake was standing on the men's side and Rachel was positioned opposite him on the women's side.

I was seized by a rage so powerful, I could barely focus on the familiar steps of the simple dance we were performing. As the parallel lines moved in opposite directions up and down the set, I eventually ended up dancing with Jake for a minute.

"What are you doing here?" I hissed. "Why did you come? Why did you bring Rachel?"

Anger flickered in his eyes. "We can't get into this now, Lee."

"Then meet me outside at the break."

After the dance ended, I made a beeline for the door. I waited outside the pavilion for what seemed like an hour before Jake came out. He looked at me warily. "What do you want, Lee?"

"You told me I could come tonight," I said, "and then you showed up with Rachel! What were you thinking?"

"I didn't tell you I wasn't going to come." Jake's voice sounded defensive. "I really wasn't planning on it, but I changed my mind at the last minute."

"Why?"

"Because Rachel wanted to come."

"Of course!" I said sarcastically. "Damn it, Jake, she ruins everything!"

Jake crossed his arms over his chest and took a step back, as if my anger was too much for him. "Well, she asked where you were going, and I told her about the dance. She got excited and wanted to see what it was all about. What was I supposed to do? Anyway, this dance is open to everybody. I've got a right to be here, and so does Rachel."

I stood with my hands on my hips, glaring at him, knowing that if I opened my mouth, I would say terrible things I would later regret.

"I don't need this from you, Lee," Jake said. "I've got enough on my plate right now."

"What? Is Rachel giving you problems?" I took wicked delight in the thought of difficulties between them.

Jake glared back at me. "I didn't come here to argue with you, Lee. I'm going back inside to dance."

As he turned his back on me and walked through the door, tears of frustration spilled from my eyes. I knew I was in no condition to go back inside, so I sat down on a bench in the shadows outside the pavilion. I heard the caller instructing the dancers to line up, and then the band began playing a lively Celtic tune. Half an hour earlier, I'd been on top of the world, but now I was feeling alienated and left out, something I'd never before experienced at the contra dance.

Then someone stepped out the door. I saw that it was Amanda, one of the dancers I didn't particularly care for, as she was a little rough around the edges for my taste. She lit a cigarette, took a drag, and then looked around as she exhaled the smoke. She startled when she saw me.

"Oh, geez, River, I didn't see you sittin' there when I came out. You scared the hell outa me. What are you doin' out here? You don't smoke."

I was glad I was sitting in the shadows so she couldn't see the tears on my face. "I'm cooling off," I said.

"Yeah," she said. "It's pretty hot in there." A moment later, she laughed when she caught the double meaning of my statement. "Oh, you're pissed off at somebody. Who? Your old man? I don't blame you. He's gettin' pretty cozy with that Rachel chick in there. People are startin' to talk. If I were you, I'd get back in there and break those two up."

"Well, Amanda," I said, "Jake's not my man any more. He's with Rachel now."

Amanda stared at me in disbelief. "Oh really? Since when?"

I didn't intend to air my dirty laundry, but it felt good to have someone sympathize with my predicament. "Jake and I haven't really been together for quite awhile."

"Seriously? I thought you and Jake were the type who'd be together forever. When did you move out?"

"I didn't move out," I said, feeling like I was getting in over my head with the conversation. "I'm just living on the other side of the house."

"And you sit there and watch Jake go runnin' out with another woman?"

"Well, not actually run out. Rachel lives there now. She and Jake live in one end of the house, and my son and I live in the other end."

"What the hell?" Amanda exclaimed. "Why the fuck do you sit there and put up with that bullshit?"

Her rude confrontation was beginning to irritate me. "I'm doing the best I can for my son," I said. "If it wasn't for Thor, I'd be long gone. I would've left years ago. But Thor doesn't want to leave, and Jake and I are trying to make the best of this. Live and let live, you know."

Amanda smirked. "Oh, I forgot. You and Jake believe in all that hippie love and peace stuff." She took another drag off her cigarette. "But if you ask me, River, you're lettin' your kid run your life. Did you ever think that's not fair to you? You got rights too, you know. And if I were you, I'd tell that son-of-a-bitch Jake to go to hell. I mean, you're a good-lookin' classy woman, and he leaves you for that skinny little twit?"

She dropped her cigarette butt on the ground and crushed it with her foot. "Take it easy, River." Then she turned and walked back into the pavilion.

Amanda's outspoken opinion served to displace my anger toward Jake and Rachel onto her. I sat on my bench fuming, kicking myself for having said anything to her. Then I sank into my dark thoughts again. *How did I get myself into such a mess? How will I ever explain this to Thor? Maybe it will be easier when he's a little older. Or maybe I should just do it now and get it over with.*

The music stopped, and I realized that while I'd been moping on my park bench, another dance had started and ended. *It's time to pull yourself together,* I scolded myself. I decided to make a quick trip to the restroom to make sure there were no traces of my crying spell left on my face. But then Rachel stepped out the door.

"This is so much fun, Leah!" she exclaimed. "I'm so glad I came. I don't think I've ever had this much fun before!" When I failed to respond to her excitement, she peered at me curiously. "Are you all right, Leah? It looks like you've been crying. Are you upset with me? Have I done something?"

It's not so much that you've done something, I thought. *It's your very existence that makes me miserable.* But I sighed and said, "No, Rachel, I'm not upset with you."

"But you're upset about something. I can tell."

"It's nothing."

She seated herself next to me on the bench. "That's not true, Leah.

Tell me the truth."

"Well, I suppose it's all these changes that have happened the past few weeks. I think it's all catching up to me."

"I know." Rachel's voice sounded wise and mature. "It's been hard on all of us." She linked her arm through mine. "We'll get through this together, Leah."

I found her words oddly comforting, and I wondered how I could be reassured by the person who was the source of my unhappiness.

"Come, Leah, let's go in and dance." When I didn't budge, Rachel gently shook my arm. "You don't let me get away with moping. The same goes for you."

By the time we walked back into the pavilion, the dancers were lined up and ready to start. There were more women than men in attendance that evening, and no male partners were left for Rachel and me.

Rachel held out her hand with a little bow. "Dance with me, Leah. I'll be the man."

I laughed in spite of my annoyance with her. "I don't think you can do the man's part, Rachel. It'll be too confusing for you. I'll be the man. I've done it before."

We muddled through the dance reasonably well, given the fact that Rachel was new at contra dancing and I wasn't entirely confident in the male role. We did a modified swing, the way two women did when they danced together, which involved us encircling each others' waists with our arms. Rachel felt so light, I was afraid I'd crush her if I squeezed her too tightly. She hung onto my waist with her skinny arm as if her life depended on it.

Then out of the blue, she tickled my side, making me jump.

"What the hell, Rachel?" I exclaimed. She didn't seem to pick up on my irritation, and giggled so hysterically that she lost her place in the dance.

After the dance ended, she bounced up and down, as if she wasn't ready to be still. "Wasn't that fun?" she chortled. "Dance with me again, Leah."

Just then, Thor ran up to me, and I used the diversion to avoid responding to Rachel's request. "Did you come to dance with me, sweetie?" I asked him as I ruffled his hair.

"No," he responded. "Dance with Dad. You haven't danced with him all night. I'll dance with Rachel."

Feeling chastened by my son, I glanced across the hall to where Jake was standing. Catching his eye, I mouthed the words, "Want to dance?" He nodded. We both walked to the lines that were forming and took our places opposite each other.

I looked across the set at my tall, well-built partner, his face glistening with sweat, his bulging biceps exposed by the short sleeves of his tee shirt, his torso tapering from his broad shoulders to his narrow, blue-jean clad hips. I was once again aware that I'd partnered up with not only the best male dancer, but undeniably the best-looking man at the dance. Suddenly, I felt a little giddy, as if indulging in a secret delight that was now off limits to me.

As we swung together, smoothly, perfectly balanced, each of us executing impeccable footwork, I gazed into Jake's dark brown eyes and saw they held a twinkle of amusement. In spite of the fact that I was trying to keep my guard up, I couldn't help but surrender to the sheer pleasure of the moment. Against my will, I smiled at him, and he smiled back.

"Are we cool, Lee?" he asked.

"I guess so," I said, still smiling.

"I don't like it when you're mad at me." His voice sounded seductive.

"I don't like it either," I said. "We never used to get angry with each other."

"I know," he said.

Memories of our habitual post-dance lovemaking flooded my mind. I reminded myself there could be no passion between us that night. Still, it was one of the most perfect moments I'd ever shared with Jake. I knew it was impossible for him and Rachel to be that good together.

I never returned to the contra dance in Elkhart. Fortunately, I found a similar group in South Bend that actually met more frequently than the one in Elkhart. So week after week, I danced joyfully with my new friends, without the pleasure-destroying shadow of Jake and Rachel hanging over me.

I'm not sure whether Jake ever went back to the Elkhart dance. I imagine he did. But I'm quite certain he never took Rachel with him again.

Chapter 12

It seems I needed one more explosion of toxic feelings to clear the resentment from my system, one final emotional outburst to make peace with the fact that Rachel had taken my place in Jake's life, that she'd captured my son's heart, and that, like it or not, she was there to stay.

One day in the middle of July, I decided to take Thor shopping for school clothing. But when it was time to leave, I couldn't find him anywhere in the house. When I couldn't find him in the front yard or the back yard, I began to panic. Then I decided to check one more location, Jake's workshop.

Sure enough, he was there with Jake and Rachel. Thor rarely ventured into Jake's workshop on his own, and I knew he was there only because he'd accompanied his friend Rachel.

I saw Rachel running her hand over one of Jake's cabinets. "This is nice," she said. "Why don't you put some like this in our kitchen?"

I didn't give her words a second thought, as I was aggravated with my son for disappearing when he knew I was ready to go shopping. "Come on, Thor," I snapped, "we need to get going."

I had to go back to school in mid-August, a week before the students started, to attend teachers' meetings and prepare for my classes. When I came home Friday evening, thoroughly exhausted from the week's activities, I was greeted by the sight of the kitchen table sitting in the middle of the living room. It was loaded with the contents of the kitchen cabinets: dishes, cookware, and containers of food. Sounds of pounding, banging, and scraping came from the kitchen.

Then Rachel appeared in the doorway between the kitchen and living room, laughing, covered with dust, holding a sledge hammer. Thor appeared behind her, dusty as well, wielding a hammer of his own.

"Come see what we're doing, Mom," he called.

They stood aside as I stepped through the door and stared aghast at the gutted kitchen. Jake, the third dust-covered party in the wrecking crew, was busy piling up scraps of wood from the old cabinets. The stove and refrigerator were gone. I glanced out the patio door and saw them sitting on the deck.

"What on earth are you doing?" I managed to ask when I recovered from my initial shock.

Rachel jumped up and down with excitement, clapping her hands. "Jake built us new cabinets," she chortled. "And last week, we went shopping to pick out a new stove and refrigerator. They should be coming any day now. We're going to have a brand new kitchen! Isn't that awesome, Leah? It will be so much fun to cook in here."

I stared at her, incredulous. I had managed to cook in that kitchen for seven years before she'd arrived on the scene, putting up with a cantankerous stove and an ancient refrigerator whose freezer needed defrosting every other week. I'd never complained, thinking that since Jake was kind enough to keep a roof over my head, I had no right to ask for anything else. But Rachel had been there for only three months, and he was already remodeling the entire kitchen for her.

"Isn't this exciting, Leah?" Rachel persisted.

"Well, I don't know what to think." I looked at Jake. "Why wasn't I consulted about this? I live here too, you know." Without waiting for his response, I turned and rushed out of the kitchen. Rachel followed me.

"I thought you'd be happy about this, Leah," she called. "I wanted it to be a surprise for you."

I turned and glared at her, my jaw clenched with rage. Her eyes flooded with tears. "I didn't think you'd be mad, Leah."

"Well, we obviously can't cook anything for dinner tonight," I said. I stepped back toward the kitchen and poked my head through the door. "Thor, go jump in the bathtub and get cleaned up. We'll go to Grandpa and Grandma's house tonight."

"But Mom," he whined, "I want to stay here. We're going to order pizza."

"You heard me!" I said, raising my voice. "Go get cleaned up!"

He crossed his arms over his chest, glowering at me. "No!"

Thor was rarely defiant with me, and I wasn't in a state of mind to handle this unusual event. "What do you mean, no?" I shouted. "Now go do what I told you to do."

Thor didn't back down. "Why are you acting this way?" he shouted back at me. "Every time I want to do something fun with Rachel, you get mad! It's not fair!"

His accusation took the wind out of my sails. I stared at him, speechless, unable to believe my son had been reading me that well. "Okay, Thor, you can stay," I finally said. But Mommy's going to Grandpa and Grandma's."

I turned to leave, and Thor grabbed my hand. "Why don't you stay and have pizza with us, Mom?"

"Please stay, Leah," Rachel called plaintively.

"I'm sorry," I said. "I just can't." I rushed out the front door without looking back.

"Where's the little guy?" my father asked in his faint, halting voice.

It had always been difficult to read my father's emotions, more so now that his facial movements were constricted from Parkinson's, but I could see disappointment in his eyes. In the two months he'd been living at my mother's house, his affection for his grandson had deepened. Several times, I'd seen him reach out a trembling hand to ruffle Thor's curly red hair.

"Where's Thor?" my mother echoed as she came into the living-room to join my father and me.

I sank wearily onto the sofa. "He's at home with Jake and Rachel."

She looked puzzled. "Why didn't you bring him?"

"I tried to. He didn't want to come."

My mother stared at me in disbelief. My father slowly turned his head to face me. "Is it me?" He gestured awkwardly toward his rigid frame. "Is he afraid of the way I look?"

"Oh Dad, no!" I jumped up and threw my arms around him, burying my face against his bony shoulder. "Thor loves you. He loves both of you. He's just angry with me."

I sat down again, trying to muster the energy to explain the reason for my son's absence. "When I came home from work today, I walked into the house to find Jake and Rachel gutting the kitchen. I was totally shocked, because I hadn't known anything about their plans. Thor was helping them, having a great time. They were going to order pizza because nobody could cook."

"Did Thor want to stay for the pizza?" my mother asked.

"Yes, he did, but there was more to it than that. I was really upset when I saw Jake and Rachel tearing up the kitchen. Rachel and Thor were excited because they'd wanted to surprise me. Thor got angry because of the way I reacted. He wouldn't do what I asked him to do. I raised my voice, and he shouted back at me. He accused me of getting angry every time he wanted to do something with Rachel."

"Might that be the truth?" my mother asked.

"Of course it's the truth!" I buried my face in my hands. "For some reason, he's really taken to Rachel. It's like they're best friends, almost like two kids together. It's like . . . it's like she's stealing him from me, just like she stole Jake. I hate it!"

"River, River, River," my mother scolded. "You know that nothing can disrupt the bond between you and your son. Just let him enjoy his new friend. It doesn't mean he loves you less."

"I know," I said. "I'm being petty."

"River, why did the thought of a new kitchen upset you?" My mother's inquiry was gentle, and I sensed she already knew the answer to her question.

"Because Jake was doing it for Rachel," I blurted out. "She's only been there three months, and he's doing this huge thing for her. I've lived with him for more than seven years, and he's never lifted a finger to do anything like that for me. I've always had to do everything for myself. Why does he love her like that? Why couldn't he have loved me? What's wrong with me?"

I burst into tears, and my mother held me in her arms. "Oh, honey, I hate to see you hurting like this. But you know as well as I do that you and Jake weren't meant for each other in that special way. Someday, there will be someone else. Someday, you'll meet the right person."

She released her embrace and lifted my chin so she could look me in the eye. "There's something I don't understand, River. Why are you still there, when it causes you so much pain?"

"Because Thor doesn't want to leave," I sniffled. "Otherwise, I'd be long gone. But Thor would never understand if I took him away now, and I don't think he'd forgive me."

My mother leaned back on the sofa and closed her eyes. "I see," she said, smiling serenely.

"What?" I asked. "What do you see?"

"There's a reason you still feel tied to that household. We may not know why until much later." She opened her eyes and gazed at me. "River, have you told Jake how you feel?"

"No, Mom, I haven't."

"Maybe you should have a talk with him. Clear the air. Then you can all live more peacefully together."

I glanced over at my father and saw a twinkle in his eyes. It was hard to tell because of his tremors, but it seemed to me he was nodding in agreement with my mother's advice.

Jake was busy over the weekend, working from early morning until late at night, painting the kitchen walls and installing the new cabinets. Then on Monday, a delivery truck brought the new stove and refrigerator and hauled the old ones away.

When Rachel wasn't helping Jake with the work in the kitchen, she busied herself with creating a food station in Jake's ceramics studio. She set up a crock pot and an electric skillet on his work table, and filled a cooler with ice for storing perishable food. Without missing a beat, she prepared three daily meals for the household, serving them to Jake and Thor on TV trays in the living room.

I spent most of that weekend in my room, trying to avoid the activity in the rest of the house. When I could no longer stand the confinement, I'd go outside and wander around in the yard, staring off into the woods. I knew I was acting like a pouting child, and I hated myself for it.

Rachel brought me a tray of food at each mealtime, a worried look on her face. "Are you okay, Leah?" she'd ask. I'd almost feel sorry for the poor girl who had to walk on eggshells around me.

"Please don't be mad at me, Leah," she said on one occasion. "If I'd known it would upset you so much to change the kitchen, I wouldn't have asked Jake to do it. I really thought you'd be happy."

Sunday morning, I told Thor that he and I would be going to McDonald's for lunch, a treat he always enjoyed. I wanted it to be a lighthearted occasion, but he sulked throughout the meal and showed no interest in exploring the playground.

"You don't like Rachel, do you, Mom?" he asked me out of the blue. "You're not very nice to her."

Once again, I was taken aback by his keen observation. "I don't dislike her," I responded. "It's just that I'm not used to having another person in the house."

"It's not that bad," he said. "She's nice. She helps a lot."

A wave of depression washed over me, and I barely had the energy to lift a French fry to my mouth. "I'm sorry, Thor," I said. I turned to stare out the window while my son picked at the remainder of his food.

My scheduled teaching days at Riverside Elementary were Monday, Wednesday, and Friday. Thor attended Harrison Elementary on the other side of town, so unless I had the extra time to drive him to school, he had to take the bus.

While I fumbled around getting ready Monday morning, Rachel fixed Thor's breakfast at her makeshift food station, and sent him off to the school bus with a packed lunch. I felt ashamed for being too inept to tend to my own child's needs. While I was angry with Rachel for acting like his mother, I had to admit I was grateful for her help.

Tuesday morning, I got up early enough to make sure Thor got off to school, and then collapsed back into bed in a state of depressive lethargy. I woke up again around 11:00 AM to find the sun shining through my window, and something inside me said it was time to kick myself back into gear.

The house seemed very still without the pounding and banging of the past four days. I decided to venture into the kitchen to look around. I couldn't help but admire the end results, which really were quite spectacular: the freshly painted walls, Jake's expertly crafted cabinets, the state-of-the-art stove and refrigerator.

Rachel had swept and mopped the hardwood floor and polished every inch of the counter tops and appliances. I opened a few cupboard doors and saw that she'd organized the dishes and cookware, stashing everything away in perfect order. Her spices were lined up in a decorative wall rack Jake had built, which included a shelf that housed her new recipe box, and I was reminded of whose kitchen this really was. I ran my hand along the granite countertop, trying to convince myself that the kitchen was for my use also, that my dishes were in the cupboards, that I should be happy about this new luxury.

Someone had brewed a fresh pot of coffee, and I reached into the cupboard for a mug. As I turned to pour the coffee, I saw Jake standing in the doorway. Our eyes met. His were unsmiling.

"For whatever reason, Lee," he said, "you're not taking this well."

Ignoring his comment, I opened the patio door and stepped out onto the deck. The warm sun shining on my gloominess felt comforting. I settled myself into one of the deck chairs and stared mindlessly at the river.

A moment later, Jake joined me with his own mug of coffee. "Lee," he said, "we have to get past this. We can't live together with all this tension in the air. You need to tell me what's going on with you." He looked and sounded utterly exhausted.

I opened my mouth to speak, but was interrupted by the creak of the patio door. Both Jake and I turned around to look. Rachel was standing there with the door open a few inches, apparently wondering whether it was safe to join us on the deck.

"Rachel," Jake said in a weary voice, "I need to have a private conversation with Lee. Give us a few minutes alone."

A hurt look crossed Rachel's face, something I'd seen a hundred times the past few days. She closed the door and backed away. I suspected she was lurking out of sight in the kitchen, trying to eavesdrop on our conversation, but I didn't care.

Jake turned back to me. "So what's eating at you, Lee? I figured you'd be happy to have a new kitchen. I don't understand your attitude."

"You didn't do it for me," I blurted out. "You did it for her!"

Jake stared at me, confounded. "What difference does it make? It got done, didn't it?"

At that moment, I resorted to behavior I despise in a woman, weepy histrionic accusations and insecure questioning. I was ashamed of every word that came out of my mouth, but I couldn't stop my outburst. I figured Jake thought I'd lost my mind.

"I lived here with you for over seven years before Rachel came," I railed at him, "and you never made a damn thing for me! You didn't do as much as paint a room for me! I had to do that myself! I cooked for years in that crappy kitchen, and you didn't care. But as soon as Rachel came, you busted your butt to fix it up. It's not fair, Jake."

On and on I went, regaling him with all his shortcomings. Then my tirade turned toward my own deficiencies. "What's wrong with me, Jake, that you couldn't love me like you love Rachel? I saw you carry her bags the day she moved in. You never did anything like that for me. I always had to carry my own stuff. You just weren't that attracted to me, were you?"

Apparently, Jake got to a point where he'd heard enough. "Knock it off, Lee!" he thundered. "You're being completely irrational."

Unaccustomed to his harshness, I stopped abruptly and stared at him. Then his voice softened and he spoke barely above a whisper, as if he, too, suspected an eavesdropper.

"You're a beautiful woman, Lee. How can you think I wasn't attracted to you? I've always been attracted to you. I still am, as a matter of fact. Any man would be. But you've never needed me. You've always been self-sufficient. You've got everything. You're intelligent, you're a fantastic artist, you're educated, you know how to make your way in the world, and you have some pretty damn fine parents who back you up when you're in a jam. What does this dumb old farm boy have to offer a woman like you?"

He took a sip of his coffee, and then sighed deeply. "Rachel came to me with nothing. Maybe it sounds a little sick, but that's part of her appeal to me. She's lost in life. She needs me, and whenever I do anything for her, it's like I've given her the world. She looks at me with those big brown eyes all full of gratitude, and I melt."

He put down his mug, then leaned back and gazed at the river. "I know you're jealous of her, Lee, and it's ridiculous. You've got so much more going for you than she does."

"Oh," was all I could say. I sank deep into my own thoughts, trying to absorb everything Jake had just told me.

He broke the silence a few minutes later when he said, "I owe you, Lee."

"What do you mean?" I asked.

"You're right. I haven't done the things for you that I should've done. Name something you want done around here, and I'll do it. It'll be for you, not for Rachel."

I stared at him, unable to believe he really meant what he'd just said. But his face looked dead serious.

"The siding," I said after a few moments of contemplation. "Please finish re-siding this house, Jake. I'm sick to death of looking at that old green paint."

He grinned. "It's a deal."

True to his word, the hardworking father of my son completed the siding project before the cold winter weather set in, transforming the mismatched ends of the house into one attractive structure. Each day when I drove home from school, I'd smile as I approached the quaint rustic cottage perched on the lovely piece of river property. Knowing that this latest renovation was done for me made the prospect of leaving even more difficult to consider

Chapter 13

Several months into the fall semester, my school principal approached me about expanding my part-time hours into a full-time teaching position. The timing of his offer, coupled with the changes in my home life, seemed serendipitous to me, and I accepted the position.

So I became far too busy with my teaching, my painting, my dancing, and my drumming circle to care about what was going on with Jake and Rachel. On the rare occasions when Jake and I spoke, we were cordial with each other. Actually, things weren't much different between him and me than they were before Rachel came.

From time to time, I'd wonder whether there was still a relationship between Jake and Rachel, as I saw no evidence that they were lovers. There were no affectionate touches, no endearing smiles, and in the course of their daily lives, they seemed just as disinterested in each other as Jake and I had been.

Once, I had the thought that Rachel was like a stray that Jake had brought into the household, a scraggly little cat that neither he nor I had the heart to put out.

But mostly, I came to think of her as a live-in housekeeper. In addition to preparing meals, Rachel busied herself with dusting, sweeping, and scrubbing every inch of our home.

For the most part, I didn't mind, as I didn't enjoy housework. But when I found her refolding the clothing in Thor's dresser drawers one day, I told her to stop. "It's my job to see that my son's room is in order," I said. "You don't have to work so hard around here."

She hung her head. "I don't have anything else to do, Leah. You and Jake make money and pay bills. I'll feel bad if I don't do something to earn my keep."

Indeed, Rachel didn't seem to have anything else to do. She had no particular interests outside of cooking and housework. However, a year after her arrival, she convinced Jake to till part of the back yard so she could grow a vegetable garden. She tended her plants with great care, as if they were her children. I'd look out the patio door and see her creeping along the garden rows, her skinny bottom in the air, pulling weeds and chatting with her seedlings.

Thor seemed comfortable in his three-parent home. But while Rachel took advantage of any opportunity to nurture him, she actually seemed more like an older sister than a mother. The interest she took in his play or his schoolwork came not from the patronizing stance of an adult, but from her own childlike nature.

While I was too busy to observe Rachel's behavior on a daily basis, I began to notice cycles in her moods. For days at a time, she'd fly through her chores at top speed, cheerful, annoyingly chatty. Then suddenly, she'd withdraw into herself.

I'd realize that I hadn't seen her all day, and I'd ask Jake, "Where's Rachel?"

He'd shrug and say, "In her room, I guess."

Sometimes, I'd find her lying morosely on the living-room sofa, huddled under a blanket. She'd say little during her down times, and since she was so unrelentingly intrusive during her good moods, I'd welcome the silence. Unfortunately, the poor girl got little sympathy from me during her depressions.

I sensed that when Rachel was feeling down, she had no confidence for dealing with the world of adulthood. When Jake would pass through a room in his busy workday mode, she'd cringe and draw back, as if the intensity of his masculinity was too much for her to bear. If I made eye contact with her, she'd avert her gaze.

When she did come out of hiding during her low moods, she'd seek out Thor. She'd sit beside him while he played on the floor, or trail after him in the yard. He seemed to sense her moods, and he knew how to cheer her up. He'd speak gently to her as he explained an aspect of a game or educated her on the nature of a bug they found in the yard. If they watched TV together on the sofa, she'd put her arm around him and draw him close, as if his presence soothed her.

As time passed, I recognized how detrimental it would be to take Rachel away from Thor. And I couldn't imagine what would happen to

Rachel if I took Thor away from her.

Just as quickly as Rachel's dark moods came, they disappeared. She'd snap back into her high spirits, flying through the house, dusting, mopping, carrying loads of laundry, fixing special meals, as if to make up for the fact that the housekeeper had slacked off for a few days.

While Thor generally shared his evening meals with Jake and Rachel, my appearance at the table was infrequent. But for Thor's sake, I made a point of showing up for dinner at least twice a week.

One evening, I witnessed an incident that made me realize how frustrated Jake had become with Rachel's instability.

Her efforts at preparing the evening meal had been desultory that day. She'd pulled some wilted salad from the refrigerator, and had warmed leftover mashed potatoes and vegetables in the microwave.

When Jake sat down at the table and surveyed the pitiful spread, he turned to Rachel and exploded. "Damn it, Rachel, we had this same crap yesterday, and the day before that, and probably the day before that! Is it too much for you to serve a guy a decent meal?"

Rachel pushed back from the table and ran down the hallway, sobbing like a little child. We heard her door slam as she retreated into the cave of her room.

Thor turned to Jake, his eyes blazing. "Dad!" he shouted. "Why are you so mean to her? She doesn't feel good today!" With that, he left the kitchen in a huff and stalked off to his own room.

That left Jake and me staring at each other across the table, and I saw profound discouragement in his weary eyes. In spite of his odious behavior, I felt no anger, only compassion.

"What the hell, Jake?" I whispered.

I could tell he was struggling to explain what he felt, but in the end all he said was, "I've worked like a dog all day, and I'm starving. I'm going into town to get something decent to eat."

He got up and headed toward the hallway, then stopped and turned to look at me. I thought he was going to ask me to come along, but he just shrugged and left the room.

That day, I realized I needed to stop taking Rachel's services for granted, that I needed to pick up the slack when she was down.

Several days later, on a warm May afternoon, I was relaxing on the deck while Rachel was showing Thor the lettuce and radishes peeking through the soil in her vegetable garden. Her spirits had lifted again. She'd made no mention of the ugly encounter at the dinner table. In fact, she'd gotten up the next morning in a cheerful mood, as if nothing at all had happened the night before.

Jake came out on the deck, coffee mug in hand, and sat down in the other cedar chair. "Thor's such an easygoing kid," I said as we watched him and Rachel on their hands and knees in the garden, chatting like best friends. "Rachel's so much more difficult."

Then I laughed. "It sounds like I'm talking about two children."

"Pretty much the way it is," Jake muttered.

I decided to use the moment to check out my hunch about his relationship with Rachel. "Why, Jacob Potter!" I exclaimed, reaching over to playfully punch his arm. "What a way to talk about your lover!"

He snorted. "Hardly a lover."

"Things not going so well?"

He turned to me, his face somber. "In the beginning, Rachel was so beautiful. She had so many complexities in her personality, and it seemed like I kept discovering new things about her. When she brought all of herself to our relationship, she was everything I ever wanted in a woman. She completed me."

Jake's eloquence stunned me, as the man generally said little more than necessary to get his point across. And I was decidedly uncomfortable with his rush of emotion.

"But you probably don't want to hear this," he said.

"No, I don't," I responded.

He continued anyway. "Then all of a sudden, it was gone, just like a switch had been turned off. It's like she's completely empty. It frustrates me, makes me downright angry sometimes."

"Like the other night?"

"Yup. I shouldn't have exploded like that. But I get so fed up with her when she acts like a helpless kid. That part of her I can't stand."

"But that's what you loved about her in the beginning, Jake. She was lost and needy, and you had the chance to be her hero."

"Yeah, but after a year, it's worn thin."

I decided Jake didn't need to hear any more of my observations on the topic of him and Rachel, and we sat in silence.

Then he said, "Lee, sometimes I don't think I can do this anymore."

I sat up straight in my chair, staring at him in disbelief. "Jake, are you going to tell her to leave?"

He looked down at the deck, slowly shaking his head. "How could I do that, Lee? Where would she go?"

My second summer with Rachel was easier than the first, as I didn't have to cope with any emotionally wrenching adjustments. While Rachel was my constant annoying shadow, her presence didn't distract me from enjoying the pleasures of the season: sunning myself on the deck, walks through the woods or along the river, long hours of painting, and reading the books I had no time for during the school year.

The warm weather, the sunshine, and the companionship of Thor and me seemed to bolster Rachel's spirits. Her days of hiding in her room were rare that summer.

Thor and I enjoyed an August tradition of attending a Native American powwow held at a park in South Bend, Indiana. Although the opening and closing ceremonies were reserved for the Potawatomi tribal members only, I'd don my fringed deerskin dress and take my son to one of the days that were open to the public.

Thor was officially one-sixteenth Ojibwa Indian, even though his curly red hair, blue eyes, and freckled complexion belied that strain of his lineage. But I enjoyed teaching him what I knew about our Ojibwa ancestors. My mother had provided him with moccasins and a tribal headdress, and he took great pride in wearing them to the powwow.

As the date of the event approached, I didn't wait for Thor to prompt me to be gracious to Rachel. "What do you think, sweetie?" I asked him. "Should we invite Rachel to go with us to the powwow?"

He threw his arms around my waist, squeezing me tightly. "That would be great, Mom. That will make her really happy."

Indeed, Rachel was thrilled by our invitation. On the car ride to the park, she plied Thor and me with questions about our Native American heritage. I allowed Thor to do most of the talking, and smiled as I listened to him described the customs of the Ojibwa tribe.

When Rachel saw the crowds at the park, she became fearful and didn't want to get out of the car. But Thor took her hand and led her to the area where people stood watching the dancers.

The drummers and singers were clustered in the center, with the dancers circling around them. We watched a traditional dance, in which men wearing beadwork and feathers told of former war and hunting expeditions. The grass dancers followed, their costumes decorated with long, colorful fringes that swayed gracefully with their movements. We were entertained by the high jumps and quick footwork of the men's fancy dance, and then women wearing brightly colored shawls danced the story of the transition from a cocoon to a butterfly.

Thor eagerly jumped into the circle for the children's dance. Rachel giggled and clapped as she watched him.

"Our little Thor is so special," she said to me. "He's the best one, don't you think?"

Her use of the word *our* jolted me. But I decided not to react, except for choosing a different pronoun in my response: "My son is always the best one to me."

Then it was time for an open dance. "It's our turn," I said to Rachel, and she followed me into the circle. As she was behind me, I couldn't see what she was doing. But I sensed she was throwing herself wholeheartedly into the dance, just as she'd done at the solstice party.

After we'd taken our places back in the audience, a Native American man in full tribal regalia approached us. Ignoring me in my deerskin dress and moccasins, he spoke to my dark-haired, olive-skinned companion in her blue jeans and sneakers. "Who are your people?" he asked.

Rachel looked startled, confused by the man's question. "She's not Native American," I explained. "She's Jewish." Then I added, "My son and I are of Ojibwa descent."

The man shot me a disinterested glance, and then addressed Rachel again. "You have the spirit of our people."

"I have the spirit?" Rachel murmured to herself as the man walked away.

Once again, I felt miffed at being overlooked while Rachel was the focus of attention. However, I summoned my most gracious behavior and said to her, "That was a nice compliment, wasn't it?"

She looked at me with large, bewildered eyes. "What does that mean, I have the spirit?"

"Think about it," I said. "It means that even if you don't have Native American blood in you, your heart and soul are like theirs."

A smile crept across her face. "Wow!" she said. Then she whispered, "I think I understand." She turned her gaze back to the dancers, appearing to be in deep contemplation.

When Thor grew tired of watching the dancers, I gave him permission to walk with Rachel up and down the rows of vendors selling an array of Native American goods: food, jewelry, beaded clothing, moccasins, pipes, and musical instruments. When they came back to me, Thor was grinning from ear to ear. He showed me a cedar flute Rachel had bought him with the spending money Jake had given her.

I turned the flute over in my hands, noting that it was beautifully crafted and, no doubt, expensive. "Rachel," I protested. "You shouldn't have done this. He's just a child."

"But I wanted to," she said.

Her generosity touched me, and since she had no money left to spend on herself, I treated her and Thor to some fry-bread. Thor wandered a short distance away while he ate, and I held the flute so it wouldn't get sticky.

Rachel stepped close to me. The traces of fry-bread around her mouth made her look comical, but the earnest look in her eyes kept me from laughing. "I can't stop thinking about what that man told me," she said. "Since you and Thor are part Native American and I have the spirit, it makes me feel like we're connected to each other. Leah, do you think there's a reason why we came into each other's lives?"

I recoiled, taking a step away from her. "I really couldn't say, Rachel."

She opened her mouth to say more, apparently to convince me of the destiny we shared, but then Thor came running up to reclaim his flute.

"I can't wait to show this to Grandma," he said. "She'll think it's really cool."

On our way home, he tested my patience as he played, over and over again, a mournful little ditty he'd composed.

"Rachel's like part of our family, isn't she, Mom?" Thor said when he and I were alone in the kitchen later that evening.

This is your opportunity, a voice within me whispered. *He's eight years old, he can understand. You can explain to him that Rachel is like a stepmother to him. He loves her. Maybe it won't upset him too much that she took my place as his father's partner.*

"Yes, Thor," I said. "She is part of our family." I gazed down at him, trying to muster the courage to utter the lines I'd mentally rehearsed a thousand times: *Daddy loves Rachel, Daddy's with Rachel now.*

I suddenly felt weak, and I sank down on a kitchen chair. "Come here, Thor," I said.

He stood in front of me, gazing at me with questioning eyes. I took his face in my hands and opened my mouth to speak.

But then another thought rushed into my head. *This old explanation doesn't apply anymore. I not sure Jake and Rachel are lovers. I don't see any evidence of that, and I'm sure Thor doesn't, either. I can't tell him they're together. That wouldn't make sense to him. Jake and Rachel aren't a couple. They don't even have as much going on as Jake and I did. Actually, they don't even communicate as much as Jake and I do now. Rachel lives here, and that's all I can honestly say.*

"What, Mom?" Thor asked.

I patted his cheeks. "You're right," I said. "Rachel's been here a long time, and I guess that makes her part of our family."

"That's great," he said. I saw relief in his eyes, and I knew what he was thinking: *My mom isn't mad at Rachel anymore. I don't have to worry about liking Rachel, because they're getting along now.*

He grinned at me and grabbed the sandwich I'd made him, then opened the patio door and went out to join Rachel on the deck.

Chapter 14

When Thor and I returned to school in the fall, Rachel's dark moods returned as well. "You're so busy, Leah," she said one day, her big brown eyes filled with sorrow. "I hardly see you anymore. I wish you'd stay home once in awhile."

She made me feel like I was neglecting her, and that irritated me. *I have no obligations toward you, Rachel,* I thought.

"You have Jake," I told her. "Jake is here with you every day. You shouldn't be lonely."

She waved her hand dismissively. "He's no fun. He's boring."

When I'd come home after a late evening meeting, I'd find her sitting in the living-room, like an anxious mother awaiting the return of a teenager out past curfew. She'd have a snack ready, something she'd baked that day, and would fix me a cup of tea.

"Tell me about your day," she'd say, her hands folded primly on her lap. Her words sounded contrived, like a needy wife trying to get her non-communicative husband to open up.

Most of the time, I'd brush her off with a thumbnail sketch of my day's activity. Then I'd yawn and announce that I was going to bed. But on occasion, I'd find myself glad to have someone to talk to, even if it was my annoying housemate.

I'd tell her the latest gossip circulating among the teachers and staff at Riverside Elementary: who was pregnant, who was having an affair, who was getting divorced, who was on the verge of getting fired. I'd complain about certain students who disrupted my classroom time and again, and how I'd run out of ideas for disciplining them. I'd grumble about how my principal had implemented some new regulation that all of us teachers found time-consuming and completely pointless.

Rachel's eyes would grow wide with alarm. "That's terrible, Leah! I worry about you."

"It's not that bad," I'd reply. "Normal stresses of the workday."

"I don't know how you it," she'd say. "You're so much stronger than I am."

In November, several weeks prior to her twenty-sixth birthday, Rachel sank even deeper into depression. When she'd emerge from her room, she'd slink around the house enveloped in a cloud of gloom, dark circles under her misery-filled eyes. I noticed that she was barely eating, and that she had transitioned from thin to gaunt.

"Jake," I said one day, "you need to do something about Rachel."

He eyed me skeptically. "Why is this on me?"

I shook my head in disbelief. "You brought her here. She's your responsibility."

"Well, what do you want me to do?"

"Take her to a doctor."

"She won't go."

"Then take her somewhere to have fun. Take her shopping. Buy her something. I don't think the poor girl has had anything new to wear in the year and a half she's lived here. She looks a mess."

"I wouldn't know what to do with her in a store," Jake said. "I don't know how to pick out lady stuff." Then he smiled coyly. "If I give you the money, will you take her?"

I grimaced. "I suppose I can. But you owe me big time!"

Several minutes later, I knocked on Rachel's door. When I heard no response, I opened it and walked in. A stale odor permeated the room, and items of dirty clothing were draped over furniture and tossed on the floor.

Rachel was lying on her bed, wearing flannel pajama bottoms and a dingy tee shirt. Her feet were bare, and the black filth on her soles told me she hadn't bathed for quite a few days. She stared at me with vacant eyes.

"Rachel," I said, "I have a surprise for you."

A spark of interest flickered in her eyes. "A surprise?"

I held out the roll of bills Jake had given me.

She looked perplexed. "Are you giving me money, Leah?"

"No," I said. "I'm taking you shopping. Jake gave me money to get you some new clothing. It's for your birthday."

She pulled herself to a sitting position. "You're doing this for my birthday?"

"Yes," I said. "We'll go Saturday."

"I didn't think you cared about my birthday. I didn't think anybody cared."

I was surprised when her statement aroused compassion in me instead of my usual irritation. I sensed her words came not from her immaturity, but from a deep wound in her heart.

I sat down on her bed and took her sticky, unwashed hand in mine. "Jake cares," I said, even though I wasn't sure that was true. "Thor cares. He misses his friend when you stay in bed all day. He worries about you."

I hesitated, knowing that I was about to take a step with Rachel I'd never taken before. I swallowed hard, and then said, "Even though you might not believe it, Rachel, I care, too. Maybe I don't always show it, but I do care about you."

Rachel threw her arms around my neck and began to sob. I forced myself to hold her for a few moments, gently stroking her bony back. Then I released her and stood up.

"Rachel, you can't do this anymore." I gestured around the messy room. "The more you live like this, the worse you'll feel. You need to shower and wear clean clothing every day. And you need to start eating. My God, girl, you're wasting away to nothing! It's starting to scare me. I won't have that going on in my house. You understand? You've got to start taking better care of yourself."

Rachel gave me a shy smile. "Okay, Leah." She got up, straightened her bedding, and began picking up her clothing.

"We're going to make a day of it," I told Rachel as I drove her to South Bend the following Saturday. "We're not leaving the mall until you've bought a whole new wardrobe."

"Okay, Leah," she said. She pulled a folded piece of paper from her jacket pocket. "I made a list of things I need: jeans, shirts, socks, underwear, and pajamas."

I smiled. "That's good, Rachel, that should make shopping easier. We'll get all that, but we'll get you something nice, too."

"Like a skirt?" she asked. "Like one of the pretty skirts you wear?"

"Sure," I said. "We'll get you a nice skirt."

"South Bend is a huge city," Rachel said as we drove into the downtown area. "It scares me."

I laughed. "Rachel, South Bend is a fraction of the size of Chicago. You used to live in one of the biggest cities in the country."

"I know," she said, "but that seems like a long time ago."

Shopping for clothing in Rachel's tiny size was a new experience for me, and I had difficulty thinking about what would be attractive on a body so different from mine. The crowds unnerved Rachel, and she couldn't focus. I ended up taking over the list, locating the items she needed, and then giving her choices of style and color. Even then, she'd defer to my opinion, saying, "I don't know, Leah. What do you think?"

As we strolled through the mall, we passed a hair salon, and I had a sudden inspiration. Rachel's hair hadn't been trimmed since she'd moved in with us, and it now hung to her waist. The ends were split and straggly.

"Want to get your hair cut, Rachel?" I asked.

"No way," she objected. "I don't want to spend Jake's money on that. I need it for clothes."

"This will be on me," I said. "My birthday gift to you. Come on, let's do it."

Rachel looked tiny and frail as she sat in the salon chair, her eyes wide with curiosity. The stylist cut ten inches off her hair, gave her bangs, and shaped the sides to form an attractive frame for her face. Then she showed Rachel how to blow-dry her hair using a styling product.

"Rachel, you look adorable," I exclaimed when I viewed the end result.

She gazed at her image in the mirror, running her fingers through her fluffy locks. "I'm a glamour girl," she said, batting her eyes. As I paid for the haircut, I asked the stylist to throw in a bottle of her product as well.

I had in mind a particular store where we would shop for Rachel's skirt. It was on the other end of the mall, and we set out on the long trek. As we passed a boutique of high-end children's clothing, Rachel suddenly stopped. She stared at the fancy little dresses displayed in the window, a faraway look in her eyes.

After a minute or two, I grew impatient. "Come on, Rachel. We've got to keep moving."

She appeared indifferent to my haste. "My mother used to take me to stores like this," she murmured. "When I was a tiny little girl, she dressed me up in stuff like this. My older brothers and sisters thought I was so cute. They made a fuss over me. Everybody loved me back then."

She sighed deeply, her shoulders sagging. "I'm tired, Leah. Can we go home now?"

"Not yet," I said, taking her arm and steering her away from the display window. "I told you we aren't going to leave until we're finished. We've got one more store to go to. We'll get you something fancy again."

Minutes later, we entered a shop stocked with exotic imported clothing. Rachel's excitement returned as she rifled through the racks of colorful skirts, caftans, scarves, and tunics. We eventually settled on a full, multicolored skirt of gauzy cotton interwoven with shimmering gold threads. The coordinating top was of a similar fabric in rich violet.

"Go try this on," I said, pointing her to the dressing room.

When she stepped out dressed in her new attire, I was so stunned I could hardly speak. The voluminous folds of the fabric added substance to Rachel's gaunt frame, and a wide gold sash cinched her tiny waist, giving the impression of an hourglass figure. Not only did she look beautiful with her new haircut and clothing, it seemed as if her personality had changed. I sensed the mysterious essence that robbed men of their senses, something alluring, other-worldly.

She twirled around so I could inspect the outfit, and the skirt flared out in a fan of glorious color. "That's it, Rachel," I said. "It's perfect. Let's get it."

"Can we buy more?" she asked, her eyes dancing with excitement.

I laughed. "Maybe another time. We're out of money now."

As soon as we arrived home, Rachel ran to her room to put on her new skirt, and then modeled it for Jake and Thor.

"Wow!" Thor exclaimed. "You look beautiful like Mom now!"

I glanced at Jake and saw a look of desire in his eyes, something I hadn't seen for more than a year. Suddenly, I felt sad for him. *Oh, Jake,* I thought. *Don't get your hopes up. This won't last. I know it won't last.*

With my coaching, Rachel styled her hair the next few days. She wanted to wear her new skirt around the house, but I convinced her that it should be saved for special occasions.

Then her depression hit full force, bringing with it the familiar pitiful figure in ragged clothing. When she emerged from her dark mood, she put on her new jeans and shirts, but made no further attempts to keep up with her hair.

Over the months, her bangs grew long and limp and hung down in her eyes, and when they became too bothersome, she fastened them back with clips. I suggested that she get her hair trimmed again, but she declined, saying "That's just not me, Leah."

Chapter 15

The cedar flute Rachel bought Thor at the powwow became his prized possession. He was never careless with it like he was with some of his toys, and he kept it in a special place, in his top dresser drawer under his folded tee shirts. I had no idea that this little flute would be his gateway instrument into the world of music.

The first time Thor took his flute to my parents' house, he insisted that we set up a drumming circle in the living room. My mother and I obligingly seated ourselves cross-legged on the floor, near my father in his recliner. Thor understood that his grandfather's impairment made it difficult for him to beat a drum. So, much to my dad's delight, he handed him a rattle and instructed him to keep the rhythm by shaking it.

Then Thor joined us on the floor, and as my mother set the beat with her drum, he played an extemporaneous flute solo. At first, the tune was slow and mournful. Then it began to pick up speed. After awhile, he couldn't contain his exuberance in the seated position, and he jumped up and strutted around the room as he performed.

Even though his playing was amateurish, I was surprised at his command of the instrument. When he was finished, he bowed while we clapped.

"I believe Thor has discovered his passion," my mother observed. "He's destined to be a musician."

At home, Thor frequently invited Rachel into his room for jam sessions, directing her to accompany him on the drum while he played his flute. She loved the activity, and allowed herself to be ordered around by her young friend. I'd hear them playing when I'd come home from school, and I'd have to poke my head in the door to remind Thor that he had homework to do.

"Aw, Mom," he'd plead. "Just one more song?"

When Thor approached his fifth grade year, he became excited about the possibility of playing in the school band. I suggested that since he loved playing his wooden flute, he could continue with a silver one. He objected, saying he wanted to try something new. He ended up choosing the trumpet, but he quickly became disenchanted with that instrument and wanted to drop out of band.

"I'm just not into horns," he told me, sounding entirely sure of himself. "I think I'm a strings man." I smiled, realizing my lanky, pre-teen son was already discovering his own identity.

When I reminded him that his father and I had made a financial investment in the trumpet, Thor grudgingly agreed to finish out the year, but only after negotiating a deal with me: if I signed him up for guitar lessons, he would stay in band and practice his trumpet faithfully.

Because the guitar lessons were right after school, I had to rush to get home on time to take him. "Why don't you let me take him?" Rachel asked one day when I was running behind schedule. "I don't have anything else to do." From that day on, transporting Thor to his guitar lessons became her responsibility.

Soon, the twang of guitar chords emanated from Thor's room during his jam sessions with Rachel. Once when I heard both the guitar and the flute, I was puzzled, knowing Thor couldn't play two instruments at once. When I peeked into the room, I saw Rachel playing the guitar.

She looked guilty, as if I'd caught her in the act of doing something wrong. "Thor taught me how to play some chords," she said defensively.

One afternoon, as I was carrying a basket of laundry to my room, I heard someone tentatively strumming guitar chords, as if trying to find the way through a new song. The playing stopped and then started again, repeating the chords and adding a few more. Then I heard singing along with the playing.

I couldn't make out the words, so I tiptoed close to Thor's room to listen. Another twang of the chords, then a plaintive soprano voice sang, *"Child of love . . ."*

That's Rachel, I thought, as it clearly wasn't my son's voice. I'd never heard her sing before.

She stopped, and then started again. *"Child of love, child of light."* Then the guitar playing went awry.

"Let me show you," Thor said. I heard the chords played with more expertise. "How do the words go?" he asked.

And while he played, Rachel sang, *"Child of love, child of light, glowing bright through the dark of the night."*

I stood mesmerized, listening to the haunting beauty of her voice accompanied by the simple guitar chords. Then, moving as quietly as I could, I ran to Jake's studio.

"Come quick, Jake, you've got to hear something," I said. "Hurry, before they stop."

Jake looked startled. "What're you talking about?"

"Just come," I said, grabbing his arm and pulling him after me. "But be quiet."

A moment later, we stood undetected outside Thor's room, listening to Rachel sing.

"Child of love, child of light,

Glowing bright through the dark of the night.

May you shine, brightly shine,

Child divine."

"Sing it again," Thor said. Then he sang along, and the soft beat of a drum joined the strumming of the guitar.

At that moment, I thought their duet was the sweetest thing I'd ever heard. I glanced at Jake, whose eyes were large with astonishment.

"She can sing!" I whispered. Jake nodded in agreement.

Suddenly, the music stopped. "Mom and Dad, are you out there listening to us?" Thor called.

I stepped into the doorway, applauding. "That was beautiful! Beautiful playing, beautiful singing, beautiful song. Where did you learn that?"

Rachel stared at me, her hands frozen on the head of the drum she'd been beating.

"Where did you get that song?" I repeated. She hung her head.

"She made it up," Thor said.

"Wow, Rachel!" I exclaimed. "That's amazing!"

Laying aside the drum, Rachel scrambled up off the floor. She brushed past me and ran through the kitchen and down the hallway to her room. I turned to Jake. "What was that about?"

He shrugged and shook his head. "Couldn't tell you."

"She just acts weird sometimes," Thor explained, as if Jake and I hadn't already figured that out.

I went back to my business of folding laundry, feeling bad about hurting Rachel's feelings, even though I hadn't the slightest idea what I'd done to upset her. After stashing the last of the clothing in my dresser drawers, I walked down the hallway to apologize to her.

"I didn't mean to upset you, Rachel," I said after she grudgingly granted me permission to enter her room. "I just wanted to let you know that I liked your song. I think it's wonderful that you write songs."

Rachel shot me an ugly look. "I don't write songs!" She spat the words at me. "I just made up one little song."

She bit her lip and pounded her thigh with her fist, clearly frustrated with me. "I know Thor's your kid, and you think you always need to know everything about him. But he means something to me, too. He's my friend. That song wasn't for you and Jake. It was a special song for Thor, something I made up about him. You butted in and ruined it. I hardly ever get to do anything with Thor without you butting in."

I was so stung by Rachel's words that I could think of nothing to say. My eyes welled with tears as I backed out of her room. I went to sit on the living-room sofa, where I turned her words over and over in my mind, trying to determine whether there was any legitimacy to her accusation.

But just minutes later, Rachel flew into the room, nearly landing on my lap as she threw her arms around me.

"I'm so sorry, Leah!" she wailed. "I don't know why I said those things to you. They're not true. I can't stand being mad at you."

"Don't worry about it, Rachel," I said as I gently pushed her off of me.

I never heard Thor and Rachel play that song again, and that saddened me. But sometimes, the simple little tune would pop into my head, and I'd find myself humming a few bars.

Thor spoke the truth when he said he was a strings man. Although he never grew tired of his guitar, he began talking about playing other stringed instruments. On his twelfth birthday, my mother, always eager to support her grandson's passion, presented him with a violin, the instrument that would become dear to him.

Chapter 16

Only my closest friends were fully aware of the complexities of my living arrangement. The situation bothered them, but as the years passed, they grew tired of prodding me to move on. With most people, I kept my personal life private in order to avoid judgmental reactions.

My coworkers at Riverside Elementary had no idea that my son and I remained part of Jake's household. Over the years, they made numerous attempts to set me up on blind dates. While a few of the potential dates sounded tempting, I knew that bringing another man into my life would require a major rearrangement of my son's world, something I didn't feel ready to do. So I routinely declined the offers, explaining that I was postponing dating until my son was older.

But one September day in the beginning of Thor's seventh grade year, that all changed. When I collapsed on the sofa in the teachers' lounge after a hectic morning, the fifth-grade teacher, Janet, looked up from the papers she was grading. "Hi, Lee. You look beat. Want some coffee?"

"Yes, please, Janet," I said.

She got up and poured two cups, handing one to me, then seated herself on the other end of the sofa. "Are you dating anyone now, Lee?"

"No," I said, feeling too exhausted to face yet another inquisition about my non-existent love life.

Janet looked at me quizzically. "How old is your son now?"

"He's twelve."

"How long do you plan to put off dating? Till he's eighteen?" Her voice held a hint of sarcasm.

I set my cup on the coffee table, then leaned back on the sofa and closed my eyes to avoid her judgmental gaze. "I really don't know, Janet."

"I'm not just being nosy," she said. "There's a reason I'm bringing this up. My brother-in-law's wife died a year and a half ago, and we've been talking to him about getting out and dating. I think he wants to.

But he's scared to death of the dating scene. He was married for almost twenty years."

I opened my eyes and shot her a stern look. "And why are you telling me this?"

"Well, I wondered if you'd be interested in meeting him. He's a really nice guy, in his early forties, vice-president of a company. Not bad-looking, either."

"Oh, I don't think so," I said. "I don't do blind dates."

"How about as a favor to me?" she persisted. "Just go out for coffee with him. Just to build up his confidence. It's not like I'm asking you to get serious with him."

I was shocked to hear a voice inside me whisper, *Why not? It can't hurt to meet him, just to talk to him. If it's nothing serious, Thor doesn't need to know about it.*

I sighed. "Okay."

Janet's face brightened. "Really? That's great! How about if I give him your number so he can call you? His name is Rick."

For the next three days, I lived in a state of nervous excitement, anticipating the phone call from my potential date. Even though I kept my cell phone near me at all times, I frequently checked for messages, thinking that somehow I might have missed hearing it ring.

When the days passed and Rick didn't call, I concluded he wasn't going to, that he'd decided his sister-in-law's description of me didn't sound enticing. While I felt a pang of disappointment, I was also relieved that my life didn't need to change right then and there, and I laughed at myself for how worked up I'd gotten.

But a week later, when I'd nearly forgotten about Rick, my cell phone rang while I was getting ready for bed. I looked at the name on the caller ID: Richard Anderson. Momentarily puzzled, I almost decided not to answer it, but then I put the pieces together. *Richard, Rick. Oh my God, oh my God! It's Rick calling!*

"Hello," I said, my heart pounding.

There was no response for several seconds. I was ready to hang up when a pleasant male voice began to speak. "This is Rick Anderson. I'm calling for Lee Jorgensen."

"Speaking."

"Hello, Lee," he said. "I hope I haven't called at a bad time. My sister-in-law Janet gave me your number. She thought the two of us might enjoy meeting."

"Yes," I said. "Janet told me about you."

"Good." He chuckled nervously. "I'm not sure what to say. As Janet probably told you, I'm out of practice when it comes to dating. Why don't you tell me something about yourself?"

I took a deep breath. "Well, I'm thirty-eight years old. I'm an artist, a painter. Of course, you already know I teach art at Riverside Elementary, and that's how I know Janet. I live in the country, close to Niles. I'm a single mother of a twelve-year-old son."

"I'm forty-four," Rick said. "Is that too old for you?"

He's Jake's age, I thought. Aloud, I said, "No, of course not. Age is just a number. It doesn't mean anything in terms of how people get along with each other."

"Good," he said. "I like your attitude." Then he informed me that he lived in South Bend, and that he had two children, a son in college and a daughter in high school. He told me he was the vice-president of finances for a recreational vehicle company in Elkhart. He sounded rather formal and proper, as if he'd been reading a manual on how to get acquainted with someone of the opposite sex.

But I found I was getting comfortable with this man. I was already in my pajamas, and I slipped under the bed covers and propped myself up against the pillows. Before I knew it, I saw by my alarm clock that Rick and I had been talking for twenty minutes. It had been years since I'd had such a lengthy personal conversation with a man, and it felt good.

"Well, Lee," Rick said, "it's been lovely chatting with you. I should probably let you go now." He paused. "I guess this is the time to ask if you'd like to get together. Would you be interested in having dinner with me?"

My heart leaped into my throat. I hadn't been on a formal date since Jake and I had met for dinner in the restaurant overlooking Lake Michigan thirteen years earlier. "How . . . how about if we start with coffee?" I stammered. "Like after work?"

"That's fine," Rick said. "I guess I was getting a little ahead of myself. I don't want to make you uncomfortable." We agreed to meet several days later, at a café in Niles.

My hand trembled as I laid my phone on my bedside stand. *What have I gotten myself into?* I wondered. I tried to console myself with the thought that, more than likely, nothing would come of this little adventure. I decided to still my nerves with a cup of tea, and I wandered into the kitchen to heat some water.

"Who were you talking to, Leah?" Rachel called from the living-room. "You sure were on the phone a long time."

"It was just a friend." I helped myself to some cookies she'd baked that day.

"What's her name?" Her voice held a hint of jealousy.

Okay, I thought. *This conversation can't go any further.* "You sure are full of questions tonight," I said as I carried my tea and cookies to my bedroom.

Two days later, as I stepped into the lobby of the Riverview Café, my knees almost buckled from anxiety. "I'm meeting someone here," I informed the hostess in a shaky voice. "He might already be seated."

When I entered the dining area, a man stood up and lifted his hand in greeting. I made a quick note of his appearance: average height, trim build, clean-shaven with sandy-blonde hair. He wore a charcoal-gray business suit, white shirt, and colorful tie. While there was nothing outstanding about his physical presentation, he was pleasant-looking and impeccably groomed. I suddenly felt self-conscious in my brightly patterned imported skirt and beaded jewelry, garishly bohemian in contrast to my date's conservative appearance.

The man remained standing as I approached. "Lee?" he asked, his hazel eyes sparkling with anticipation.

"Yes," I said. "You must be Rick."

"Yes, I am." He shook my hand, and then pulled out my chair so I could be seated. I couldn't remember the last time any man had treated me that graciously, and I enjoyed the gesture.

"I'm so glad you came," he said after seating himself. "I've been looking forward to this meeting. I'm a little nervous, to be sure, but excited."

"I'm nervous, too," I admitted. "Very nervous."

"Don't be," he said. "I don't want to make you uncomfortable in any way."

He gazed at me, smiling. "My sister-in-law was right. You certainly are a beautiful woman."

I felt myself blushing, and my embarrassment seemed to worry him. "I hope that wasn't too forward. It's not that I think physical attraction is the most important thing in a relationship. There's communication and trust and shared interests, those sorts of things."

I nodded in agreement.

"I tend to talk too much when I'm nervous," he said. "You can stop me any time."

I thought about the distant silence between myself and my former lover. "No problem," I said. "I like a man who communicates."

The waitress brought our coffee. As Rick reached across the table to pass me the creamer, I noticed the crisp white cuffs peeking out from the sleeves of his expensive jacket. *He must get his shirts professionally laundered,* I thought.

I couldn't remember a time in my entire life when I'd been on a date with a man who was dressed so formally. I compared his polished appearance with Jake's rugged earthiness. *Since it didn't work out with Jake, could I make it with a man like this?*

Rick took a sip of his coffee. "I can't believe how much ground we covered in our phone conversation two days ago. But of course there's so much more to talk about. Tell me something else about yourself, Lee."

"This might surprise you," I said. "My name isn't actually Lee. My full name is River Leah Jorgensen. Some people call me River. Others call me Lee, short for Leah." I paused, thinking of Rachel. "And once in awhile, someone calls me Leah."

"What do you want me to call you?" Rick asked.

"Take your pick," I said. "It doesn't matter to me."

He smiled. "I'll call you River. It suits you. You look like a child of nature. My full name isn't nearly as exciting as yours. It's Richard Allen Anderson."

"It sounds important," I said. "Like an executive." We both laughed.

Then Rick asked how I came by my unusual name. He listened with rapt attention as I launched into the story of my unconventional upbringing by my professor father and my flower-child mother.

"Fascinating," he said. "You grew up in an entirely different world than I did. I don't think I've ever met a woman like you before."

I must have looked concerned, because he said, "That's a compliment, you know. You're like a queen from some foreign country I know nothing about."

He then regaled me with a description of his strict Catholic upbringing, telling me how the nuns in the Catholic schools he attended were the bane of his existence. "I hated it then," he said. "But looking back, I know it was good for me."

"Are you still Catholic?" I asked.

He looked at me quizzically, as if trying to ascertain the motive for my question. "Yes I am, although I'm not as dogmatic as some. I might look like a straight-laced kind of guy, but I'd like to think I'm open-minded. Does my being Catholic put you off?"

"Not at all," I said. "I was raised to respect everyone's personal beliefs. My mother used to say there are many paths to finding God, and I agree with her. Religion isn't something I hold against anyone."

"Good," he said.

I realized Rick was already speculating on how compatible we'd be in a relationship. In my mind, I tried to fit the two of us together, to

bring all the puzzle pieces of our lives into one coherent picture. I couldn't quite see it, but I wanted to believe it was possible. I liked this man.

Rick suddenly grew quiet, lowering his eyes, as if preparing himself to tell me something difficult. Then he looked up at me again, a somber expression on his face. "I suppose my sister-in-law told you my wife passed away eighteen months ago."

"Yes," I said. "I'm sorry for your loss. How are you doing with it?"

Pain flickered in his eyes. "I'm okay now. But it was a long, difficult ordeal. She died of breast cancer. She was diagnosed in her late thirties and passed away four years later."

"You must've really loved her," I said.

"I did," he replied. "But that's not to say our relationship was perfect. We married young, and we both had a lot of growing up to do. There's a lot I'd want to do differently the next time around."

While I was thinking about how impressed I was with his intentions, Rick jolted me by asking, "How about you? Have you been married? Are you widowed? Divorced?"

"I've never been married," I said. I saw Rick wince ever so slightly, and I realized I'd just informed him my child was born out of wedlock.

But he made no comment on that fact, and gracefully steered the conversation toward more lighthearted topics. After many good laughs and several refills of coffee, I glanced at my watch and saw that two hours had passed. "Oh!" I said. "I've got to get going."

"I apologize for keeping you so long," Rick said. "I'm sure you have things to do." He reached for the bill, and I lingered in the lobby while he paid it.

"Well, this was lovely, River," he said when he joined me. "May I call you again?"

"I'd like that," I said, genuinely hoping he would.

He looked at me like he didn't know what to do next. He held out his hand for a parting handshake, and then said, "What the heck, can I give you a hug?"

"Sure," I said. The hug was brief, but sweet. I caught a whiff of his pleasant-smelling aftershave.

On the way to my car, the air began to leak out of my euphoric mood. Each step toward my vehicle brought me closer to the reality of what I'd need to do if I pursued a dating relationship with Rick. I'd have to explain myself to Rick, to Thor, even to Jake and Rachel. My heart grew heavy at the thought.

"Why does this need to be so difficult?" I whispered as I turned my key in the ignition.

The next day, which was Friday, the school secretary came to my classroom on the noon break. "These came for you," she said, setting a vase containing a dozen red roses on my desk.

After she left, I plucked the card from the bouquet and read the message: *To a beautiful woman. Thanks for spending time with me. Rick.*

Like a giddy little girl, I squealed with delight. I was glad no one was around to witness my silly outburst.

At the end of the school day, I sat at my desk staring at the roses, wondering what to do with them. I knew if I left them at school, they'd be wilted by the time I came back on Monday, and I'd miss out on enjoying them in their prime.

Well, I'm not going to waste these, I said to myself. *It isn't every day that I get roses.* I picked up the vase and carried it out to my car, knowing that by doing so, I was introducing my relationship with Rick into my home life.

Chapter 17

Thor must have heard me drive up to the house, because he was at the door waiting for me. "Hey Mom, can I . . . ?" He stopped short when he saw the roses. "Where'd you get the flowers?"

"From a friend," I said.

"Oh." He sounded unimpressed. "Can I go to Tyler's house? He invited me. His mom's ordering pizza."

"I suppose so," I said. "Let me put my things down, and I'll take you."

"Rachel said she'd take me, if you said it was okay."

Just then, Rachel appeared in the doorway between the kitchen and living room, jangling Jake's truck keys. Her eyes grew round with surprise when she saw what I was carrying.

"Who gave you the roses, Leah?"

"A friend," I repeated.

She shot me a look that said, *I don't think you're telling me the truth.* Then she headed out the door with Thor.

I stepped into the kitchen and set the vase of flowers on the counter. As I reached into the refrigerator for a bottle of water, I jumped when I heard a voice behind me.

"So who's this friend of yours?"

I turned around to face Jake. He stood with his arms folded across his chest, an inscrutable expression on his face.

"Just someone I had coffee with," I said, trying to sound nonchalant. I started to head toward my bedroom, but Jake stepped in front of me, blocking my way. I'd never before seen him behave that aggressively.

"Are you dating someone, Lee?" he demanded to know.

My jaw clenched with anger. "How is that your business, Jake? Why should you care?"

His expression softened, and I was surprised to see pain in his eyes. "I just don't like the idea, okay?"

I laughed bitterly. "After what you've done, you object to me dating? After bringing another woman between us?"

"I know what I did," he said. "I'm not claiming to make any sense." He stepped aside to allow me passage through the door.

I carried the roses to my room and placed them on my dresser. Then I sat on my bed gazing at them, my emotions in turmoil. "He's jealous," I murmured to myself. "I can't believe it. Jake is actually jealous."

I thought about Rick, clean cut, articulate, mannerly, and I smiled as I considered the possibility of a fresh start with someone new. Then the face in my mind's eye changed to Jake's ruggedly handsome visage. Pain stabbed my heart, while my body ached with old desire.

I buried my face in my hands. "God, I hate this," I muttered.

Then I heard tapping on my door frame, and I looked up to see Rachel standing in the doorway, still holding Jake's truck keys. "Leah, can I come in?" she asked.

"I guess so," I said wearily.

"I just have a bad feeling."

"About what?"

"About that friend of yours." She sat down beside me on the bed, her slight frame barely weighing down the mattress.

"Rachel," I said. "How can you possibly have a bad feeling about my friend? This has nothing to do with you."

She hung her head. "I don't know why I feel this way." A moment later, she said, "Okay, I'll admit it. I'm jealous. You're so busy that you don't even have time for our friendship, and now you have this other girl you're talking to all the time."

I turned to face her. "Don't you get it, Rachel? This friend is a man. Yesterday, I had coffee with him, and today he sent me the roses."

She stared at me, an incredulous expression on her face, as if the idea of me having a relationship with a man was something she'd never considered. "Oh," she said as she got up to leave my room.

Rick called me Saturday evening. "Did you get the roses I sent?" he asked.

"Yes," I said. "Thank you so much, Rick. They're beautiful! I didn't expect anything like that."

"I just want you to know that I like to treat a woman right."

Once again, a pleasant half-hour chat with Rick lifted my spirits, carrying me away from the reality of the awkward household relationships, making my dilemma momentarily fade into oblivion. We discussed the possibility of going out for dinner, but both of our schedules were too busy to arrange a date before the following Saturday.

"I want to get together when we're not pressed for time," Rick said, "when we can have several leisurely hours with each other."

After I hung up the phone, I went to the living room to watch television. It was dark, and I didn't see Rachel curled up on the loveseat until I turned on the lamp beside the sofa.

"You've been talking to that man again, haven't you, Leah?" she scolded.

"So what?" I retorted.

"I hate him."

I laughed. "How can you hate him, Rachel? You've never met him."

"I hate him because he's going to take you away from me. He's going to make you fall in love with him, and then he'll take you and Thor out of my life."

"I think that's a premature assumption, Rachel," I said. "I've only met Rick once. It's not like we're planning on getting married."

"So his name is Rick." Rachel spat out the name like it was the ugliest word in the English language. "Well, I hate Rick."

Refusing to respond to her little tantrum, I reached for the remote to turn on the television. But she continued.

"Why do you think you need a man, Leah?"

"That's not a fair question coming from you, Rachel. You have Jake. Why do you need a man?"

"I don't need a man, and I don't need Jake. If you need a man that bad, Leah, you can have Jake. Then you can tell that Rick guy to go to hell."

I put down the remote and got up to leave the room. "Rachel, that's disgusting. You're just talking crazy."

"Don't be upset, Leah," she called after me. "I was just kidding."

Rick called on Tuesday evening and then again on Thursday to finalize our date plans. "I'd like to make dinner reservations at Madison Gardens in South Bend," he said. "And if I may, I'd like to pick you up at your house."

I froze. *This is it,* I thought. *This is the time to come clean with him.*

"Rick," I said, "I don't think it's a good idea for you to pick me up. I'd rather meet you at the restaurant."

"Oh." He sounded defeated. "If that's what you prefer." He paused. "Maybe I'm being overly eager. I guess I should back off a little bit."

"Oh, no, Rick," I said. "That's not it at all. There's something I need to tell you. And it's not easy."

"Go ahead. I'm listening."

"My son and I live in the same house as his father."

"What?" Rick's voice sounded sharp. "You mean you're still with him?"

"No, no, no!" I protested. "Definitely not! Jake and I haven't been together for years, and he has another girlfriend. Actually, I'm not sure you can say she's his girlfriend. I don't think there's much of anything between them anymore. But they live in one end of the house, and my son and I live in the other end. It's for Thor's sake."

"I see." Rick's voice was calm, but cool. "I guess you're doing what you think is best. You must be trying to protect your son's attachment to his father."

"Yes," I said, knowing I wasn't exactly telling the truth. *It's not his attachment to his father. It's his relationship with Rachel.*

"How's that arrangement working out?" Rick asked.

"It's okay. We all get along pretty well." Then I said something I hadn't said in several years. "Of course, my son and I will be moving out some day. Soon, I hope."

"That's good," Rick said. He moved on to finalize our date plans, but the enthusiasm was gone from his voice. I mentally berated myself for not having been honest with him from the beginning.

I knew before I even left the house that my dinner date with Rick was destined to go poorly.

The restaurant was elegant, the food was delicious, and I felt confident that I looked my best. But while Rick was as gracious as ever, he seemed tired and distracted. I knew he was slipping away from me.

As we ate our salads, I worked hard to keep the conversation buoyant. But midway through the entre course, I couldn't bear the tension any longer. "Rick," I blurted out, "is something wrong? You don't seem like yourself tonight."

He forced a smile. "I guess I'm a little tired."

"I think we need to clear the air," I said. "It hasn't been the same between us since I told you about my living arrangements."

Rick sighed deeply. "Well, I have to admit it threw me for a loop. I didn't see that one coming."

"I'm really sorry," I said. "I'm so sorry I didn't tell you up front."

He looked at me intently. "I wish you had. I feel like . . . like I've been deceived."

His words jolted me, and tears welled in my eyes. "I didn't mean to lie to you," I said.

He made no response, just gazed at me wearily.

At that point, I knew for certain that the budding relationship between Rick and me couldn't bear the weight of the issues I'd been hiding from him. Irreparable damage had been done. Now I had nothing left to lose, and words poured out of my mouth before I could stop myself.

"I never meant for things to end up the way they did. Jake and I had drifted apart, and then he started a relationship with another woman, Rachel. I was getting ready to move out of the house. But then my plans fell through, and I had nowhere to go. Jake said I could stay, so I just moved to the other end of the house.

"Then my son became attached to Rachel, and they're really close now. All these years, I've been afraid my son would never forgive me if I moved him out of that house, so I've stayed. We all get along okay. I'd even say we're friends. I haven't tried dating until now, because I thought it would be too complicated. I guess I was right."

"River." Rick's voice sounded compassionate. He reached over and took my hand. "Your son doesn't know you're on a date tonight, does he?"

"No," I whispered, staring down at my plate. I slid my hand out from under Rick's and began twisting the dinner napkin on my lap.

"I figured that's why you didn't want me to pick you up at your house," he said. "Why didn't you tell him about me?"

My face burned with shame. "It's just complicated. That's all I can say."

I can't tell you the full truth, Rick, I thought. *I can't tell you that Thor doesn't know about the nature of Jake's relationship with Rachel. I can't tell you that my relationship with Jake isn't any different than it was prior to Rachel's coming. I can't tell you that Rachel clings to me in a weird way that makes me afraid of what would happen to her if I left the household.*

"I appreciate your being honest with me," Rick said. "And now I'll be honest with you. River, I can't do this."

I glanced up, but I couldn't bear to see the sadness on his face, so I lowered my eyes again. "I figured you'd say that," I mumbled.

"I wish I didn't have to say it," he said. "Believe me, I don't want to. Last night, I didn't sleep a wink, because I kept turning the situation over in my mind. Part of me wants to pursue this relationship, to see where it goes. I think I've already fallen for you. I'm enchanted by you, River, and I hate the idea of letting you go."

He focused on cutting a bite of steak, but instead of eating it, he laid his fork down and continued talking.

"I tried to be open-minded about your situation. I know you're doing what you believe is right, and I'm not in a position to judge. But I'm a traditional man. I can't help it, those values run deep. And I've got to think about my children. I can't put them or myself through anything messy, not after what we've all been through with my wife's death."

I stared at the table, twisting my napkin into a tight cord.

"And I don't want to be the man who upsets your son's life," he added. "I'm not that kind of guy, River."

A volcano of emotions welled inside me, years of pent-up feelings threatening to erupt. I was so angry, I could've thrown myself on the floor, kicking and screaming. But more than that, I was sad. I was heartbroken because my life circumstances held me prisoner while I watched an opportunity slip away, an opportunity to be with a good man who genuinely cared for me.

Through the roar of emotions in my head, I was dimly aware that Rick was still speaking. His every word and movement seemed surreal, in slow motion. He took out his wallet, pulled out a business card, and reached over to lay it beside my plate. "If you ever move out, River, call me. I hope you will."

The waitress stopped by our table to ask if we wanted dessert, jarring me back to the present moment. Rick looked at me questioningly, and I shook my head.

"Are you sure?" he asked. "They have some wonderful cheesecake here."

"No thanks," I said. Rick declined as well, and the waitress left our bill on the table.

"I need to go, Rick." My voice sounded harsh in my own ears. I reached into my handbag and pulled out several bills. "Here's for my meal."

Rick held up his hand in protest. "I wouldn't think of taking it. This is on me."

I shoved the money back into my bag and stood up to leave. Tears spilled from my eyes and began streaming down my cheeks. By the time I reached the door, I felt ashamed of my abrupt departure, and I turned back to look at Rick. He was sitting in a dejected slump, eyes downcast, toying with his silverware. When he glanced up and saw me looking at him, he lifted his hand in a final farewell gesture.

A bit of humor burst through my tortured thoughts. *The poor guy was scared to death to start dating. His first time out, he hooks up with a woman with a boatload of issues. It'll probably be another five years before he works up the nerve to try again.*

It wasn't until I was halfway home that I realized I'd left Rick's business card on the table. I knew I had no need for it.

The minute Rachel heard me open the door, she rushed into the living-room. When she saw the traces of tears on my face, she flew to my side to comfort me.

"Oh, Leah, what happened? What did Rick do to you?"

"Nothing," I said. "He didn't do anything. It's just not going to work out between us."

She wrapped her skinny arms around me and hugged me tightly. "I knew that guy was no good. You're better off here with us."

It felt strange to seek comfort from someone who was partly to blame for my dating failure, to be consoled by one of the very people who were holding me hostage. But at that point, I needed something to boost my sagging spirits, and when Rachel was done fussing over me, I walked down the hallway to Jake's studio. He was standing at his kiln, removing recently fired pieces and placing them on a shelf.

"It didn't work out, Jake," I said as I stood in the doorway.

"Huh?" he said, his eyes still on his work.

"My date. I won't be seeing him anymore."

He turned to look at me, and I could see the relief on his face. "I'm sorry to hear that, Lee. You deserve . . ." His voice trailed off as he lifted another piece from the kiln. "Damn it," he said, holding the bowl up to the light. "This one cracked."

"Deserve what, Jake?" I demanded to know. "What is it that I deserve?"

He continued to examine the bowl in his hands, seemingly ignoring me. But as I turned to walk away, he said, "Someone to love you, Lee. You deserve someone to love you."

Chapter 18

No doubt, my failed attempt at dating set me up for what happened next. I'm sure my grief and frustration clouded my thinking, rendering me vulnerable.

It started with an ordinary problem. Thor needed money for a school field trip the next day, and I didn't have the cash on hand. So I decided to ask Jake for help.

I poked my head into the living-room. "Do you know where your dad is?" I asked Thor.

"Nope," he responded, not looking up from the video game he was playing.

Rachel, in one of her dark moods, was lying on the sofa watching Thor play. "Do you know where Jake is, Rachel?" I asked.

She shifted her position, pulling her blanket around her shoulders. "How would I know?" she replied sullenly. "It's not my job to keep track of him."

I walked down the hallway to Jake's studio and found it empty. I looked out the side door to see if his truck was in the driveway. It was, so I knew he was somewhere on the property.

Without bothering to put on a jacket, I ran through the October chill to the workshop. The light was on and the door was unlocked, so I stepped inside. A quick glance around both rooms assured me Jake wasn't there. But a few tools were lying on his workbench, so I knew he'd recently been in the building.

I stepped outside. "Jake? Where are you, Jake?"

"I'm back here," he called. "Behind the shop."

I walked around the building and found Jake seated on a wooden bench. He was leaning forward with his forearms on his thighs, gazing at the view of the river against the backdrop of the brilliant autumn colors.

"Oh," I said, "I didn't know there was a bench back here."

"I built it a couple of months ago," he said, glancing up at me. "I needed a place to take a break." He grinned. "I'm getting to be an old man. I have to sit down once in awhile."

I waved my hand dismissively. "Jake, you're not old. You're barely middle-aged." My voice sounded coy, and I felt embarrassed, so I switched to another topic. "This is a perfect place to take a break, with the view of the river and the woods. Aren't the colors gorgeous this year?"

"They're awesome," he said. "Come sit down and enjoy them."

Jake's invitation surprised me. *Should I be doing this?* I wondered. *Isn't this a little too intimate?*

I looked at my former lover sitting there in his faded jeans and work boots, his long tail of hair, now mostly white, contrasting with the green of his well-worn sweatshirt. The sensuality this rugged man exuded was so strong, its pull was irresistible. I took several steps toward him, hesitating only a moment before seating myself on the bench beside him.

He glanced sideways at me. "So what do you need, Lee?"

"I almost forgot what I came for," I said. "Money. Thor has a field trip tomorrow, and I'm short on cash."

"No problem," he said. "I'll bring it by later this evening."

The breeze picked up, making me shiver, and I rubbed my arms to warm myself.

"You silly thing," Jake said. "What are you doing out here without a jacket? Come here." He put his arm around me and pulled me close to the warmth of his body.

Oh, my God! I thought. *What is he doing?* Jake hadn't touched me in ages. The familiarity of his body and the scent of his skin took me back to our early years together. Without thinking, I laid my head on his shoulder. A strand of my curly hair popped up and brushed against his face.

"That tickles," he said, chuckling. He shifted his position to tuck my hair back where it belonged, then tightened his arm around me and drew me even closer.

We must have sat like that for five minutes without speaking, taking in the splendor of the trees, the river, and the setting sun. It felt like we'd melted together, breathing as one person.

Jake was the first to break the silence. "This reminds me of the first time you came here, Lee. Remember? How long ago was that? Twelve, thirteen years?"

"Thirteen," I said. "Thor's twelve, so it would've been thirteen years ago."

He laughed. "We sure didn't expect him to come along, did we? It's funny how things work out."

He moved his hand up and down my arm as if to warm me, and the next thing I knew, his fingers were caressing my neck. My entire body tingled. I wondered if he was aware of what he was doing.

"Jake," I said, "do you think we should be doing this?"

"Doing what?" he asked.

"Being this close."

"Why not?"

"You know. Because of Rachel. You and Rachel."

Jake blew his breath forcefully through his lips. "Me and Rachel? That ship sailed a long time ago."

I drew back and looked at him. "You mean you aren't . . . ?" He interrupted me with a kiss.

"Jake, what are you doing?" I asked as he kissed me again and again.

Reluctantly, he released his embrace. "Sorry for getting carried away, Lee. Guess I've been a little too lonely lately."

I stared at him, my head reeling. "Me, too," I said. "I've been lonely, too."

"So we've both been lonely."

"Yes. But we shouldn't . . . we shouldn't . . ." I couldn't think of a way to finish my sentence, so I stood up to leave.

"I'll bring the money later," Jake called after me.

On my way back to the house, I willed myself to keep my emotions in check. I walked through the side door, down the hallway, through the kitchen and into the living-room, as if nothing at all had happened since I'd left the house ten minutes earlier. Thor was still playing his game, and Rachel looked as if she'd fallen asleep.

"Time to get ready for bed," I said to Thor. "Is your homework done?"

"Yes, Mom," he grumbled. He reluctantly put down the game controls and headed off to his room.

I walked over to the sofa and shook Rachel's shoulder. "Better get to bed, sleepyhead." She opened her eyes and stared at me, then slowly got up and stumbled off to her room, her blanket draped around her skinny body and dragging on the floor.

I went to the bathroom to brush my teeth, gazing at my reflection in the mirror, thinking about the kisses I'd shared with Jake. Then I closed my eyes, trying to reign in my runaway fantasies.

"Be careful, River, be careful," I whispered to myself.

I put on a short red satin nightgown, pretending the choice was random, refusing to admit to any motive for looking alluring. Leaving the door slightly ajar so Jake could enter with the money, I climbed into bed and read until I was too sleepy to keep my eyes open. I was disappointed that Jake hadn't shown up, but decided I would catch him first thing in the morning.

Just as I reached over to turn off the lamp on my nightstand, I remembered several items I wanted to take to school the next day. *I'd better put them in my bag so I won't forget them in the morning,* I told myself.

So I got up and packed my bag, and when I turned to climb back into bed, I saw Jake standing in the doorway, looking at me with hungry eyes.

I froze, feeling naked in my skimpy gown. "Oh. I didn't think you were coming."

"I told you I'd bring the money," he said. He took several steps into the room and laid two twenty-dollar bills on my dresser.

We stood there, staring at each other.

"You're beautiful, Lee. You know that?" Jake's voice was husky.

As if on cue, we moved toward each other, and Jake enfolded me in his arms, covering my lips, my neck, and my shoulders with kisses, all the while easing me toward the bed. A horrifying, yet amusing, thought raced through my mind: *what would straight-laced Rick think of me now?*

There have been plenty of times in my life when I've made mistakes, but didn't realize until later that I'd done the wrong thing. This time, I knew up front I was doing wrong, but I didn't stop myself. I couldn't stop myself.

Later, as I lay with my head on Jake's chest, it seemed like nothing had ever changed between the two of us, except for the fact that he now seemed more open, more tender. If it hadn't been for Rachel sleeping in her room at the other end of the house, I would have completely surrendered to our closeness.

Jake sighed deeply. "Guess I'd better get going, although I don't want to." He stroked my cheek with his fingers, and then kissed me one last time. "Thanks, Lee. You have no idea how much I needed this."

In the dim lighting, I watched him pull on his jeans and tee shirt. I wanted to ask questions. *What happens now, Jake? Are we together again? What do we do with Rachel?*

But I didn't.

I overslept the next morning. As I rushed around getting ready for work, I refused to let myself think about what had happened the night before. It wasn't until I was driving home from school that I allowed myself to savor the memories of making love with Jake, and to ponder the questions brewing in my mind. *Was this a one-time event? Will Jake come to my room again? Should I talk to him about what happened between us?*

It occurred to me that I hadn't been on birth control pills for five years, and I wondered whether I should call my doctor for another prescription. I decided to wait and see what happened next.

Rachel fixed a nice pasta dinner that evening, with a green salad and garlic bread. I felt uncomfortable with the idea of sharing a meal with her and Jake, but when I declined her invitation, she pouted.

"I don't understand you, Leah," she said. "I work so hard to please you. Evidently, what I do just isn't good enough."

I gave in to her petulance, and seated myself across the table from Jake. The two of us said little during the meal. Rachel quizzed Thor about the events of his school day, and scolded him about the book report he hadn't finished.

Jake and I both declined dessert, claiming we were too full. While Rachel stood at the counter with her back to us, cutting a brownie for Thor out of the batch she'd baked that day, Jake caught my eye and smiled ever so slightly. I felt myself blushing, and hoped my normal complexion would return before Rachel turned around.

Jake didn't come to my room that night. The next evening, I had a meeting and didn't get home until late. But whenever I had a moment to myself, my mind turned to thoughts of Jake. I felt excited, but confused and unsettled. When three days went by without a nighttime visit from him, I concluded our evening of passion was a random event.

Needless to say, I felt lousy every time I looked at Rachel. I suppose it was my guilt that made me offer to wash the dinner dishes the fourth evening. Rachel protested, but I was insistent, so she ran off to play music with Thor.

I was elbow deep in sudsy water when I felt a hand on my back. I turned and looked up to meet Jake's gaze. "Can I see you later tonight, Lee?" he whispered. I smiled. He brushed my cheek with a kiss and left the room.

He came around eleven o'clock, waking me up when he slid into my bed. After our lovemaking, he lingered until midnight, lying beside me holding my hand.

"We don't have much time to talk anymore, Lee," he said. "I miss that." I stifled a laugh, thinking Jake must have forgotten that we'd never spent much time talking.

He asked me how my job was going, and appeared to listen intently as I described the joys and challenges of my teaching position. He told me about his new business ventures, his new customers, and a new line of ceramics he'd envisioned.

Then he glanced at the clock on my nightstand. "I'd better let you get some sleep, Lee. Sorry for keeping you up so late."

"No problem," I said.

As I watched him dress, I knew I had to ask a question. "Jake?"

"What, Lee?"

"Are we together again?"

He sat back down on the bed and took my hand. "Were we ever really apart?"

His response confused me, and I didn't know what to say. He got up to leave, but just when he placed his hand on the doorknob, I said, "Shouldn't we work this out with Rachel?"

"What do you mean?" he asked.

I wasn't sure what I meant. *Are we supposed to announce to Rachel that Jake is switching partners? Have her sign a document, turning him over to me like the title of a car?*

I sighed. "It's just confusing to me, Jake."

"Don't worry about it, Lee," he said. "You worry too much." He opened the door and left the room.

The next day, I called my doctor's office and asked for a new prescription for birth control pills.

For the next month, Jake and I carried on a secret nightlife, a routine of passionate lovemaking followed by intimate conversation. Years earlier, I'd been satisfied with Jake as a lover, but this time around, our connection was even better. This time, he demonstrated a capacity for friendship. Whenever something important happened at school, I'd smile to myself, thinking, *I can't wait to tell Jake.*

One night, I mustered the courage to broach a sensitive topic with him. "Have you seen your folks recently?" I asked as I lay in his arms.

He stiffened slightly, then said, "I stopped by their place a couple of months ago."

I decided to venture another question. "Do they know about your life, Jake? Do they know you have a son?"

"No, they don't."

"Why not, Jake? Why have you kept Thor a secret?"

He was silent for awhile, and I wondered if I'd pushed him too far. But when he spoke again, he didn't sound upset. "In the beginning, it was just too difficult, Lee. I wasn't on good terms with them, and I knew they wouldn't take the news well. They probably would've disowned me. Now, it seems like there's too much water under the bridge."

I was seized with sadness, and Jake must have sensed it. "I know I screwed up, Lee. I should've told them right off the bat. I'm sorry. I don't want you to think I'm ashamed of you and Thor."

"You know, Jake," I said, "Thor's going to ask questions some day. I'm surprised he hasn't already."

"I've thought about that," he said. "I guess I'll deal with it when the time comes."

What seemed so right between Jake and me at night created an enormous amount of guilt for me during the daytime. I could hardly look at Rachel, and found excuses to leave any room she entered. She noticed this.

"Are you angry with me, Leah?" she asked. "You hardly talk to me anymore. It feels like you're avoiding me." She seemed oblivious to any change in the dynamics between Jake and me, and I knew he hadn't said anything to her.

That night, I brought the subject up to Jake a second time. When he retreated into silence, I rolled over with my back to him, feeling hurt and abandoned. But after a few minutes, he gently pulled me back into his arms. "I've been thinking about how to handle this," he said. "I realize it's my problem to deal with. I'll take care of it. I promise, Lee."

I made myself believe him.

Several nights later, I woke up in the early hours of the morning, and was momentarily confused when I discovered an arm around me. The next instant, I realized Jake had fallen asleep before he could make his usual late-night departure.

It was the first time he'd ever spent the night with me, and I was delighted with this new level of intimacy. But then I thought about what might happen if we were to be discovered by Rachel, who was sometimes an early riser.

I nudged him. "Jake, wake up! You'd better leave."

Apparently as alarmed as I was, he stumbled out of bed in a daze, fumbling to get his clothes on. In the process, he banged into my dresser, creating a terrible racket. I sat up in bed, cautioning him to be quiet.

When he opened the door to leave, I saw my sleepy-eyed, rumpled-haired adolescent son standing in the hallway outside my room.

"Oh, it's just you, Dad," he said. "I thought a burglar was trying to come through Mom's window." A wide grin spread across his face. I could only imagine what he was thinking, catching his parents in the act. But I thought I saw relief in his eyes. If he'd had any doubts about the viability of his parents' relationship, this incident offered him proof that his mother and father were still involved with each other.

"It's okay, Thor," I called. "Go back to bed."

I lay down again, my mind racing. I thought about all the times I'd almost told Thor about his father and Rachel, but hadn't. At that moment, I was glad I'd never had that talk with him. How would I ever explain to him that his father was cheating on his girlfriend with me?

Then a fearful thought struck me: *What if Thor innocently mentions this early morning encounter to Rachel?* "I thought I heard a burglar this morning," I imagined him saying. "But it was just Dad coming out of Mom's room."

Jake had to tell her about us. We couldn't wait any longer.

The next time he came to my room, I pushed the point. "Jake, have you said anything to Rachel?"

I felt his body tense up, and I turned away from him. The silence between us felt heavy and ominous.

"Come back to me when you've worked it out," I finally said.

"Lee, don't be this way," Jake pleaded. When I made no response, he got out of my bed and left the room.

Chapter 19

When I missed one monthly period, I told myself not to worry, that such things happen to women my age. With all the strength of my will, I demanded my period to come the next month. When it didn't, anxiety seized me and held me in its grip. I realized my responsible action of getting back on birth control had occurred too late.

It had been nearly a month since I'd given Jake the ultimatum about talking to Rachel. He hadn't returned to my room since then, and had avoided contact with me during the day. For a week, I grieved the ending of my love affair and the loss of my friend and confidante.

Then my feelings toward Jake settled into bitter resentment. I realized he hadn't really changed, that he was the same avoidant, non-communicative man he'd always been and always would be. His brief period of openness with me had been an aberration, an exception to the norm.

How could I have been so deluded? I asked myself. *How could I have possibly believed a relationship between me and Jacob Potter could work out?*

The consequences of my ill-advised affair left me feeling nauseated, ashamed, and in the clutches of a paralysis I'd never before experienced. I knew I had to face the fact that I was having another baby, and that this would create an explosion in the life of our household. While Thor might take having a sibling as a normal event, I was sure Jake wasn't interested in having a second child. And Rachel would be presented with the incontrovertible evidence that Jake had been unfaithful to her.

I really didn't want to talk to Jake, but I knew I had to. I finally succeeded in cornering him one cold December evening, in the finishing room of his workshop.

"Jake," I said. "Got a minute to talk?"

"Of course." His voice was polite but flat, and he kept his eyes glued to the cabinet he was finishing. The odor of the varnish offended my pregnancy sensibilities, making me feel violently ill.

"Can we go into the other room?" I asked, inching toward the door, waving my hand in front of my nose. "I can't stand the smell."

Jake looked at me suspiciously, then laid down his brush and followed me into the main room of the workshop.

"What is it, Lee?" He sounded guarded and impatient, and I knew I needed to be direct with him.

"I'm pregnant."

The room was deadly silent, except for the popping and crackling in the wood-burning stove. I studied Jake's face for a reaction. His eyes narrowed, and his jaw clenched ever so slightly.

He finally spoke, irritation in his voice. "Again?"

Rage coursed through my body. In my mind's eye, I saw a steel door slam shut between Jake and me. I knew with a certainty that it would never re-open, that I'd never again be intimate with Jacob Potter.

"Again?" I mimicked. "You view this as a mistake, don't you, Jake, just like our first child. Thor was nothing more than an accident to you."

"You know that's not what I mean, Lee." He looked away from me and glanced around the room, seemingly studying the details of the partially finished cabinets, the workbench, the tools hanging on the wall. "Are you sure it's mine?"

The rage surged again. "Of course it's yours, Jake! I haven't been with anyone but you for the past thirteen years!"

"Well, I didn't know what you'd done with that guy you were dating."

"I didn't do anything with Rick. This baby is yours, Jake. There's no way around that fact."

"I thought you were on birth control, Lee. If I'd known you weren't, I wouldn't have started anything. Why didn't you say something?"

I glared at him. "Neither of us was thinking very rationally when we started having sex. I don't believe you had the subject of birth control on your mind." Then I hung my head, staring at the swirls of sawdust on the concrete floor, feeling degraded and ashamed. "I hadn't taken birth control pills for years, not since Rachel came. There was no reason to. But after you and I had been together twice, I got back on them again. Evidently, it was too late."

I raised my head and met Jake's gaze, but I couldn't read the expression on his face. "You're absolutely sure you're pregnant?" he asked.

"Absolutely sure," I said. "I've missed two periods, and I have all the symptoms. I took a home pregnancy test, and it was positive."

He shrugged. "Okay, then." Abruptly, he turned his back on me and headed toward his finishing room, as if impatient to get back to work. His seeming indifference to my plight enraged me all the more.

"What are we going to do about this, Jake?" I shouted. "You can't just ignore this."

He turned to face me again. "I need some time to think about it, Lee."

"Of course you do," I said sarcastically. "You have to think about everything, don't you, Jake?" I turned and ran out the door, hating him, loathing myself.

As I hurried toward the house, I saw Rachel standing by the side door in her flannel pajamas, hugging herself to ward off the cold. "Is something wrong, Leah?" she asked, eyeing me quizzically.

"No," I said, brushing past her.

"You're lying," she said as she followed me down the hallway. "Something is wrong. I can feel it. Something is terribly wrong. You need to tell me, Leah."

"Not now, Rachel," I said. "I need to be alone." I entered my room and closed the door, then locked it for good measure.

I waited and waited for Jake's response. The days turned into weeks, with me growing more frustrated by the hour. The house seemed confining, and the tension involved with guarding my secret from Rachel and Thor made me feel crazy. So I stayed away from home as much as possible.

I knew that in the end, the problem of my pregnancy would be mine to deal with, as Jake had clearly chosen the path of avoidance. As I ruminated on my dilemma, I came up with only one option. I would move out of the house and start a new life with Thor and the baby, leaving Jake and Rachel behind for good.

Rachel seemed to sense my despondency. She took it upon herself to imbue the house with holiday cheer, enlisting Thor's help in decorating the tree and baking holiday goodies. She must have wrangled money out of Jake, because she came home from shopping trips with bulging bags. Soon, beautifully wrapped gifts appeared under the tree.

I didn't have the heart to ruin Christmas for everyone by announcing my pregnancy, and I convinced myself I could make it through the holidays with my secret intact. I promised myself that once New Year's Day was past, I'd break the news to my mother and revisit the idea of moving Thor and me into her home.

The resolution to my problem came quicker than I expected, in a painful and unanticipated way.

It was New Years Eve, and I'd almost made it through the holidays with my secret intact. *Tomorrow,* I told myself, *I'll go see my mom, and we'll have a chat. Then I'll break the news to Thor that I'm having a baby, and that we'll be moving. He'll have several days left of his holiday break to adjust to the idea before he returns to school.*

I had no definite plans for that evening. I thought about accepting an invitation to a friend's party, in order to avoid another night of solitary brooding. Rachel wanted me to stay home, and she fluttered around me, chattering about what we could do to usher in the New Year. She prepared a special meal, a new seafood dish, and persuaded all of us to join her around the dinner table.

"I know this is going to be a great year for all of us," she announced as she filled our plates. "The best year ever."

You couldn't be more wrong, Rachel, I thought. I glanced at Jake. His face was expressionless, and he averted his gaze when he saw me looking at him.

I took a bite of shrimp and rice. "How do you like it?" Rachel asked, eager for my approval.

Just when I was ready to pronounce her culinary creation delicious, I was seized with terrible cramps. I dropped my fork and pushed back my chair, clutching my abdomen. I knew immediately what was happening.

"Oh, Leah!" Rachel gasped. "Is something wrong with the food?"

I shook my head.

"You okay, Lee?" Jake asked.

I shook my head again, and then succumbed to another wave of cramping. As I struggled to my feet and headed toward the bathroom, I could feel warm blood running down my thighs.

I heard Rachel say to Jake, "I'll go help her."

I closed myself in the bathroom and sat on the stool, breathing through wave after wave of agonizing cramps, feeling hot one minute and chilled the next.

The door opened and Rachel stepped in. "Leah, I hate to see you like this. Is there anything I can do?"

"I'll be alright in a few minutes," I moaned.

"You're having a miscarriage, aren't you?"

I nodded and began to sob. I felt so weak I thought I might collapse and fall off the stool.

Rachel placed her hand on my shoulder to steady me. "I'm taking you to the emergency room. Stay right here. I'll be back in a minute." Her voice carried unusual authority, and I nodded in mute consent.

I heard her talking to Jake in the hallway. "I need the keys to the truck. I'm taking Leah to the hospital."

"I can take her," Jake said.

"No!" Rachel's voice sounded angry. "She doesn't need you, she needs a woman."

On the way to the hospital, I huddled in the passenger seat, feeling drained and helpless. Rachel periodically glanced over at me and patted my arm, murmuring, "It'll be okay, Leah."

Even in my foggy state of mind, I was struck by the reversal of our roles. She'd become the mother figure, and I was now the needy child.

In the emergency room, Rachel confidently took care of business at the reception window, and then stayed by my side while hospital staff situated me in a bed and started me on IV fluids. When we were alone, she smoothed my hair back from my face and crooned, "Don't worry, Leah, I'm here with you. I'm not going to leave you."

I was beginning to recover my senses by then, and the sweetness in her voice irritated me. As she stroked my hair, I felt the urge to smack her hand away.

"I'm okay, Rachel," I said a little too gruffly. She leaned back in her chair and clasped her hands together in her lap, a hurt look in her eyes.

After a few minutes, she said, "It was Jake's, wasn't it."

Her matter-of-fact observation caught me off guard. I'd expected that she would initially attribute my pregnancy to the man she despised, the infamous Rick. But I felt enormously relieved that my secret was now in the open.

"Yes," I said, "it was Jake's." I forced myself to turn my head and make eye contact with her. "I'm sorry, Rachel. I'm so sorry. I never meant for this to happen."

"It's okay, Leah." Her voice was calm.

I was puzzled. "No, it's not okay, Rachel. You should be angry with me. I betrayed you."

"How can I be mad at you, Leah? After everything you've done for me, how could I hold anything against you?" Her face darkened. "I'm sure it was Jake's fault, anyway. He's like that, you know."

I wanted to jar her out of her complacency. "It wasn't just Jake's fault. I'm to blame, too. What I did wasn't right. You should be angry."

"Jake doesn't belong to me, Leah. You were here first. I was the intruder." Rachel got up and wandered slowly around the small room, fingering my IV tubing, running her hand along my bed railing, straightening the covers over my feet. She stopped to gaze at a picture hanging on the wall, her back to me. "I kind of figured you and Jake would do it once in awhile."

"And that didn't bother you?"

"No." Rachel turned around and laughed, as if a ridiculous idea had occurred to her. "Leah, do you still think I love Jake?"

"I really don't know, Rachel. I've never been sure about the two of you. I know at least in the beginning, Jake was in love with you, very much so."

"I know." Rachel's eyes took on a faraway look. "But I'm not in love with him. I'm in love with someone else."

Her revelation mystified me. I couldn't imagine how she could have met someone new. She virtually never left home except to run errands, and that was usually done in the company of Jake or me. Was she pining for an old lover?

"Who?" I asked. "Who are you in love with, Rachel?"

She stared at me for a long moment, chewing her lip, her brow furrowed. Then she looked away. "Oh, never mind."

"Rachel," I said. "I know I've told you this before, but this time I really mean it. I'll be leaving soon. Thor and I will be leaving. The only reason I've stayed so long is for Thor's sake. But it's time for us to go, and he'll have to adjust to it. Then maybe you and Jake can get things straightened out between the two of you."

Fear flickered in her eyes. "Don't leave me alone with Jake, Leah. Please don't. Let me be the one to leave."

After a lengthy wait in the emergency room, I was given an ultrasound, which confirmed the fact that I'd lost the fetus I'd been carrying. Then I had to undergo dilation and curettage of my uterus, an unpleasant procedure that further drained my strength and dampened my spirits.

After the procedures were over, Rachel rushed back to my bedside. "I feel so sorry for you, Leah," she said, her eyes brimming with tears. "I hate to see you suffer like this."

Finally, after giving me a list of discharge instructions, the emergency room doctor pronounced me ready to go home. His nurse helped me into a wheelchair, while Rachel left to bring the truck around. As I sat by the exit door waiting for my ride, feeling exhausted and bedraggled, I heard the emergency room staff noisily counting down the seconds before the clock struck midnight. Then they burst into raucous whooping and cheering.

I felt a tear slide down my face. I don't think there's been another moment in my life when I've pitied myself more. Instead of ushering in the New Year with champagne and kisses, I was being sent home to recover from the ending of an ill-fated pregnancy.

As Rachel pulled up in the truck, the nurse came to wheel me out the door. "I'm sorry," she said as the cheers resounded in the background. "This isn't a good time for you, is it?" I had to give her credit for her sensitivity.

When we got home, I went to Thor's room to check on him. He was in bed, wide awake, reading a comic book. He looked relieved to see me. "Are you okay, Mom? I was really worried about you."

"I'm fine," I lied. "I just had a really bad stomachache. I'll probably need to rest for a few days."

Just after I'd settled into bed for the night, I heard a tap on the door. "Come in," I said, thinking it was Rachel checking on me one last time. But the door opened to reveal Jake standing there.

"Come in," I repeated.

He didn't move. He looked like he was scared to death to approach my bed, a place where he'd spent so much time just weeks ago. He seemed to know it was off limits to him, now and forever.

I remembered the conversation I'd had with him behind his woodworking shop, when he'd referred to himself as an old man. *He's right,* I thought. *He looks old.* The strain of the past few hours seemed to have aged him ten years.

"I just want you to know how sorry I am, Lee," he said.

"What for, Jake?"

"Everything. Everything."

Chapter 20

After the miscarriage, I fell into a depression, the likes of which I'd never before experienced. When my holiday break ended a few days after the traumatic event, I didn't feel ready to return to work. So I took a week of sick leave, allowing the school to believe the plausible story that I had a bad case of the flu.

I stayed in bed most of that time, overcome by spells of weeping, trying to make sense of the chain of emotional challenges I'd recently experienced: the failed relationship with Rick, the harsh reality check following my affair with Jake, the misbegotten pregnancy, and the loss of the baby.

I'd never desired a second baby, as having a single child had seemed perfect to me. But before the miscarriage, I'd begun to view my baby as someone who deserved consideration. I'd find my imagination wandering. *Would it be another boy, or would I have a daughter this time? Would it be another redhead, or a blonde like me? Would it be artistic like Jake and me, or musically inclined like Thor? Or would it carve out its own niche as an athlete, a scientist, an entrepreneur?*

In spite of its regrettable conception, I grieved for this unborn soul, this child whom I would never know.

When my depression became too much to bear, I turned to the solace of sleep. When I'd wake up, I'd feel so dark and heavy, so dead inside that I'd close my eyes and sleep again.

Somewhere within me, I knew that the darkness would pass, that change would come. It had to come, because I could no longer tolerate the weird status quo of my household relationships. I had no idea what form that change would take, but I prayed for it to come quickly.

My mother, with her unconditional acceptance of me, could have been helpful during that time. But even though I knew she wouldn't judge me, I felt too ashamed to tell her about my recent mistake and its unfortunate consequences.

As she usually did, she called me at least once a week. I'd listen to her chatter about my father's condition, and how her most recent discovery in the realm of herbal remedies had perked him up.

But she noticed I was deflecting the conversations away from myself. "River, honey," she said one day, "I sense something is amiss in your world."

"I'm just going through a bit of a slump," I said. "You know how it is this time of the year."

"It could be a dark night of the soul. You need to embrace it, River. Discover the wisdom it offers you. A dark passage always precedes a period of growth."

I sighed. "I know, Mom."

I was glad she didn't push me for details. I felt it was best if the secret of my pregnancy and miscarriage was kept by just three people, Jake, Rachel, and myself. I knew Jake wouldn't tell anyone else, and Rachel had no one outside of the household to confide in.

But I needed to make sure. One morning when she dutifully brought me orange juice and scrambled eggs on a tray, I said, "Rachel, you won't tell anybody about this, will you?"

"Of course not, Leah," she said. "It isn't my business to tell."

"Not even Thor? Promise me you won't tell Thor."

Rachel sat down on the edge of my bed, gazing at me solemnly. "Leah, I wouldn't think of telling Thor. It would hurt him. You know I would never hurt Thor."

I reached out to squeeze her hand. "Thank you, Rachel."

During my days of recovery, Rachel hovered over me as much I would allow. I had to tell her repeatedly that I needed solitude.

"I just want you to know I don't hold anything against you," she said. "I hate Jake for what he did to you."

"Have you and Jake talked about what happened?" I asked.

She shook her head. "No. Why should we?"

The Saturday before the Monday I was due to return to school, I woke up with a flicker of light illuminating the darkness in my mind, a feeble ray of hope. I suddenly knew what I needed to do to work my way through my emotional quagmire. I needed to paint.

My creative energy was ready to flow, eager to be released. I envisioned a series of watercolor paintings, and I set up my work station as soon as I got out of bed.

My first painting depicted a meadow strewn with wildflowers. A path running through it came to a fork where it split into two paths that wound through the meadow in opposite directions. A man and woman who'd apparently been traveling together were just beginning to walk their separate ways. Their hands were extended in a lingering touch, their final contact.

"What are you doing, Leah?" Rachel asked when she came to my room to check on me.

I was surprised that her question didn't annoy me, that I wasn't irritated when she stood close to me and peered at my canvas. "I'm painting," I responded.

"Why?"

I put down my brush and gave her my full attention. "Sometimes, expressing feelings through art can help a person get through difficult times. The past few months have been hard on me."

"I know," she said. "I've felt so sorry for you. What are you painting?"

"What do you think?"

"Well, it's a man and a woman. They're walking away from each other. What does it mean?"

"That's Rick and me. Our paths crossed briefly, then we said goodbye and went our separate ways."

Rachel wrinkled her nose in disgust. "Why do you want to paint that guy? Are you sad over him?"

"Yes," I said. "I'm sad over Rick. He wasn't a bad guy. He was actually a very nice man. We just weren't right for each other. But I'm still sorry I had to say goodbye to him."

Rachel sighed. "I know he wasn't bad. I was just jealous, that's all."

I knew what she meant, that she'd resented the attention I'd given to Rick, wanting it for herself. But I decided to tease her by assuming the other possible interpretation of her statement. "So are you interested in dating Rick? I could call him and tell him, if you want."

Rachel shot me a look of outrage. "How could you say such a thing?" she wailed as she ran from the room.

I completed my second painting the next day. It portrayed images of a man and woman separated by a wall, each wearing frustrated, melancholy expressions. When Rachel came to view the finished product, she exclaimed, "Oh, this one's dark and gloomy." She studied it carefully. "That's you and Jake, isn't it?"

"You're right," I said.

"That wall between you won't let you be together. Is that wall me?"

"Oh no, Rachel! That wall was there before you came along. Jake and I have never really connected. It's just our personalities. We don't fit with each other."

Rachel nodded, looking thoughtful. "The reason you don't fit with Jake is because you're too good for him, Leah. You deserve someone better, someone even better than Rick."

"I don't know about that," I said. "I appreciate Jake. We had a purpose in each other's lives. We made Thor, and I wouldn't trade my son for anything in the world."

"If it wasn't for Jake," Rachel observed, "I would've never met you. I hate to think how sad my life would be if I'd never met you. Jake brought us together."

Her words made me uncomfortable. I smiled at her, but made no comment.

Getting back into my routine at school consumed all of my energy, and I didn't paint during the week. But the following Saturday, I completed my third painting. A sleeping infant lay curled in the center of a large daisy. Several of the petals folded over the baby, forming a coverlet.

"Oh, Leah," Rachel said when she saw it. "This is your baby, isn't it?"

I watched a tear slide down her face, and I blinked back my own tears. "Yes. This painting represents the baby I lost."

"This is the most beautiful picture I've ever seen. This is our baby girl."

"We don't know whether it was a girl, Rachel."

"It was a girl. I'm sure of it." She seated herself on my bed in a cross-legged position, gazing at me with a contemplative expression on her face. "You know what, Leah? We never had a funeral for the baby. That isn't right."

Her words made me think. I knew there was truth in what she'd said. My mother had raised me to understand the importance of a ceremony, and many transitions in my life had been marked by ceremonies. But other than painting the picture, I'd done nothing to commemorate the child I'd lost.

"You're right," I said. "We should have a funeral."

"What should we do?"

"I don't know. Do you want to do something Jewish? Read something out of the Tanakh?"

Rachel waived her hand. "No, Jewish funerals are too complicated. Too boring for a baby. Let's do something from your religion."

"I don't really have a religion, Rachel."

"Make something up."

"I supposed we could light some candles, maybe some incense, and do a little drumming."

"That's perfect," Rachel said. "We'll do a drumming circle for our baby girl."

That afternoon, Rachel and I made a pilgrimage into town to purchase supplies for the evening ceremony. We bought a bouquet of delicate flowers, pink rosebuds with baby's breath. We chose candles in pastel colors, and I found a type of incense with a light, sweet scent.

As we were preparing for our ceremony that evening, Thor poked his head into the room. "Are you doing a drumming circle?"

"Yes, we are," I replied.

"Good," he said. "I'll play the flute."

I was caught off guard by Thor's assumption that he'd be included in what we were doing. While I racked my brain for an explanation as to why he couldn't participate, Rachel stepped in.

"This is a women's circle," she explained. "It's about female stuff."

Thor made a face. "Okay, I'm outa here!"

As Rachel and I decorated my bedroom with the flowers and candles, it occurred to me that this was the room in which the baby had received its life. It seemed fitting that the funeral ceremony should also take place here. The flickering candlelight bathed the room in a soft glow, illuminating the portrait of the baby, and the sweet smell of incense wafted through the air. The setting was perfect.

Rachel and I seated ourselves opposite each other on the floor. Her face was solemn, her dark eyes serious. For the first time in all the years I'd known her, I was glad to have her there with me, to feel her sisterly support as we commemorated the child I'd lost. No one in the world but Rachel could have known exactly what I'd been through, and exactly what I needed to ease my pain.

"We need to drum very softly for a baby," she said. She closed her eyes and began tapping the head of her drum, barely brushing the surface with her fingertips, humming a sweet, melancholy tune of her own creation.

Later that evening, Jake walked into the kitchen while I was putting away the dishes I'd just washed. I tensed up, wanting him to get what he came for and leave the room.

But he lingered. I continued with my task, trying to ignore his brooding silence. Finally he spoke. "What was going on in your room this evening?"

"Rachel and I were having a memorial service for the baby," I said.

"The baby?"

I turned to look at him. "The baby I lost."

"You didn't say anything about it to me. Did you even consider that I might . . . ?"

I stared at him, dumbfounded. I'd never before seen wounded feelings reflected on his face. "What, Jake?"

"You don't think I care about anything, do you, Lee? You just think I'm some coldhearted prick."

I felt much better after the ceremony for my baby. But something still seemed unfinished, and I realized I needed to do one more painting.

"This is beautiful," Rachel observed as she watched me render the colors of a brilliant sunrise on my canvas. "You're so good at this, Leah." Then she peered closely as I painted the tiny figure of a woman walking toward the sunrise, arms outstretched. "Who's that?"

"That's me," I explained, "walking into my future. It symbolizes that I've passed through my difficult time. Now I'm moving forward with my life."

Rachel studied the painting, her head cocked to one side. "This picture is about you leaving, Leah. I don't like it. It scares me."

I couldn't disagree with her. Leaving was definitely on my mind. But once again, I convinced myself that I needed to wait until the end of the school term and make my big move over the summer. *In a month or two,* I told myself, *I'll start talking to Thor about it.*

It seemed that as my outlook improved, Rachel's state of mind deteriorated. I was accustomed to her mood swings, the episodes of sluggish gloom alternating with periods of energetic cheerfulness. But this was different. She seemed extra sensitive and fragile, fumbling through household chores she normally completed with expertise.

One day, she dropped a cup while drying dishes and cried out in anguish when it shattered on the floor. Then she sat down at the kitchen table and wept with her face buried in her folded arms. Another day, she forgot to put detergent in a load of laundry. When she realized her mistake, she sank to the floor and sat with her back against the washing machine, staring into space, seemingly unable to figure out how to correct her error.

I attributed this change to her realization that Thor and I would be leaving the household in the near future. I felt genuinely sorry for her, regretting that the anticipated improvement in my life would take place at her expense. I imagined her living alone with Jake, overcome with sorrow, wandering around the house like a phantom, withering away to nothing.

I forced this dreadful image from my mind, as I knew I couldn't stop my forward momentum for her sake. But because of my guilt, I put aside my reservations when she became emotionally distraught and gave her comforting hugs. She'd cling to me, weeping like a desperate child.

One evening in early March, I walked into the living room and found her huddled on the sofa, sobbing. "What is it, Rachel?" I asked as I sat down beside her. "You've been crying so much lately."

She said nothing, but moved toward me, and I didn't protest as she crawled onto my lap and threw her arms around my neck. I hugged her tightly.

"Ouch!" she exclaimed.

"I'm sorry, Rachel." I released my embrace and gently pushed her away from me. "I didn't mean to hurt you."

"It's okay," she said. "It's just my boobs. They've been so sore recently." She wrapped her arms around me again. "Hold me, Leah. I need you to hold me."

"Is it your time of the month?" I asked. "Your breasts are sore, and you're so emotional."

"No," she said. "Just hold me." She nuzzled her face against my neck, then reached up and caught the corner of my mouth with a kiss.

Startled by her display of affection, I recoiled and pushed her away. "No, Rachel. Don't do that." With a little sob, she let go and lay limply across my lap.

Suddenly, I suspected a possibility I hadn't considered before. I place my hand on her lower abdomen and felt the hard bulge of her growing uterus through the flimsy fabric of her pajamas.

"Rachel, you're pregnant."

"I thought I might be." She reached up to kiss me again.

"No, Rachel. You can't do that."

"But I love you, Leah," she protested. Then she began to cry again. "Don't leave me, Leah. I want to go with you. Put me in your painting so I can walk into the sunrise with you. We can be a family together, you and me and Thor and the baby."

At that moment, Thor appeared in the doorway of the living-room. "What's going on?" he asked. Rachel startled and quickly sat up.

My face burned with embarrassment, and I breathed a prayer of gratitude that my son hadn't walked in a minute earlier. "Rachel's just having a bad day," I explained.

"Rachel's always having a bad day." The sarcasm in Thor's voice told me he'd run out of patience with the erratic behavior of his childhood friend.

Rachel looked as if Thor's sharp words had stabbed her in the heart. "I'm sorry," she cried as she jumped up and ran from the room.

Anger burned in Thor's eyes. "Why is everything around here so depressing? Why can't things be normal for a change?"

I wanted to capitalize on the moment, to use Thor's expression of discontentment as a platform for introducing the subject of future plans. But before I could speak, he muttered, "I'm sick of this," and stalked out of the room.

I felt terrible about the abrupt ending of my conversation with Rachel, and I worried about her emotional state. I knew she'd experienced a double dose of rejection, my refusal of her overture followed by Thor's criticism. I went to her room, and as I listened outside her closed door, I could hear muffled sobbing. When she didn't respond to my knock, I attempted to open the door, but it was locked. I gave up, resolving to talk to her later.

To my relief, she responded to my knock the following morning with a feeble, "Come in." I found her curled up in bed in a fetal position, her long hair fanned out over her pillow. Her eyes were red and puffy, and I imagined her night had been as sleepless as mine.

I sat down on the bed and took her hand, but instead of clutching like she usually did, her hand lay limply in mine. "Rachel," I said, "we need to finish the conversation we started last night."

"I don't want to," she whimpered. "I'm embarrassed. Just forget about it, Leah."

"No, Rachel," I said. "We're not sweeping this under the rug. We've got to deal with your pregnancy and . . . your feelings."

Rachel closed her eyes, wincing at my words. "Just go away, Leah. Why do you care? You hate me anyway."

I felt so frustrated, I almost shouted at her. "Rachel! Sit up and talk to me like a grown-up!"

Startled, she opened her eyes and slowly pulled herself to a sitting position. "Okay," she said, brushing the hair out of her face.

"How did this happen?" I asked. "All these years of being with Jake, and now all of a sudden you're pregnant? Did the two of you plan this?"

Rachel hung her head, trying to avoid eye contact with me, but I raised her chin and forced her to look at me. "No," she mumbled, "we didn't plan it. Jake was using those things to keep me from getting pregnant. He said he didn't want us to have children."

"You were using condoms?"

She nodded, contorting her face in disgust. "He kept them here in my room. But last year, we stopped having sex." A defiant expression crossed her face. "Because I didn't want to. That's probably why he went to you, because I didn't want to."

Of course, I thought. *That makes perfect sense.*

"So I threw those nasty things away," she continued, "because I told myself I would never have sex with Jake again. I made that promise to myself. Then in November, he came to my room, out of the blue."

I bristled, recognizing this as the same time I'd issued Jake the ultimatum about talking to Rachel. *He couldn't face the messy challenge of telling her what was going on between us. He couldn't handle the pressure I was putting on him. So he walked away from me and forced himself back into her life. That spineless, selfish son-of-a-bitch!*

"He made me do it," Rachel said. "I was afraid to say no to him. I was afraid he'd make me leave."

"Is he still coming to your room?" I asked.

She nodded, looking repulsed. "I don't love him, Leah."

"I know. You told me that."

"I've never loved Jake, Leah. I love you. I've loved you for a long time. I thought you were starting to love me back. You stopped being so grouchy with me, and you were giving me hugs. I thought you might be happy about my baby, because it would make up for the one you lost. I thought we could raise it together. But that was all just a big stupid idea. I'm such an idiot."

"You're not an idiot, Rachel," I said. "I do care about you, but it's like a sister thing. I don't love women in a romantic way. Not that it's a bad thing. I'm just not made that way."

"I know, Leah. I should've known that all along." Rachel turned away from me, staring out her bedroom window. I could tell she wanted the conversation to be over. But I wasn't finished.

"Does Jake know you're pregnant?"

She shook her head.

"Surely he can tell. Your body's changing."

"He hasn't said anything."

"Then you need to talk to him about it. Don't wait any longer, tell him today. Make him take you to a doctor. The two of you should start making plans for this baby. And then you and Jake need to explain things to Thor."

Rachel's eyes widened with fear. "I can't! Thor will hate me!"

My voice softened. "I'll stand by you, Rachel, the same way you stood by me when I had the miscarriage. But I can't do this for you. This is your responsibility, yours and Jake's."

Then, to convince myself as well as her, I added, "At the end of the school year, Thor and I will be moving out. Then you and Jake can focus on raising your child."

"No, Leah," she whispered.

"Yes, Rachel," I said.

Chapter 21

Over the next two months, a cloud of gloom hung over our home. I knew Thor sensed it. He grew surly to the point of disrespect, and when he wasn't escaping the house by hanging out with his friends, he secluded himself in his room. I didn't have the heart to discipline him for his adolescent rebellion, since the adults in the household were guilty of far more serious crimes.

I wanted so badly to take my son aside, to explain to him what was going on, and to offer hope that in a few short months, things would change for him and me. But I knew that announcing Rachel's pregnancy wasn't my responsibility, and I was determined not to allow Jake and Rachel to avoid what they needed to do.

So I waited. I watched as Rachel began wearing extra-large tee shirts to hide her growing abdomen. I rarely spoke to Jake, as he managed to stay out of my sight. No doubt, he knew my respect for him had dwindled to nothing.

From time to time, my concern for Rachel overrode my resolve to mind my own business, and I'd ask whether she'd seen a doctor. "Not yet," she'd say. "I'll have Jake take me soon."

I grew increasingly worried about her, and came close to telling her I'd take her myself. But I knew if I became her partner in prenatal care, I'd refuel her fantasy of her and me raising the baby together. So I bit my tongue and continued to wait.

Then one evening in early May, the life we'd known in our household for the past six years came crashing down around us. I was busy with schoolwork in my bedroom, vaguely aware that Rachel was cooking dinner. Suddenly, I heard a shriek, a crash, and the splash of water. I ran to the kitchen to see what mishap had occurred.

What I saw will be forever etched in my mind, three figures frozen in mid-action, like a scene captured in a photograph. Rachel stood in front of the stove, her arms flung in the air. A large pot lay on the floor in a puddle of water, apparently having just slipped out of her hands.

The front of her tee shirt was drenched and clinging to her body.

Thor stood about four feet to Rachel's side, staring in open-mouthed horror at the bulge of her abdomen outlined under her wet shirt. Jake, who'd just entered the kitchen from the hallway, stood like a hulking statue, one hand resting on the doorframe.

Then the action resumed. Thor's face contorted into an expression of outrage, and words he never used in my presence began flying from his mouth. "What the hell?" he shouted, pointing at Rachel's belly. "You're pregnant! What the fuck is going on here?"

I could almost see his brain churning, events from the past six years falling into place, the disturbing picture coming into focus in his maturing mind. He turned to glare at Jake, jabbing his finger in the air. "You son-of-a-bitch! You did this to her!"

None of us adults said a word as Thor stood there shaking with fury, his fists clenched at his sides. He glanced around and saw me standing in the doorway to the living-room.

"You're liars!" he shouted, including me in his condemnation. "This house is full of liars! You guys are sick, you're all crazy! I'm not staying here anymore! I'm going to Grandma's!" He pointed at me. "Mom, tomorrow you're taking me to Grandma's!"

I stood aside as he brushed past me and stalked out of the house, slamming the front door behind him.

That night, for the first time in almost thirteen years of parenting, I stayed up waiting for my son to return home. Too frightened to read or watch TV, too immobilized to pace the floor, I maintained a silent vigil, sitting motionless on the living-room sofa.

I wasn't angry at my rebellious son, as I knew full well he was the victim of a massive scheme of deception the adults in the household had perpetrated for years. I could only imagine how he felt.

He came quietly through the front door around 11:00 PM. He glanced at me sitting on the sofa, and then looked away.

"We're leaving first thing in the morning," I said. "I've got most of your things packed. You don't need to worry about school tomorrow.

I've already called in for both of us."

He nodded and walked past me to his room.

I spent most of that night lying awake, staring at the ceiling of a room I knew I'd never sleep in again. The day of change had finally arrived, not in the reasonable way I'd envisioned, but in the form of a bomb exploding in the middle of our household.

I had just fallen into a restless sleep when I was awakened by the sound of knocking on my bedroom door. A glance at my alarm clock told me the time was 6:30 AM. Reluctantly, I slid out of bed and wrapped my robe around me. When I opened the door, I found Jake standing there, his face white with shock.

"She's gone, Lee," he said. "Rachel's gone."

"Huh?" My dazed mind couldn't comprehend what he'd told me.

"I woke up about an hour ago. Something didn't feel right to me. I went to her room to check on her. The door was open, her stuff was cleared out. She's gone."

"Oh my God, Jake!" I exclaimed. "What are you going to do?"

"I don't know."

He headed toward the kitchen, and I followed him. I sank onto a chair and watched him make a pot of coffee. He stood with his back to me, silently waiting for the coffee to brew. His muscular physique looked as if all the strength had been drained from it, and he propped up his sagging frame by leaning heavily on the hand pressed against the countertop.

Finally, he reached into the cupboard for two mugs, filled them with coffee, and brought them to the table. He sat down across from me, worry etched in every line of his face. "I spent forty-five minutes driving around looking for her," he said. "I figured she might've gone to the train station, so I went there. I even checked inside, but she wasn't there. My wallet was lying out on the table in the studio. I'm missing some money, forty or fifty bucks. She didn't take it all. I figure she took what she needed to get to wherever she's going. She's never stolen from me before."

His frightened eyes appealed for my help. "What should we do, Lee?"

"Call the police, I guess. That's all I can think of. Make a missing person report."

"I suppose we should."

"But you know what, Jake," I continued, "Rachel's an adult, and she has the right to go anywhere she wants to go. She has no obligation to stay here. Did you think about the fact that she probably doesn't want you to find her?"

He stared at me with misery-filled eyes.

Just then, Thor walked into the kitchen. His lip curled in disgust when he saw his father, and he turned around and headed back to his room.

The sight of Thor reminded me what my priority needed to be. I'd promised my son we would leave that morning, and that's what we would do. The crisis of Jake's missing girlfriend would have to be his to deal with. I got up, grabbed a granola bar from the cupboard, poured a glass of juice, and took the food to Thor's room.

"Here's your breakfast," I said. "Get dressed, and then we'll load the car. We can't take everything today. We'll come back for the rest later."

As I stepped out of Thor's room and closed the door behind me, Jake confronted me in the hallway.

"Please don't leave now, Lee," he begged, tears pooling in his eyes. "I can't take all of you leaving at once."

"I'm sorry, Jake," I said. "Thor and I need to go."

For the first ten minutes of the drive to my mother's house, Thor stared out the car window in silence. I made no attempt to engage him in conversation, and waited until he finally spoke.

"How could you even talk to him, Mom?"

"What do you mean, Thor?"

"How could you sit there at the table drinking coffee with Dad, like nothing was wrong?"

I took a deep breath. "Thor, I had to talk to him. Your dad came to me this morning and told me Rachel was gone. She left some time during the night. Your dad was really worried. We were talking about what he needed to do."

"Oh!" Thor turned and stared out the window again. "Well, I don't blame her for leaving." A few minutes later, he turned back toward me, crossing his arms defiantly over his chest. "Tell me why you put up with this, Mom."

"Put up with what, Thor?" I asked, even though I knew full well what he was talking about.

"You put up with Dad cheating on you. You didn't do anything about it."

"It's not quite the way you think it is, Thor."

"Then what is it? Tell me the truth. I don't want to hear any more lies."

I kept my eyes on the road in front of me, choosing my words carefully. "Do you remember when you were six years old, and I told you Rachel was coming?"

"Yes. You told me a friend was moving in because she didn't have anywhere else to stay."

"Well, Thor, I should've been more honest with you from the beginning. Rachel wasn't just a friend. She was your dad's lover."

I glanced sideways at my son, meeting his horrified stare. "You mean you let Dad have another girlfriend? You just sat there and let him move her into our house?"

"Don't you remember, Thor?" My voiced sounded defensive. "I was planning to move us to Grandma's house. But you didn't want to go, and I didn't want to upset you, so we stayed."

"You should've made me move," he said. "I would've gotten over it. You shouldn't always do things because of me. You should do them for yourself, too. You shouldn't have let Dad treat you like that."

"It wasn't quite that simple, Thor. Your dad and I . . ." Tears welled in my eyes, and I almost choked on my words. "Your dad and I were never really a couple. We dated a little bit, and I was thinking about breaking up with him, but then I found out I was pregnant with you. If it wasn't for you coming along, your dad and I wouldn't have stayed together. He was kind enough to let me live at his house while I was pregnant, and I ended up staying longer than I ever thought I would. So in a way, I couldn't blame your dad for having another girlfriend. He and I have always lived our separate lives. I suppose it seemed normal to you, because that was the only kind of family you knew."

"No, it didn't seem normal!" Thor nearly shouted the words. "What do you think I am, stupid? I've been around my friends' parents, and I see how normal families live." He turned away from me, retreating into an offended silence.

"I'm sorry, Thor," I said, tears streaming down my face. "I'm so sorry."

"I'll get over it, Mom. Not today, but some day. I'm just freaked out that Rachel was Dad's girlfriend. I can't believe I didn't know that. I always thought she was just a friend."

He looked down, fingering the bottom of his tee shirt, appearing to be in deep thought. "She really was a good friend. We had lots of fun together." His voice sounded wistful.

"Yes, Rachel was a good friend," I said. "She loved you, Thor. I'm sure she still does."

"It's weird," he said. "It's like I had two moms and no dad. Dad never cared about me. I don't think he ever wanted me to be born. He won't care about Rachel's baby, either. He's too selfish."

Thor's words hit me hard, left me reeling. I could no longer concentrate on driving, so I pulled off the road into the parking lot of a grocery store.

"Why didn't you ever tell me you felt like that, Thor?" I asked.

"Because it didn't seem like something you'd want to hear."

Then he brought up the subject I dreaded the most. "Mom, if Rachel was Dad's girlfriend, why did I see him coming out of your bedroom?"

I felt the energy draining out of me, while a dark, burning shame washed over my entire being. "That was a mistake, Thor. A big mistake. There was a period of time when I thought your father and I could be together again. He told me he wasn't with Rachel anymore."

"Of course he did," Thor said scornfully. "He's a big fat liar. I don't know why you put up with him, Mom. You're just like Grandma. You don't get upset about anything. Grownups should get upset about some things."

"I'm upset now, Thor," I sobbed. "Believe me, I'm upset." I fumbled in my handbag for tissues. When I saw that my son was sniffling as well, I handed him one. "I want you to know, Thor, that no matter how you think your father feels about you, I'm so glad I have you. You're the most important thing in this world to me."

"I know that, Mom."

A police officer drove through the parking lot and stopped when he spotted us. No doubt, the bags and boxes piled high in the back seat caught his attention.

"Is everything okay here?" he asked as he approached my window.

I tried to nod and smile reassuringly at him, but his question provoked another round of deep sobbing.

The officer looked at Thor. "Why aren't you in school, young man?"

"We're having a family emergency," Thor explained.

"Where are you going?"

"To my grandma's house in Mishawaka."

"Oh," the officer said, "you're almost there, then. Well, drive safely, ma'am."

When I regained enough composure to drive again, I pulled back out onto the highway. We rode in silence until we reached my mother's house. As we pulled into her driveway, Thor said, "I might be mad for a little while, Mom, but I'll get over it. We'll just have to start over and live a new life."

"We'll do that, Thor," I said. "We'll start right now.

Chapter 22

I had called my mother the previous evening to inform her of the crisis in our household. "I'm so sorry for springing this on you," I said, "but Thor and I need to get out of here immediately." Then I told her about Thor's reaction to discovering Rachel's pregnancy.

She seemed unperturbed. "Sometimes it takes a bolt of lightning or a clap of thunder to disrupt an intractable situation," she observed. "It took Thor blowing up to set you free." She assured me it was fine for Thor and me to stay with her as long as we needed to.

Moving into her home wasn't easy. My father's hospital bed and medical equipment filled one of the bedrooms, and my mother slept in the second bedroom. Thor and I piled our belongings in her treatment room. The treatment table became my bed, while Thor slept on the living-room sofa.

Everything had happened so quickly: the blowup at Jake's house, Rachel's disappearance, and the move to my mother's home. I felt dazed and disoriented.

But my first dinner in my new home helped me comprehend the fact that my life had truly changed. When Thor and I joined my mother and father at the kitchen table, it seemed like my son and I had belonged to that household forever. For the moment, our recent lives with Jake and Rachel seemed distant and unreal.

Thor and I had a month of school left, and the daily commute to our Michigan schools was arduous. Our morning routine was hectic, competing for the single bathroom, trying to stay out of my mother's way while she completed my father's care. Sometimes, we had difficulty finding what we needed in our hastily packed bags and boxes. But Thor never uttered a word of complaint about our crowded quarters and lack of privacy.

After several days in my mother's home, I broke down and told her about my affair with Jake, my pregnancy, and my miscarriage. She shed a few tears over the loss of my baby, but informed me that my child's soul would be born into another body.

"Nothing in the universe is ever lost," she said. "You child will reappear in your life at some point."

But when she closed her eyes to access her inner vision regarding my affair with Jake, her faced darkened. As she spoke, her judgmental tone surprised me. "Jake is not an honest man. He hides from his obligations, and when faced with difficulty, he becomes a master of deception. He keeps his world small and limited, and he limits the lives of those close to him. Rachel instinctively knew to run from him when she realized you were removing your protective presence from the home. You were wise to let her go. And you were wise not to let this crisis distract you from your own course of action."

She shifted in her chair, as if feeling ill at ease. "You stayed in Jake's world far too long, River. It's good that you're out of it now."

My mother's words aroused defensiveness in me. *He can't be that bad*, I thought. *He has his good points.* But aloud, I said, "I know, Mom."

"He wants you to come back," she continued, "because you provide what he lacks. You take care of matters he doesn't want to address. You may be tempted to succumb to his seduction, but it's important that you don't. He isn't good for you, River."

But I can't completely turn my back on him, something in me protested. *He's the father of my son.*

My mother seemed to read my thought. "And he's not good for Thor, either. He models traits that are alien to your son's spirit."

I shuddered at the severity of her words.

Even though I resolved to continue my forward movement, I grieved for my old life. Lying on the narrow treatment table at night, I missed my comfortable bed in my beautifully decorated room at Jake's house. I missed every room of my former home, the remodeled kitchen, the rustic living-room with the wood-burning stove, the smell of clay emanating from Jake's studio. I missed walking through the patio door and stepping out onto the deck. I longed to see the view of the river one last time.

I missed Rachel, her annoying chatter, her flighty moods. I

wondered where she was, whether she was safe, whether she was receiving care for her pregnancy. I couldn't imagine how the girl who'd rarely left the house was managing to negotiate the challenges of the outside world. "Please watch over her," I fervently beseeched her Jewish God.

I missed Jake's strong, silent presence in the home. Sometimes at night, I'd call up the memory of his muscular arms around me, the sweetness of our lovemaking. But then I'd force myself to remember his shortcomings, his deception. Anger would churn inside me, enough to keep me from becoming immobilized by my backward glances.

One evening, my mother asked me to stay with my father while she and Thor went to the grocery store. I lay forlornly on the sofa, while my father sat in his chair gazing out the window. I remembered how quiet his house had been when I visited him during my childhood, how the silence made me feel lonely.

Suddenly, he spoke, making rasping sounds I couldn't understand.

Startled, I sat up. "What is it, Dad? Do you need something?"

He repeated the words, and I still couldn't understand them. So I went to his chair and knelt on the floor in front of him. I looked up, my eyes meeting his. "Tell me again, Dad."

And this time I understood. "It's . . . hard . . . on . . . you." He clasped my hand in his rigid grip.

My eyes flooded with tears. "Yes, it's hard, Dad. It's really hard." And with that, the dam holding back my sorrow burst. I leaned my head against my father's bony knee and wept. He laid a trembling hand on my head, and it remained there until my tears subsided.

When I stood up, I leaned over to kiss the cheek my mother had shaved that morning. "You'll . . . be . . . fine," he rasped.

"I know, Dad," I said.

Two weeks after Thor and I moved to my mother's house, Jake called me on my cell phone. I stepped out into the back yard so I could talk with him in private.

"Sorry for bothering you, Lee," he said.

"It's okay." I felt ashamed of the fact that I was happy to hear his voice.

"I thought you might want to know this. Rachel called me today. She told me she lost the baby."

His news hit me hard, and I sank down on the bench by my mother's pond. "I'm sorry, Jake. I'm so sorry. How are you doing with this?"

I could picture him shrugging, as he usually did when he didn't want to deal with emotions. "I suppose it's just as well," he said. "It's less complicated this way."

"Did she say whether the baby was a boy or a girl?"

"No."

"You didn't ask her?"

"I didn't think it was necessary to know that."

I cringed as Thor's words echoed in my mind: *He won't care about Rachel's baby, either.*

"Where is Rachel?" I asked. "How's she doing?"

"She's at her parents' house in Chicago. She said she's okay."

"Good." Relief washed through me. Even though I knew her parents were the last people Rachel would want to stay with, at least she'd be safe in their home.

"She told me not to come looking for her," Jake said. "She doesn't want anymore contact with me."

"So are you going to leave her alone, then?"

"Yup. I'm not going to bother her. I think that'll be best for all of us."

His last sentence puzzled me, but I didn't question it. "Well, thanks for passing on the information, Jake. I'm sorry about the baby, but I'm glad Rachel's okay. It's a load off my mind."

"Wait, Lee," he said.

"What, Jake?"

"When are you coming home?"

His plaintive question tugged at me powerfully. I forced myself to remember my mother's words of caution.

"I don't know, Jake."

"I miss you, Lee."

Suddenly, I was aware of Jake's lack of reference to his son. *He didn't say he missed Thor. He didn't ask when Thor was coming home.* My mood changed abruptly.

"I have to go now," I said, barely able to control my anger. "I'll talk to you later."

After ending the call, I sat gazing at the mesmerizing fountain in my mother's pond, trying to wrap my mind around Jake's news. *Poor Rachel,* I thought. *She's been through so much. Was the stress more than she could handle? Is that why she lost the baby?*

I got up and went inside to look for Thor. I found him doing his homework, sitting cross-legged on the floor in the treatment room surrounded by the clutter of our bags and boxes.

"What's up, Mom?" he asked.

"I have some sad news," I said. "Your dad just called me and told me Rachel lost her baby."

"Lost her baby?"

"Yes. The baby was born too early to survive."

"Oh." His shoulders sagged, and his blue eyes clouded with sorrow. "That's awful. Rachel must feel terrible. Should we do something?"

"There's nothing we can do, Thor. Except send her our love."

He looked at me, puzzled. "How do we do that?"

"Just imagine sending loving feelings from your heart."

He nodded. "I can do that. Where is she?"

"She's staying with her parents in Chicago."

"Good," he said. "They'll take care of her. She needs someone to take care of her."

He turned his attention back to his math assignment, but as I was leaving the room, he said, "Mom, you're not getting back together with Dad, are you? I know he wants you to."

"No, Thor," I said. "I'm not going back to your father. You and I are moving forward with our lives. I don't know where we're going, but it will be forward, not backward."

I walked into the kitchen to help my mother clean up the dinner dishes. "Mom," I said, "Jake called to tell me Rachel lost her baby."

"Oh," she said. "I'm sorry to hear that." She closed her eyes for a moment, and then shook her head. "Something doesn't feel right about this, River. Something's wrong."

"What is it, Mom?"

"I don't know. Time will tell."

Chapter 23

When the daze resulting from all the changes finally cleared from my mind, I began seriously pondering the question of what I needed to do next. My first line of thinking ran toward stabilization. I reasoned that Thor and I had already been through enough upheaval, and that it would be best to stay in our same community and schools.

I searched for apartments in Niles and found several vacancies in Timberwood, a fairly new complex in a nice neighborhood. Feeling confident that I could afford the rent on my teacher's salary, I arranged with the landlord to see one of the apartments, and Thor and I stopped by one day on our way home from school.

"Isn't this lovely?" I exclaimed as we walked into a freshly painted, newly carpeted living-room, considerably larger than the one in Jake's house. The two bedrooms were spacious as well. To my delight, the kitchen included a dishwasher and garbage disposal, amenities missing in Jake's kitchen.

"Wow!" I said when I saw the small balcony overlooking the Saint Joseph River. "Look at this, Thor. We'd have a view of the river, just like at our old place. Maybe this apartment was meant for us."

Thor shrugged and turned away from me.

"So what do you think?" I asked him. "Can you picture us living here?"

He hung his head, tracing the pattern of the kitchen floor tiles with the toe of his shoe. "I don't know," he mumbled.

His lack of enthusiasm surprised me. "I'll get back to you," I informed the landlord.

When we were back in the car, I turned to face my son. "What's wrong? That apartment is just as nice as your dad's house, actually nicer in some ways."

"But it's just the same old thing," he said. "I thought you told me we were moving forward. I thought we were going somewhere else. I didn't think you wanted to stay in Niles."

I stared at him, dumbfounded. "I thought you'd want to stay in your school and be close to your friends. If we stay in Niles, we'll be close to Grandpa and Grandma, and you can even see you dad."

Thor winced when I made reference to Jake.

"If you want to," I added.

He shook his head. "I've lived in the same place all my life. I want to go some place different. I want to try something new."

Thor's words made me wonder whether I was setting my sights too low, whether I was underestimating what he and I could take on. I knew I wanted to stay within a few hours' drive from my parents' home, in case they needed me in a crisis. Thor agreed that these limited parameters were reasonable, and together we poured over an atlas to look at possibilities within our range: Saint Joseph, South Haven, Holland, Kalamazoo, and Grand Rapids in Michigan; anything as far south as Indianapolis in Indiana; Chicago and the surrounding communities in Illinois.

The first two weeks of our summer break, I spent long hours on my computer, looking for job opportunities in all the school systems within our designated range. I found a handful of openings for art teachers, and sent out resumes.

But the process felt tedious and uninspiring. None of the possibilities excited me, and nothing seemed like an improvement on our life in Niles.

When I didn't get a single nibble on the resumes I sent out, I called the landlord at Timberwood to inquire whether he still had vacancies. He informed me all the apartments had been leased.

Something inside me was on the verge of caving in. My thoughts returned to an option I knew was always available: going back to Jake's house.

My mother must have sensed I was giving up. "Maybe you need to make a leap of faith," she said. "Just go where the Spirit leads, and trust that things will work out the way they should. You know that saying: *If you can barely stand, leap.*

"I never heard of that saying, Mom," I snapped. "It doesn't make sense."

"It just came to me," she said. "So I know it's relevant to your situation."

"Well, the Spirit doesn't seem to be leading me anywhere. That's the whole problem."

"Then we need to do something about that. Let's petition the Universal Intelligence for guidance."

That evening, my mother, my father, Thor, and I formed a circle in the living-room. My mother burned incense formulated to enhance intuition, and chanted a few mantras for the same intent. As Thor and I got up to go to bed, she expressed confidence that the Spirit was already moving on our behalf.

I woke up the next morning in an irritable mood. "I got nothing," I said as I sat across the kitchen table from my mother.

She smiled serenely. "Nothing came to me, either, honey. But don't give up hope. The Spirit has its own timing."

"Well, I hope it's quick," I grumbled.

Thor wandered into the kitchen in his pajamas, looking sleepy and dazed.

"Would you like some granola, Thor?" my mother asked. "I made a fresh batch yesterday."

"Sounds good, Grandma." He reached into the refrigerator for milk.

"Boy, I had a crazy dream," he said as he pulled his chair up to the table. He chewed a mouthful of granola, then closed his eyes and shook his head, as if to clear his mind. "I can't get that stupid dream out of my head."

My mother's eyes lit up with interest. "What was it about, Thor?"

"I was standing on a beach looking at a really big lake. It was so surreal, like I was really there. I could see the big rocks, and I could hear the waves and the sea gulls. I could even feel the wind blowing. And a voice in my mind kept saying, *R C, R C, R C.* Pretty weird, huh?"

My mother furrowed her brow. "R C, R C, R C," she repeated. Then she and I exclaimed in unison, "Racine!"

We burst into laughter. Suddenly, I felt charged up, a sense of purpose flowing through my veins. "Oh, my God!" I said to Thor. "The Spirit spoke to you!

He stared at me, bewildered. "What are you talking about, Mom?"

"The Spirit is telling us to move to Racine, Wisconsin. Racine is on Lake Michigan. That's where you were standing in your dream. You were looking at Lake Michigan."

A grin spread across Thor's freckled face. "Awesome!"

"My grandson is receiving guidance," my mother murmured, her face glowing. "Thor, you are destined to become a holy man."

The next few days, I focused all my efforts on creating a plan for moving to Racine. I checked for teaching positions in the school system. Even though there were no openings for art teachers, I sent my resume to the superintendent's office, along with a cover letter announcing my plans to move to Racine within the next few weeks.

At that point, I wasn't concerned about whether or not I landed a teaching job. I had enough money in savings to get us by for several months. I'd sell furniture or wait on tables if I had to. I didn't care. I knew everything would work out.

I researched rental properties on the internet, and ended up calling the manager of an apartment complex. He agreed to hold an apartment for me until the middle of July. I felt no trepidation about leasing the apartment sight unseen. I trusted the Spirit was working on my behalf.

I worked rapidly on my plans, making a list of things I needed to do: *contact Riverside Elementary to tender my resignation, rent a moving truck, round up boxes for packing, call Jake to set up a time to get the rest of our things.*

The thought of Jake's reaction to our move dampened my spirits, but I kept working. *When we arrive in Racine, I'll need to enroll Thor in school, get a Wisconsin driver's license, open a bank account, locate a doctor, a dentist, a hair salon.* My thoughts flowed quickly, efficiently, bringing into focus the hazy outline of my future.

On the morning of our move, a Monday in early July, Thor and I loaded the car with the belongings we'd brought to my mother's house. The moving van was scheduled to arrive at Jake's house around noon, and we had only a few hours to pack up the things we'd left there.

I hugged my parents as we said goodbye, promising to return for frequent visits. My mother smiled through her tears as she pressed a check for five hundred dollars into my hand.

"This is from your father," she said. "He knows moving is expensive, and he wants to make sure you don't run short on money. He says if you need anything else, don't hesitate to ask."

She looked at me intently, as if wanting to make sure I got her point. "That's his way of showing love, River."

"I know that, Mom." I ran across the room and covered my father's face with kisses one last time.

My stomach churned with anxiety as I drove the twenty miles to Jake's house. It had been two months since Thor and I had moved out. I would have preferred to steer clear of the sentimental feelings triggered by seeing my former home, as my emotional circuit was already overloaded. But it would have been foolish to leave all of our belongings behind just for the sake of avoiding pain.

Thor was silent, and I sensed his tension. "Ready for this?" I asked.

He nodded, then said under his breath, "I hope Dad's not there."

I pretended I hadn't heard what he'd said. Inwardly, I agreed with him, as I knew facing Jake would be even more emotionally wrenching than seeing the house.

I turned off the highway onto the long lane. As we approached the house, I sighed with relief when I saw that Jake's truck wasn't parked in the driveway. Apparently, he wanted to avoid an emotional encounter as much as I did.

I'd called him three days earlier, to tell him we were moving, and to let him know when we'd be coming to pick up the rest of our things.

"Okay, Lee," he'd said, his voice sounding weary. "Whatever works for you."

The house, which had previously bustled with activity, seemed devoid of life when we walked through the front door. I looked around the dusty, abandoned living-room, formerly kept spotless under Rachel's diligent care. The throw pillows lay askew on the sofa, unmoved since my last evening in the house when I'd sat there waiting for Thor to come home. I suspected Jake hadn't set foot in that room since all of his household companions had left.

Thor stood motionless in the doorway of his former bedroom. I walked up behind him and laid a hand on his shoulder. "This is so weird, Mom," he said. "It's unreal."

I blinked back the tears as I entered my own bedroom. A few items of clothing still hung in my open closet. Several of my dresser drawers were open, spilling out their remaining contents. In my hasty departure two months earlier, I'd shoved my box of paintings and my art supplies into one corner. My bed was unmade, and I could barely resist the urge to crawl in, pull the covers over my head, and weep. But I turned away from temptation and stepped back out into the hallway.

"We don't have any time to waste," I said to Thor as I handed him several empty boxes. "The moving van will be here in two hours."

We worked silently in our separate rooms, stripping away all traces of our former lives and packing them in boxes. I remembered the things I'd stored in the third hallway bedroom, and against my will, I entered the wing of the house previously occupied by Rachel. I couldn't resist taking a few more steps down the hallway to peek into her room.

Jake had turned it into a storage space. He had stacked boxes of inventory against the walls, and several large ceramic pieces lay on the bed Rachel had once slept in. It seemed disrespectful to the space that had been hers for six years.

What did you expect? I asked myself. *Did you think he'd make her room into a shrine?*

When we'd finished with our bedrooms, Thor and I moved into the kitchen, which was cluttered with dirty dishes. A sticky film covered the stove and counter tops, something Rachel never would have allowed when she lived there. As I sorted my things from Jake's, I discovered Rachel's recipe box shoved to the back of a cupboard. Evidently, Jake hadn't wanted to see it sitting out in the open as a daily reminder of her.

A wave of sadness washed over me. *She said she always took her recipes with her. Why hadn't she taken them this time?* I opened the box and flipped through the cards, noticing particular recipes stained from frequent usage.

On a whim, I tucked the box in with the dishes I was packing. I felt guilty, like I was committing a petty theft. But I reasoned that if Rachel had any say in the matter, she'd want me to have her recipes rather than leaving them behind with Jake.

Just as we were finishing up in the kitchen, I heard the rumble of the moving van pulling up in the driveway. I greeted the movers at the front door, directing them to load our beds and dressers and the loveseat in the living-room. Thor busied himself carrying boxes out to the van.

I was so preoccupied with the project that I didn't realize Jake had come home. I jumped when I heard his voice behind me.

"Got a minute, Lee?"

I turned to face him. "Oh! I didn't hear you come in."

"Can we talk?"

I glanced at Thor, who was heading out the front door, arms laden with boxes. He looked over his shoulder, eying the two of us suspiciously.

"Sure," I said to Jake.

You shouldn't do this, something inside me whispered as I followed my former lover into the kitchen, through the patio door, and out onto the deck. Hesitantly, I seated myself on one of the cedar chairs. Jake pulled his chair around to face me, gazing intently into my eyes.

"I wanted to let you know, Lee, that I told my parents about you and Thor."

He couldn't have stunned me more if he'd hit me on the head with a sledge hammer. "You did what?" I asked, incredulous.

"I told my parents the whole story. It caught them off guard, and they were upset at first. But then they came around. They said they figured I'd been hiding something. They said I'd been acting secretive for years."

They sure got that right, I thought.

"And now they want to meet you and Thor."

My mind reeled back to the day thirteen years earlier when Jake and I had driven past his parents' farm. I recalled the image of his Mennonite mother in her long dress, bending over her flowerbed, gardening tool in hand. I remembered the urge I'd felt to get to know her.

Closing my eyes, I imagined holding Jake's hand as he led Thor and me through the front door of the farmhouse. I envisioned his elderly parents greeting us, inviting us to sit down to a home-cooked meal.

I shook my head to clear the images from my mind. "Why now, Jake? Why now, of all times?"

He stared down at the boards of the deck, and then lifted his head to look at me. His eyes expressed more sincerity than I'd ever before seen in them. "Because I've done nothing but screw up with you, Lee. For fourteen years, I've been nothing but a screw-up. I wanted to prove to you that I can step up and do the right thing."

His earnest gaze melted my guard, and I felt my heart turning to mush. "Oh, Jake," I whispered as tears spilled from my eyes.

He reached for my hand, and I allowed him to hold it. "Remember, Lee, when our son was a baby and we talked about getting married?"

I nodded.

"We can do that now. Rachel's out of the picture. We can start over and get it right this time. I promise you I'll put everything I have into the relationship."

He caressed the back of my hand with his thumb. "I've never said this to you before, Lee, because I've been too much of a coward. But I'm going to say it now. I love you. I fell in love with you the day I met you, and I kept on loving you. Even when Rachel was here, I loved you. When you started dating Rick, it made me crazy, and I realized how much you meant to me."

He looked at me imploringly, his dark eyes begging for my understanding. "I don't want to lose you, Lee. That would be the worst thing that ever happened to me."

I closed my eyes again, allowing his words to sink in. I could have easily thrown myself into his arms, promising him one more attempt at a future together. But my mother's words of warning echoed in my mind: *You've stayed in Jake's world far too long.*

I pulled my hand from his. "Jake, I have plans in motion."

He leaned back in his chair, sighing deeply. "I know. Maybe you need to be on your own for awhile. But it's never too late to come back, Lee. Never."

I heard the creak of the patio door opening and turned to see Thor standing behind us. "We're done loading, Mom," he said. "Is there anything else you want to put on the truck?"

"I don't think so, Thor." I stood up and walked with him back through the kitchen and into the living-room. Jake followed us, and the three of us watched in silence as the moving crew closed up the back of the van, then headed down the long drive to the highway.

"Well, I guess this is it," Jake said. I nodded.

He reached into his pocket, pulled out a roll of bills, and handed it to me. "I owe you this, Lee."

I unrolled the money and counted ten one-hundred-dollar bills. "Thank you, Jake," I said. "I didn't expect you to do this. But it will help."

"I want to make sure you'll have everything you need," he said. "Let me know your address, and I'll send something every month. I told you I'm going to do the right thing."

He looked at Thor. "He's my son, too. It's my job to support him."

I watched the expression in Thor's eyes change from dull resentment to hopeful interest as he met his father's gaze. Never in Thor's thirteen years had I seen father and son engage in such direct, albeit silent, communication.

"I have something for you, Thor," Jake said. "Let me go get it. I'll be right back."

My son and I exchanged bewildered glances as Jake left the room. He returned a moment later, carrying a skateboard. I could tell it was an expensive model, top of the line.

Thor looked startled. I knew he'd expected nothing from his father.

"I guess this is what guys your age like to do," Jake said as he handed Thor the skateboard. "You're going to be a city kid now. I figure they'll have skate parks somewhere around."

"Thanks, Dad." Thor clutched the skateboard in one arm and gave his father an awkward half-hug.

"Take care of yourself," Jake said, "and look out for your mom."

Thor turned abruptly and headed out the front door. He stood by the car, waiting for me.

Then Jake reached for me, wrapping his arms around me in a lingering embrace. I laid my head against his shoulder, clinging to his strong, sensuous body one last time. "Remember, Lee," he whispered in my ear, "it's never too late to come back home."

"Do you want me to put the skateboard in the trunk?" I asked Thor as I approached the car.

"No," he said, "I'll hold it."

As we drove down the long lane, I watched my son from the corner of my eye. He was running his fingers around the edges of the skateboard and gently rotating the wheels.

"It's a pretty nice gift, isn't it?" I said.

"Yes," he sniffled. I realized he was trying not to cry.

"Are you sad, Thor?"

My words triggered him into full-blown sobbing. We'd reached the end of the lane, and I stopped the car so I could give him my full attention. "What's wrong, Thor?"

"I . . . I . . . just wish . . . he'd been a better . . . dad," he choked out between sobs.

"Do you want to stay?" I asked, temptation pulling on me one last time. "Your dad would like for us to stay. He'd like for us to be a family."

Thor wiped his face on the sleeve of his tee shirt. "No. We're supposed to go to Racine."

"You're right," I said as I pulled out onto the highway.

Chapter 24

That evening, I called my mother. "We're here in Racine," I told her. "We made the trip in four hours. We didn't run into any major problems. The toughest part was getting through Chicago, but we did it."

"Wonderful!" my mother exclaimed. "You must be exhausted."

"I am. I feel like I'm ready to drop, but I'm too excited to sleep."

"How do you like your new apartment?"

"It's pretty small. But it's cute and clean, in good condition. It'll do for now. It's on the third floor, and we have a nice little balcony. The moving men were kind enough to set up our beds, so at least we can be comfortable tonight. After the truck left, Thor and I drove around and found a restaurant for dinner. Then we found a grocery store, and I picked up some things to get us through the next couple of days. We got a bit of a feel for the neighborhood. We're not that far from the lake. A few blocks, I think."

"It sounds perfect," my mother said. "You'll have your work cut out for you the next few weeks, getting settled. But I know Racine has good things in store for you. I can feel it."

The next few days, I worked from the time I got up to the time I dropped into bed at night, unpacking boxes, putting things away, arranging furniture. For the most part, Thor worked steadily beside me, but from time to time, I'd tell him to take a break.

On the afternoon of our second day in the apartment, I stepped out onto the balcony for a breath of fresh air. I saw Thor on the sidewalk below, trying out his new skateboard. He seemed undaunted by his lack of skill, and in spite of his awkwardness, he kept practicing. I noticed he'd already attracted the attention of other boys in the neighborhood. He stopped to talk to them, and then let them take turns on his skateboard.

Smiling to myself, I went back to my work. *I'm so lucky to have such a good kid,* I thought. *In spite of all he's been through, he's doing great.*

Fifteen minutes later, Thor bounded up the stairs and burst through the door. "Mom, some kids told me there's a skate park just a few blocks away!"

The next afternoon, our doorbell rang for the first time. I opened the door to find two adolescent boys standing there, awkward in their gangly bodies, as if they hadn't adjusted to their recent growth spurts.

"Is Thor here?" one of them asked in a cracking voice.

My equally gangly son came tearing out of his bedroom. "Hi, guys!" he said to his newly acquired buddies. Then he turned to me. "Can I go to the skate park with them?"

"Sure," I said. "Be back in two hours." I smiled as the apartment door closed behind the boys. My country-born son was adjusting to city life without missing a beat.

Within a week, I felt like I was getting my bearings in my new neighborhood. I made several trips to the grocery store and filled my pantry and refrigerator. Thor and I located the hospital and the middle school where, in seven weeks, he'd start his eighth-grade year. I arranged for telephone service. I opened a bank account and deposited the check from my father.

I discovered a second-hand furniture store, and with Jake's money, I bought a recliner, a coffee table, and lamps to complete my living-room ensemble. I also found a pretty little kitchen table at a discount price. While it wasn't nearly as grand as Jake's oak table, it was perfect for my new apartment and my new lifestyle.

After six days of constant work, I decided it was time for a break, and Thor and I set aside our projects in favor of a walk to the beach. As we approached the lake, I caught my breath, taking in the limitless expanse of shimmering water. Frothy waves gently slapped the shore, while screaming sea gulls circled overhead. The hot July sun beat down on our skins, but a pleasant breeze provided a cooling balance.

"Does this look anything like your dream?" I asked Thor.

He stopped to survey his surroundings. "Pretty much." He turned to me and grinned. "I think this is where the Spirit wants us."

"Do you like it here?" I asked.

"What do you think?" he responded. He pulled off his tee shirt and dropped it on the hot sand, then ran at top speed toward the lake, yelping loudly as he plunged into the cold water.

As I gazed out over the vast expanse of Lake Michigan, I remembered the view from the other side when, fourteen years earlier, I'd sat with Jake in the restaurant in Saint Joseph, Michigan. I recalled his words: *Did you know if you sailed straight across the lake from here you'd end up in Wisconsin?*

Was he already writing the end of our story? I wondered.

I searched my mind and heart for any remnants of sentimentality for my life in Michigan, but found none. I felt more alive than I had in years, eager to embrace the unknown of the new life I'd started, joy dancing in every cell of my body.

Two days later, my mother called. "The universe is working on your behalf, darling," she announced cheerfully. "You won't believe what just happened. I received a call for you this morning." She paused, as if trying to heighten my curiosity.

"Who was it, Mom?"

"Mr. Douglas, the principal of Parkside Elementary School. He said he received your resume. He'd like to speak with you."

"Oh my God, Mom!" I exclaimed. "I wasn't expecting to hear anything from him. There weren't any openings."

"I told him you'd moved to Racine a week ago," my mother said. "He gave me his office number. You should call him right away."

I grabbed a pen and scribbled down the number while she read it to me. "I'll call him as soon as I hang up with you," I promised.

"Good luck, honey," she said, "although I don't think you'll need it."

I could feel my heart palpitating in my chest as I dialed Mr. Douglas's office. A secretary put me through to him.

"Thank you for calling back." Mr. Douglas's voice was deep and resonant. "I know this is very short notice, considering the school year starts in six weeks. But our art teacher just resigned. This leaves us very little time to fill the position, and we're trying to set up interviews as quickly as we can. Would you believe your resume showed up on my desk the day after I received her letter of resignation?"

I almost laughed out loud. I could imagine what my mother would say about this coincidence.

"Are you interested in interviewing for the position?" Mr. Douglas asked.

"Absolutely!" I said.

Can I do this? I asked myself after I hung up the phone. *Can I get my bearings quickly enough to start a new teaching position in a new school? Can I manage this in a span of a few weeks?*

Then, from somewhere unknown, a clear, calm thought floated through my mind. *Of course you can.*

Chapter 25

Butterflies danced in my stomach as I pulled up in front of Parkside Elementary School. I surveyed the expanse of the long brick building, wondering whether I would soon be fortunate enough to call it my place of employment. Some of the large windows were still decorated with colorful artwork from the previous academic year, and I imagined what projects I'd have my students do if I were offered the art teacher's position.

Taking a deep breath, I got out of my car, walked through the front entrance, and announced to the secretary at the reception desk that I was scheduled for an interview. She immediately ushered me into the principal's office.

Mr. Douglas, a gray-haired, big-bellied man in his late fifties, greeted me enthusiastically, again making reference to the serendipitous timing of my resume's arrival. The interview was short and rather routine. Mr. Douglas informed me that he had a few other applicants to screen, and that he'd then decide who to call back for a second interview.

"Obviously, we need to move this process along quickly," he said. "You'll hear from my secretary one way or the other, within a week."

I left the interview in a buoyant mood. I told myself that even if I didn't get this job, my son and I would be fine. Something else would work out. I'd come too far for things to fall apart on me.

Nevertheless, waiting for the second call kept my nerves on edge. As I continued to work around my apartment, I left my cell phone within easy reach. Two days later, it rang while I was standing on a chair hanging curtains in my bedroom.

"Thor, honey, can you bring me the phone?" I called to my son, who was watching TV in the living room.

Thor jumped up, ran to the kitchen, and grabbed the phone off the table. "I hope it's Mr. Douglas," he said as he handed it to me.

But in response to my enthusiastic hello, I heard a timid, childlike voice whisper, "Leah?"

My heart sank. "Hello, Rachel," I said.

Inwardly, I cried out in protest. *Why are you calling me, Rachel? I've worried about you, I've gotten over that, I've put you behind me, I've moved on. Why are you intruding into my life a second time? Why can't you leave me alone?*

Thor had headed back to the living room, but at the sound of Rachel's name, he appeared in my bedroom doorway, listening intently.

"Where are you, Leah?" Rachel's voice sounded sorrowful. "Jake told me you and Thor moved out. Where did you go?"

I thought about telling her we were in Seattle, Washington, or Augusta, Maine, or even Anchorage, Alaska, somewhere out of her reach. But I couldn't bring myself to utter such a lie, especially not in front of my son. "We're in Racine, Wisconsin," I said.

"Oh, good!" she chortled. "That's not very far from Chicago. I can come see you, Leah."

"How'd you get my number, Rachel?" I asked, trying unsuccessfully to hide my irritation.

"I memorized it a long time ago, in case I needed you."

Of course you did, I thought.

"And I need you now, Leah."

I felt her spinning a sticky web around me, from which I couldn't extricate myself. I sank down on my bed, feeling defeated. "Why do you need me, Rachel? You're at your parents' house, aren't you? You told Jake you were okay."

"But I'm not, Leah." Urgency rose in her voice. "I need to come see you."

"Now's not a good time, Rachel. We just moved here. We're not even completely unpacked."

"Please, Leah." It sounded like she'd begun to cry.

Thor waved his arms at me, trying to get my attention. "Just a minute," I said to Rachel. Then I turned to my son. "What is it?"

"What's going on?" he asked.

"It's Rachel. She wants to come visit us."

"Is something wrong?"

"Maybe. It kind of sounds like it."

"Then why are you telling her she can't come? That's not very nice."

I sighed deeply, and then spoke into the phone again. "Okay, Rachel."

"Can I come today?"

I knew I was fighting a losing battle. "That's fine."

At 7:00 o'clock that evening, Thor and I stood at the train station watching the rail passengers disembark, looking for our skinny, dark-haired houseguest.

Thor spotted her first. "Mom!" he exclaimed, nudging me. "I thought you said Rachel lost her baby. I don't think she did!"

He pointed at the young woman making her way toward us, her protruding abdomen overpowering her tiny frame. She was carrying one of the ragged duffel bags she'd brought to Jake's house six years earlier.

My mother's words echoed in my mind: "Something doesn't feel right about this." *Yes, something was terribly wrong. It was all a big lie.*

As Rachel approached, I saw that she was wearing the same threadbare, low-rise blue jeans she'd worn for the past six years, now riding even lower to accommodate her late-stage pregnancy. Her once-oversized gray tee shirt stretched tightly over her massive belly. She shuffled toward us in a pair of ungainly flip-flops.

When she saw us waiting for her, she tried to run, her arms outstretched, her face beaming. "Oh, it's so good to see the two of you again! I've missed you so much!"

I returned her embrace, then stepped back and looked at her pointedly. "Rachel, you told Jake you lost your baby. That's what all of us have been thinking."

She looked down, caressing the curve of her abdomen. "I know I said that. But it's not true. The baby's still in there." She laughed, like she expected us to appreciate the joke.

"Why, Rachel?" I asked. "Why did you lie to Jake?"

"Because I don't want him to have anything to do with the baby. He didn't want it in the first place. Why should he have it now?" She cocked her head, searching my unsmiling face. "Don't you understand that, Leah?"

"No," I said. "I don't understand that, Rachel."

She looked stricken, like I'd just slapped her face, and her dark eyes glistened with tears. But I was in no mood to deal with her pitiful weeping. "Let's go," I said. "I've got things to do at home." Abruptly, I turned and headed back toward the lot where our car was parked.

A minute later, I realized my anger had quickened my gait, and that I'd left Thor and Rachel far behind. I looked over my shoulder and saw Thor take Rachel's arm to steady her as she made her way down a short flight of steps. Sighing, I waited until they caught up with me.

"This is nice," Rachel said as she followed Thor and me into our apartment. She seemed exhausted from climbing the stairs, and was breathing heavily. "You bought some new things, didn't you, Leah?"

"Yes," I said. "I had to."

She tossed her duffel bag on the floor and sank into the recliner. "This is new," she said, caressing the leather arm of the chair. Then she leaned back, groaning with pleasure. "It feels so-o-o good to my aching body."

"Have you had anything to eat, Rachel?" I asked. Although deeply resentful of her presence, I felt duty-bound to do the right thing by her.

"Not since breakfast," she informed me.

When I served her a tuna salad sandwich several minutes later, she said, "This is different. It's usually me making food for you."

I winced. *She thinks our relationship is picking up where we left off.*

She took a bite of her sandwich, and then set her plate down on the table next to her. "Look at this, Leah." She pulled up one leg of her blue jeans to reveal an alarmingly swollen ankle. "Isn't this awful? I can't even wear my shoes anymore. I have to wear these flip-flops."

I recoiled at the disturbing sight, but in spite of my concern, I tried to remain nonchalant. "That happens when you're pregnant, Rachel. When I was pregnant with Thor, I had to keep my feet up all the time at the end."

"Okay," she said. "I thought it was just me.

Thor was sitting on the loveseat, silently taking in my conversation with Rachel. I sat down next to him, and then leaned forward to give our guest my full attention. "Rachel, have you gotten prenatal care?"

She nodded. "I went to the doctor twice when I was in Chicago. My mother made me."

"Good," I said. "You should keep going. Do you have another appointment?"

She hung her head. "I don't want to go back there," she mumbled.

"You don't want to go back to that doctor?"

"No, I don't want to go back to Chicago. I don't want to go back to my parents' house."

"Why not?"

Rachel's eyes welled with tears. "Because it's the same old thing. They try to run my life. They treat me like I'm an idiot. They act like I don't know the right thing to do. They'll try to take over the baby when it's born. I don't want them to treat my baby like they did me."

I didn't respond to her statement, because I knew if I did, my words wouldn't be kind. *Somebody has to tell you what to do, Rachel, because you never know the right thing to do. You insist on having your freedom, but when you get it, you don't know the first thing about taking care of yourself.*

"They even asked me if I wanted to put my baby up for adoption," she continued. "Can you believe it? How could they think I'd give away my own child?"

Adoption's not a bad idea, I thought. But I knew better than to second her parents' opinion. "Have you gotten anything for the baby yet?" I inquired.

"My mom bought a bassinette and some blankets and stuff. She didn't ask me what I wanted. She just did it."

"Rachel," I said, trying hard to keep my tone even. "You need to go back home. Even if you don't like it, your parents are helping you with what you need. You have your doctor there, so that's the best place for you to be. You don't have to stay there forever, but right now, you need your parents' help."

She stared at me, sorrow in her big brown eyes. "I should've known better than to come, Leah. I should've known you wouldn't want me here."

"That's not the point, Rachel," I said, now feeling completely exasperated. "I'm just not in a position to help you like your parents can. I don't even have a job yet. Do your parents know you're here? Did you tell them you were leaving?"

She hesitated, a strange look in her eyes. Then she shook her head.

"That's not fair to them, Rachel. They're probably worried sick. You should call and let them know where you are. Tell them you're visiting a friend for a day or two, and that you'll be back soon."

A defiant look crossed her face, and she slowly shook her head from side to side.

Anger welled in me, and I wanted to smack the smug expression off her face. Instead, I stood up, picked up the plate holding her half-eaten sandwich, and carried it to the kitchen. I paced back and forth in front of the patio door, staring at the city lights below, trying to calm myself.

This is so unfair, I fumed, clenching my fists so hard my fingernails dug into my palms. *Just when I'm starting to feel like I have my head above water, she shows up and drags me down again.*

Taking a deep breath, I walked back into the living-room. "I'm tired, Rachel. Let's go to bed. We'll talk about this in the morning." Then I realized I hadn't even thought about sleeping arrangements.

Thor must have sensed my frustration. "Rachel can sleep in my room," he said. "I'll sleep on the recliner."

He grabbed the battered duffel bag, and Rachel followed him to his bedroom. I went to my own room and sat down on my bed, trying to think. Then I picked up my cell phone and looked up the number Rachel had called me from, the home of her father, Isaac Rosenbaum.

Thor appeared in my doorway. "I need a blanket, Mom."

I glanced up. "I'll get you one in a minute."

"What are you doing?" he asked.

"I'm thinking about calling Rachel's parents. They need to know where she is."

"She doesn't want you to do that," he objected.

"But her parents are probably worried sick."

"But if you call them, Rachel will be really upset."

I sighed and laid my phone on my nightstand. "I guess I'll deal with this in the morning."

Chapter 26

Thankfully, Rachel slept late the next morning, giving me time to collect my thoughts. As I tidied up my kitchen, I mulled over the predicament that had been thrust upon me. Once again, I came to the conclusion that the only reasonable course of action was for Rachel to return to her parents' home. I knew full well I had no capacity to meet her needs.

She came shuffling into the kitchen around 10:00 AM. "What are you doing, Leah?" she inquired, instantly irritating me by the childish question she'd asked so many times at Jake's house.

"Just cleaning up the kitchen," I responded. "What do you want for breakfast?"

"I'm not hungry."

I turned to face her, ready to confront her nonsense. "Rachel, you're pregnant and you need to eat, for your own sake and for your baby's. I insist! Now what do you want? Eggs? Cereal? Waffles?

Apparently sensing my frustration, Thor stepped into the kitchen. "We've got three different kinds of cereal, Rachel," he announced. He reached into the cupboard and set the boxes on the table in front of her.

Giggling, Rachel chose a cereal, and Thor supplied her with a bowl and spoon. I marveled at how my son still possessed the ability to coax his friend out of an obstinate mood.

I hung up my dish towel and sat down at the table with her. "We need to talk about your plans, Rachel," I said. "I still believe the right thing is for you to go back to your parents' house. You don't need to stay there forever. But you're going to need some security for a little while, and they're the best people to give it to you. You need to call them and make arrangements to go back. If you don't, I'm going to."

Rachel continued to eat, staring at the back of the cereal box, pretending she hadn't heard what I said.

"Rachel, look at me," I demanded. She raised her eyes to meet mine. "I can't take care of you right now. I don't have the room. I don't have the money. I'm sorry, but that's the way it is."

She gave an exasperated sigh, then put down her spoon and held out her hand. "Give me your phone, Leah."

I handed her my cell phone, and she busied herself with it for a few moments. At first, I thought she was complying with my demand to call her parents, but a moment later, I realized she'd just deleted her father's number from my phone.

"There!" she said. "Now you can't call them."

I stood up, outraged. "There are other ways I can get their number," I barked. "I can call directory assistance, you know."

She looked up at me, smirking. "Leah, it's no big deal, really. I've run away from my parents' house a hundred times. They're used to it. They know I never stay."

"You mean you ran from them like you ran from Jake's house?"

"Pretty much."

Suddenly, I felt foolish for all those weeks of worrying about her. I suspected her parents were past the point of getting riled up over her comings and goings.

"Well, Rachel," I said. "If you're not going back to Chicago, where are you going?"

Her cocky attitude vanished, and she stared at me with the eyes of a frightened child. "I don't know, Leah. I haven't figured it out yet."

"You don't have a lot of time to figure it out. How far along are you, anyway?"

"I'm not sure. About eight months, I think."

The shrill ring of my cell phone startled both of us. I grabbed it off the table and headed toward my bedroom so I could talk in private.

"This is Mrs. Walton from Mr. Douglas's office," the caller announced. "He'd like to know if you're still interested in the teaching position. If you are, he wants me to schedule you for a second interview."

"Oh yes, I'm still interested," I assured her. We agreed on an interview time for three days later, at 10:00 AM.

I hung up the phone and sank down on my bed, my body trembling with excitement. Things were opening up for me. I was moving forward, and I couldn't allow the crisis at hand to distract me. I had to get rid of Rachel. There had to be a way to get her out of my home.

"Who was it?" Thor and Rachel asked in unison as I walked back into the kitchen.

"The secretary at Parkside Elementary School," I said. "I've been invited back for another interview for the teaching position."

"That's awesome, Mom!" Thor exclaimed.

"That's awesome, Leah!" Rachel echoed. The expression in her eyes had changed from fear to relief.

Damn it! I thought. *She thinks that if I get the job, I'll be in a position to take care of her.*

I sat down at the table and buried my face in my hands. I knew my words sounded harsh, but I had to make my point. "Rachel, we've got to find somewhere else for you to go. I just don't have the time or energy to take care of you and a baby and start a new job all at the same time. There's only so much of me to go around. Do you understand that?"

I lifted my head to see her staring at me, white-faced, perfectly still. "I understand, Leah," she whispered.

I stood up and paced around my small kitchen, overwhelmed by my conflicting feelings. Anger toward Rachel seethed from every pore in my body, yet I was afraid for her. I felt terribly guilty, even though I hadn't the slightest inkling of how to help her.

Then a thought popped into my mind. "There's got to be some kind of crisis pregnancy center here in the city," I said. "Thor, bring me the phone book."

Rachel stared down at the table, looking defeated, while I scanned the ads in the Yellow Pages. "Here's something," I said. "Hannah's House. An organization dedicated to helping pregnant women in crisis."

I looked up at Rachel and smiled. "That's what we're going to do, Rachel. I'm going to call right now to see if we can stop by later today."

Her face registered no hope, only resignation. "Okay, Leah."

That afternoon, Rachel and I drove fifteen minutes across town to the pregnancy center. We pulled up in front of a shabby bungalow with a sagging porch.

Rachel wrinkled her nose in disgust. "This doesn't look like a very nice place."

"The outside doesn't mean anything," I reassured her. "It's a charitable organization. They probably don't have much money for maintaining the property."

A gracious elderly woman greeted us at the front door. "I'm Lydia," she said. "I'm part of the volunteer staff here." She ushered Rachel and me into the living room.

"Have a seat," she said, gesturing toward a well-worn sofa with an old-fashioned floral design. She handed each of us a brochure. "You might want to look this over. It tells about our mission and the services we provide. Our director is Mrs. Jenkins. She'll be in to talk with you in a few minutes."

The brochure stated that women were accepted into Hannah's House at any stage in their pregnancy, and that they could remain in the facility up to sixty days post-partum. They had a counselor on staff, and a social worker who helped the women find housing and other services in the community. Through donations, they were able to provide their clients with cribs, car-seats, and baby clothing.

"Looks pretty good," I murmured to Rachel. "This could be just the thing for you."

Mrs. Jenkins, a tall, thin middle-aged woman, entered the room and seated herself in a chair facing us. "What brings you to Hannah's House?" she asked Rachel, smiling warmly.

Rachel looked panicky. I waited for her to respond to Mrs. Jenkins' question. When she didn't, I decided it wasn't the time to insist on her independence. I launched into a brief account of her unexpected pregnancy, her alienation from the baby's father and from her parents, and my inability to house her and the baby in my small apartment.

Mrs. Jenkins nodded in understanding and answered my questions about the operation of the facility. She informed us Hannah's House was a small organization with room for only five women at a time.

I glanced at Rachel. She was watching three young women milling around in the kitchen, two of them pregnant. The third one cradled a sleeping infant in her arms.

"We're full right now," Mrs. Jenkins said. "But one of our residents, Kimberly, is scheduled to move out in a week."

"That's me," called the young woman with the baby. She walked into the living-room, lifting her infant over her shoulder and gently patting its back.

"Are you moving in?" she asked Rachel. "You'll like it here. They've been really good to me. I don't know what I would've done without them. They're helping me get my own apartment."

"Would you like for me to reserve that bed for you?" Mrs. Jenkins asked. Rachel looked at me questioningly, and I realized she hadn't uttered a single word since we'd entered the facility.

"Rachel, I think this is what you need right now," I said.

She hung her head. "I guess I'll take it," she whispered.

"Good," Mrs. Jenkins said. "We'll look forward to having you join us." She then went over the rules of the house, and Rachel signed a form stating that she agreed to abide by them.

"Call us in a week to make the final arrangements," she said as she handed Rachel a copy of the form."

I stood up and shook the director's hand. "Thank you so much. I'm sure you'll take good care of my friend." I turned toward Rachel. "Are you ready to go?"

Rachel attempted to struggle to her feet, but collapsed back down on the sofa. I noticed that her face looked pasty and bloated.

"Honey, you don't look like you're feeling well," Mrs. Jenkins observed. "Have you seen your doctor recently?"

Rachel stared at her, a blank expression on her face.

"She had a little bit of prenatal care when she was living in Chicago," I informed Mrs. Jenkins. "But we need to find her a doctor here. Do you have any suggestions?"

"I have a list," she said. "Let me get it for you." She left the room, then returned a minute later and handed me a sheet of paper. "These are the doctors we work with. They're usually quite accommodating with our clients."

"Thank you," I said. "We'll set something up as soon as we can."

"Where will I live while I'm waiting to go to Hannah's House?" Rachel asked on the drive home.

For the first time since she'd arrived in Racine, I felt my heart opening to Rachel, and compassion replaced my exasperation. I reached over and squeezed her hand. "You can stay with me until the room opens up. We'll manage."

"Thanks, Leah." Wearily, she reached up to brush a tear off her cheek. It seemed as if the gesture took all the strength in her body.

"Remember, Rachel," I said, "even when you're at Hannah's House, I'll still be your friend."

"Really?"

"Yes."

"Will you be my friend forever?"

I willed myself not to hesitate. "Of course."

She leaned her head against the passenger side door, and I thought she'd dozed off. But then she spoke again. "Having a baby hurts, doesn't it, Leah?"

"Of course it hurts," I replied. "Childbirth is difficult."

"I've been worrying about that."

"You'll be okay, Rachel. We women have a special strength that gets us through it."

"Will you be with me when it happens?"

"I'll do everything I can to be there, Rachel."

It seemed like the outing to Hannah's House drained Rachel of all her energy. When we got home, she went straight to bed.

Phone in hand, I sat at my kitchen table trying to arrange a doctor's appointment for her, systematically working my way down the list Mrs. Jenkins had given me. Fear gripped me as one clinic after another declined taking a new patient in late pregnancy, or told me they had no appointments available for weeks.

Just as I was giving up hope, a receptionist chirped, "You may be in luck. Dr. Thompson has a cancellation three days from now. One of his patients delivered early, so her appointment slot is available. Let me ask if he'll see your friend."

I waited impatiently while the receptionist put me on hold. Five minutes later, she was back on the line. "Dr. Thompson normally doesn't do something like this. But he said that since your friend was referred by Hannah's House, he'll consent to see her. Should I book her for 2:00 PM?

"Yes, please do," I said, relief washing through my tired body. "I'll have her there."

"I'm so sorry," I said to Thor as he spread his blanket and pillow out on the recliner that night. "I feel so bad about booting you out of your bedroom. I wanted us to have a peaceful place of our own, and now everything is turned upside down again. It's not fair to you, sweetie. I'm really sorry about that."

"No problem, Mom," he said.

"Rachel won't be here long," I told him. "Just another week. Then we'll have our lives back."

Chapter 27

The next morning, I tackled the job of organizing my bedroom closet, trying to find a way to store as many items as possible in the limited space. While I was in mid-project, Rachel wandered into my room wearing a pair of faded pajama pants, the frayed hems dragging on the floor.

I glanced up from my work. "You're looking better this morning, Rachel. Did you sleep well?"

"Fabulous!" She stretched dramatically, her old gray tee shirt riding up to reveal her swollen belly. I caught a glimpse of her stretch marks, ugly furrows gouged into her delicate skin.

"Want me to help you, Leah?" she asked.

"I can manage," I said. "This won't take me long."

Ignoring my words, she began poking through the unpacked boxes sitting along my bedroom wall. "Oh, Leah!" she exclaimed, holding up her recipe box. "I forgot to take this with me when I left Jake's house. But you remembered it!"

She opened the lid and flipped through the cards, then grinned at me mischievously. "You knew I was coming. You were waiting for me."

"I had no idea you were coming," I said.

But she didn't seem to hear me, and continued to pull items out of the boxes. I gritted my teeth in frustration, and was just about to tell her to stop when she suddenly sat down on my bed.

"I don't feel well," she whispered.

"Go lie down," I said. "You're at the end of your pregnancy, and you need lots of rest."

She shuffled out of the room, and I continued my work in peace.

Ten minutes later, she was back. "Leah, promise me something."

"What, Rachel?"

"Promise me you'll never let Jake know about the baby."

"It's not my business to tell Jake," I said. "It's yours. It's between you and him."

"But promise me you won't tell."

"Okay," I said as I reached up to shove a box to the back of my closet shelf.

"Say it, Leah. Turn around and look at me, and say it so I know you're telling me the truth."

I sighed and turned to face her. "I promise I won't tell Jake about the baby."

Our conversation had caught Thor's attention, and he appeared in the bedroom doorway.

"Do you promise not to tell your dad about the baby?" Rachel asked him.

"Rachel, don't bring Thor into this!" I scolded.

"Don't worry, Rachel," Thor said. "I promise not to tell my dad."

"Go lie down, Rachel," I said.

An hour later, I took a break from household chores, hoping for some time to myself. I situated myself on the loveseat, computer on my lap, emailing friends about my move to Wisconsin. Because I was so engrossed in what I was doing, I didn't realize Rachel had entered the room. I startled when she spoke to me.

"Leah, will you be my baby's godmother?"

I felt like screaming at her. *Can't you give me just a few minutes of peace without making some demand on me?* "I suppose so," I said without looking up from my computer screen.

"If you're the godmother, it means you have to do special things. Like having birthday parties and buying presents on holidays. Maybe even starting a savings account for college. You know what I mean?"

"Yes, Rachel," I snapped. "I know what it means to be a godparent."

"You'll always have to be there for my child. And if anything happens to me, you'll have to take care of it."

"Nothing's going to happen to you, Rachel."

"I know. I'm just trying to be a responsible mother, Leah. A mother should think about these things. "

I tried not to let sarcasm creep into my voice. "Good for you."

She stood watching me as I finished an email message. "Should we put that in writing?" she asked.

"Put what in writing?"

"That you'll be my baby's godmother."

"It doesn't need to be in writing."

"Yes, it does. We need an official document. That way, you can't back out of your agreement."

I looked up at her, no longer able to control my irritation. "Then for God's sake, Rachel, write something up!"

"Do you have paper?"

"In the kitchen, top drawer on the left."

She went to the kitchen, got what she needed, and shuffled off to her bedroom.

Twenty minutes later, she emerged from her room. "Look at these, Leah."

She proudly handed me two sheets of paper, identical documents written in penmanship so neat and ornate, they looked like they'd been rendered in calligraphy.

I, Rachel Rosenbaum, appoint River Leah Jorgensen to be the godmother of my child.

I, River Leah Jorgensen, agree to be the godmother of Rachel Rosenbaum's child. I will be there for the child while it is growing up, and I promise to do everything that a godmother is supposed to do.

She had drawn lines at the bottom of the pages for our signatures.

"Pretty good, huh?" she said. "My father's an attorney, so I know a little bit about these things. I made one for you and one for me. Now we just need one of those people to sign it. You know those people who punch their seal on things to make them legal?"

"You mean a notary?"

"Yes. Where can we find a notary?"

I handed the documents back to her. "Rachel, you're taking this too far. We don't need a notary to sign these."

"Yes, we do."

I eyed her suspiciously. "I think you're up to something, and I don't like it. Are you planning on running away and leaving the baby with me? Because unless you absolutely convince me that you're not going to take off and run after this baby is born, I'm not going to sign these documents."

Rachel grinned at me. "Would I do anything like that?"

"I'm dead serious, Rachel."

"I'm not going to run away, Leah. Really. I always run away from my parents, and I ran away from Jake. But I'd never, ever run away from you. And I won't run away from my baby, either. I promise."

While her heartfelt response reassured me that she wasn't planning on abandoning her child, the thought of Rachel clinging to me for life was terrifying. But I said, "Okay, then. Give me the pen, and I'll sign the papers."

She held the pen and paper behind her back, out of my reach. "No. You have to sign the documents in front of a notary."

"Rachel, you're getting on my last nerve!" I shouted.

She contorted her face into an exaggerated pout. "You never wanted to do this in the first place, did you, Leah? You just want me and my baby to disappear out of your life."

I heard Thor laughing in his bedroom. "Mom," he called, "you might as well give in. She's going to wear you down. She always does."

I sighed. "Okay, Rachel. We'll go to my bank after lunch. They'll have a notary there."

What am I getting myself into? I wondered. *Why do I feel like she's systematically spinning a web around me? I've got to draw a line somewhere!*

"Leah, where am I going to live when I leave Hannah's House?" Rachel asked me that evening.

"I can't tell you that," I replied. "The staff at Hannah's House will help you find a place. They'll probably help you get on welfare so you can support yourself and the baby."

"Oh." She sank wearily into the recliner and closed her eyes. I could almost hear her thoughts churning.

A minute later, she asked, "Wouldn't it be easier if we just got a bigger apartment, with three bedrooms? If I go on welfare, I can help pay the rent. And I can take care of everything while you work, like I did at Jake's house."

The sneaky little spider is still spinning, I thought. *She's determined to get her way.* "We can't do that, Rachel," I said. "I can't move for a long time, because I signed a year's lease on this apartment."

"Oh." She sounded dejected. "I guess I'll have to be on my own, then." She leaned her head against the back of the chair. "I'm so tired, Leah."

The next day, Rachel slept all morning and into the early afternoon. Just when I began to worry about her, she waddled out into the living-room and collapsed into the recliner. She refused my offer of food, complaining that she felt nauseated.

"I can run out and get you some crackers," I suggested. "Maybe some soda to settle your stomach?"

"I don't want anything to drink," she said. "It will just make me swell up more."

She pulled up one leg of her pajamas. I cringed at the sight of her swollen foot and ankle, which looked decidedly worse than when she'd arrived at my home three days earlier.

With considerable effort, she crossed one leg over the other and poked her puffy ankle. "See?" she said. "The hole stays there after I take my finger out. Isn't that awful?"

Without saying a word to her, I picked up the phone and took it to my bedroom, where I shut the door and called the office of the doctor she was scheduled to see the next day. "My friend has an appointment with the doctor tomorrow," I told the receptionist, "but is there any way she can be seen today? She's not feeling well."

"I'm sorry," the receptionist replied. "There's nothing available today. But I can let you speak with the nurse."

"Please," I said. When the nurse came on the line, I described Rachel's symptoms.

"Make sure she keeps her feet elevated and gets plenty of rest," the nurse advised. "Have her drink lots of water and keep her away from sodium. That should help flush out some of the edema. If her symptoms get worse, take her to the emergency room."

"I just called your doctor's office and talked to a nurse," I informed Rachel when I went back out to the living-room. "She said to stay off your feet and drink plenty of water. And if you start feeling really sick, tell me, and I'll take you to the emergency room."

"I'm okay, Leah," Rachel protested. "I'll be fine until I see the doctor tomorrow."

I went to the kitchen, got a bottle of water, and set it on the table next to her chair. "You just stay right there with your feet up. Don't get up unless you need to."

"My head hurts," Rachel said later that afternoon. "It hurts so bad I can't even see straight."

"That's not good, Rachel," I said. "Let's go to the emergency room."

"No, Leah, I'm fine. I'll be fine until tomorrow."

I stood in front of the recliner, bending down toward her, one hand on each arm of the chair. "I need to get this straight with you, Rachel. You are going to the doctor tomorrow. You're not getting out of it."

I paused, trying to think of a way to get my point across. "If you won't cooperate, I'll call the police, and they'll make you go."

Rachel looked at me like I was crazy. "You're being ridiculous, Leah. Why are you getting so worked up? I already told you I'd go."

The next morning, before I left for my interview with Mr. Douglas, I slipped into Thor's room to check on Rachel. She was lying motionless in bed, flat on her back, eyes closed.

"Rachel," I said, gently shaking her arm. "I'm leaving for my interview. I'll be back in a couple of hours. Remember, we have your doctor's appointment this afternoon. If you can, try to get up and get in the shower. Okay?"

"Okay, Leah," she whispered, smiling slightly without opening her eyes. "Good luck on your interview. I hope you get the job."

"Keep an eye on Rachel," I told Thor before I stepped out the door. "I'll be home as soon as I can, and right after lunch, I'll be taking her to her doctor's appointment."

Mr. Douglas had just asked me to describe my philosophy of teaching when I felt the rumble of my vibrating cell phone in the pocket of my slacks. *It's probably Rachel,* I thought, *wanting to ask some silly question about her doctor's appointment.*

Trying to ignore the rumbling, I began answering Mr. Douglas's question. "Instead of just teaching techniques, I believe the most important part of being an art teacher . . ." The rumbling stopped, and then started again.

Annoyed and distracted, I tried to recapture my train of thought. "I believe it's important to help each student discover and express their unique creativity . . ."

Once again, the rumbling stopped and started again. "I'm sorry, Mr. Douglas," I said. "My cell phone keeps ringing, and I need to see who it is."

"That's fine," he said.

I checked my phone and saw that three calls had been made back to back from my home phone. "I think I'd better see what's going on," I said. "May I step out into the hallway to make a call?"

He nodded. "Go ahead."

I dialed my home number, and Thor answered, panic in his voice. "Mom! I went in to check on Rachel, and I can't wake her up! She's breathing kind of funny."

"Call 911!" I almost shouted. "Right away! They'll take her to the emergency room. Ride with her in the ambulance if they'll let you. I'll meet you at the hospital as soon as I can."

I stepped back into the principal's office. "I'm so sorry, Mr. Douglas, but I have to leave. My friend's going to the ER, and I need to be there for her. I'm so sorry to cut the interview short. I really am very interested in the position."

"Do what you need to do," Mr. Douglas said. "And don't worry. The job is yours. We'll talk about the details later."

Chapter 28

I circled the crowded lot near the hospital emergency room, praying fervently for a parking space to appear. I breathed a sigh of relief when I saw a vehicle backing out, and quickly pulled into the space it had vacated. Then I jumped out of my car and ran to the emergency room entrance.

My heart pounded wildly as I stood at the reception desk. "I'm here to be with my friend, Rachel Rosenbaum," I said, trying to catch my breath. "Can you tell me what room she's in?"

The receptionist glanced up at me, an irritable expression on her face. "They took her upstairs just a minute ago. If you go sit in the waiting room, someone will be down to let you know what's going on."

"Do you know where my son is?"

The receptionist frowned and shook her head. "How would I know?"

Ignoring her rudeness, I pressed on. "The red-haired boy who came in the ambulance with her. Have you seen him?"

"Oh," she said. "He's in the waiting room." She pointed down the hallway.

I found Thor sitting alone in a corner of the room, his blue eyes large and scared in his white face. I sat beside him and took his hand, which was trembling.

"What happened, honey?" I asked. "Do you know what's going on?"

"They were doing things to her in the ambulance, trying to wake her up," he said in a shaking voice. "They were calling ahead to the hospital, saying things about her blood pressure and stuff like that. They took her away as soon as we got here."

"You were brave," I said. "You were so brave. You did the right thing by calling me. Now all we can do is to wait."

It wasn't long before a nurse came to speak with us. She was wearing a nametag inscribed with *Bonnie Scott, RN*. "Your friend has been taken to surgery for an emergency C-section," she informed us.

"If you'd like, you can come up to the surgical waiting room. I'll show you where it is."

Thor and I followed the nurse down a maze of hallways, and then rode with her on the elevator to the third floor. She ushered us into a half-filled waiting room, where people sat in clusters, reading magazines or conversing quietly with their companions.

"I'll let you know when Rachel's out of surgery," she said.

I sat down and picked up a magazine, trying to distract myself from my anxious thoughts. Thor sat leaning forward with his forearms on his thighs, staring at the floor, jiggling one leg. Then he jumped up and went to look out the window, nervously shifting his weight from one foot to the other. A few minutes later, he sat down beside me again, sighing deeply.

"What's going on, sweetie?" I asked him.

"What if I screwed up, Mom?"

"You didn't screw up," I reassured him. "You did exactly what you needed to do. Everything will be all right. Rachel's in good hands now."

"I hope so," he said.

Half an hour later, I looked up to see Nurse Bonnie Scott approaching us, accompanied by a tall man in green scrubs and a shorter man in a black suit. The nurse and the black-suited man stood in the background, while the man in scrubs stepped forward and addressed me.

"I'm Dr. Peterson. Are you the family of Rachel Rosenbaum?"

"We're her friends," I responded. "We're the closest thing to family she has in this area."

Dr. Peterson pulled a chair around and sat down to face me. "We delivered a baby girl by caesarean section," he informed me. "She had a bit of a rough time to start with. She's a few weeks early, but she's stable and doing fine now."

He gazed intently at me, his eyes filled with sorrow.

Why is this man looking at me like that? I wondered. *Why should he be so sad?*

"I'm so sorry," he said.

Sorry for what? They almost lost the baby, but she made it. She's fine now.

"I'm sorry to inform you that we were unable to save the mother. She died on the operating table. She'd developed eclampsia, and her organs were shutting down. She was too weak to make it through the surgery. We did everything we could."

A thick, heavy fog swirled around me, filling my head, clouding my thoughts, numbing my senses. I heard Thor cry out in agony, his voice sounding far away. The surgeon continued to speak. His mouth seemed to move in slow motion, and his words sounded garbled.

"Most of the time, we can save women in her condition. But Rachel didn't put up much of a fight to survive. It seemed like she was ready to let go of her life. She went peacefully."

My son leaned against me, his body heaving with sobs. I could scarcely lift my arm to encircle his shoulders. I opened my mouth to speak, but no words came.

"I feel . . . like this . . . is my fault." Thor choked out. "I should've checked . . . on her earlier. If I would have . . . checked on her . . . she might still . . . be . . . alive."

Dr. Peterson laid a hand on Thor's knee. "You can't blame yourself. A few minutes wouldn't have made any difference. The two of you did everything you could to make sure Rachel got to the hospital. The baby survived because of your quick response to this crisis. Otherwise, we would've had two mortalities."

He stood up, placed his hand on my shoulder, and then walked out of the room.

The nurse took the seat vacated by the surgeon, and the black-suited man pulled up a second chair. "This is Reverend Lawrence," the nurse said. "He's the hospital chaplain."

"I'm here to help in any way I can," Reverend Lawrence said.

"They're cleaning up Rachel's body right now," the nurse continued. "Would you like to see her?"

I nodded mutely.

She glanced at the chaplain. "Reverend Lawrence will take you to her. I'll be here on the surgical floor. If you have any questions, let me know."

She left the room while the chaplain stayed with us, patiently waiting for a cue that we were ready to view Rachel's body.

I pulled Thor close to me, and we held each other tightly. "We did everything we could, Thor," I said. "Both of us did everything we could."

"I'm sure you did," Reverend Lawrence murmured in a consoling voice.

I walked with my arm around my son as the kindly chaplain guided us to the recovery room. He gestured toward a bed surrounded by a green curtain. "I'll leave you alone with her now," he said. "I'll be waiting in the hallway. If you need me, let me know."

I braced myself as we rounded the curtain, not wanting to lay eyes on Rachel's lifeless form. But there she was, covered up to her chin with the hospital blanket, the sheet neatly folded over the top. Her hair, which had been carefully brushed back off her face, made a dark contrast against the white pillowcase. Her eyes were closed, and her face looked soft, innocent, and childlike. Only the faint creases in her forehead and around her mouth suggested her actual age of thirty. Her enlarged womb, recently delivered of its precious contents, bulged slightly under the covers.

A wave of dizziness passed over me, and I felt myself swooning. Thor grasped my arm to steady me.

"I can't believe this," I whispered. "How can this be? How can this possibly be?"

"It's so weird," Thor said. "I talked to her just two hours ago. The first time I checked on her, she told me she was fine. She said she was going to get up and get ready. But she didn't get up, so I checked on her again. That's when I couldn't wake her up. And now she's dead."

He looked at me, his blue eyes large and round, his brow furrowed. "How can someone be alive one minute, and then all of a sudden they're dead?"

"I don't know, Thor," I said. "I don't understand this either."

His shoulders sagged, and he hung his head. "I feel so terrible, Mom. I was a little bit mad at Rachel for coming to stay with us. It felt like she was getting in our way. But now she's gone, and I wish she'd come back. I'd do anything to make her come back."

Overcome with weakness, I walked around to the one available chair on the other side of the bed. I watched my son as he gazed at the body of his childhood companion, a river of tears running down his stricken face. It seemed that in the space of a few minutes, his soul had aged by a thousand years. I knew that the last remnants of his childish naiveté had taken flight.

"Thor, do you want some time alone with Rachel?" I asked him.

He nodded.

"I'll step outside. I'll be back in a minute."

I walked out into the hallway and stood next to Reverend Lawrence, leaning against the wall for support.

"It's so difficult to lose a dear friend," he said.

I felt disconnected from the words that came out of my mouth, and my voice didn't sound like my own. "I hardly ever thought of Rachel as a friend. Mostly, she was a source of frustration to me. But yes, it hurts. It hurts to lose her."

With that, my tears found an outlet and began streaming down my face.

Nurse Scott stepped into the hallway. "I'm sorry to disturb you," she said, "but do you have any information about Rachel's next of kin?"

"Her parents live in Chicago," I said. "Her father's name is Isaac Rosenbaum." I thought about the number Rachel had deleted from my cell phone. "I'm sorry. I don't know their address or phone number."

"That's okay," the nurse said. "I'll see if I can locate them."

Thor came out into the hallway, his eyes red from crying. "It's your turn, Mom," he said.

I watched the chaplain put a protective arm around my son's shoulders. Then I walked back into the recovery room and around the green curtain.

I pulled the chair up to the bed and sat down. Ever so carefully, I uncovered Rachel's thin arm and held her hand, now cold to the touch, in both of mine.

"Rachel," I whispered. "If your spirit is still nearby, I hope you hear me. I know it's been difficult between us at times. You needed so much from me, and I didn't always have it to give you. I'm so sorry, Rachel. I'm sorry I failed you. I did the best I could. You loved me so much. I want you to know that I love you, too."

Burying my face in my folded arms, I leaned against the bed and wept.

When I walked back out into the hallway, I felt weak and disoriented, with no idea of what to do next. But the chaplain surprised me with a question: "Do you want to see the baby?"

The baby. I hadn't even begun to consider the baby.

Chapter 29

Thor and I followed Reverend Lawrence up to the nursery on the hospital's fourth floor. The three of us stood in front of the large window, gazing at a dozen swaddled infants lying in their bassinettes. Reverend Lawrence waived at a nurse, and she came to see what he wanted.

"We'd like to see the Rosenbaum baby," he said.

The nurse looked at us curiously, and then wheeled one of the little beds up to the window. Its tiny occupant was red-faced and squalling, with a thick shock of unruly black hair. One little arm had escaped the swaddling of her flannel blanket, and her fist flailed angrily in the air.

The nursed stepped out into the hallway to join us. "The poor little thing has been crying nonstop for the past hour," she informed us. "We can't seem to calm her. But I guess her crying is a good sign. She's got some healthy lungs. It was touch and go with her at the beginning, and the doctors thought they were going to lose both the mother and the baby."

She bit her lip, shaking her head slowly. "It's so sad about the mother. Did you know her?"

"Yes," I said. "We were friends."

She laid a hand on my arm. "I'm so sorry for your loss."

"Thank you," I said. "It's such a shock. It doesn't seem real to me yet." A wave of dizziness swept over me as I pictured Rachel's lifeless form in the hospital bed.

But the crying infant pulled my attention back to her, and the words popped out of my mouth before I could think. "May I hold her?"

"Sure you may," the nurse said. "Let me get you some gloves and gowns."

A few minutes later, Thor and I, swathed in our protective gear, entered the nursery. The nurse placed the wailing infant into my arms. Instinctively, my body began to sway in an effort to soothe her. "It's okay, it's okay," I crooned to the motherless child.

After a minute, she stopped crying and opened her eyes. I could see they were dark like Rachel's. Then she closed them again, yawned, and fell asleep.

"Wow!" the nurse exclaimed. "I guess you have the magic touch."

"She's so tiny," I said. "How much did she weigh?"

The nurse looked at the card taped to the bassinette. "Six pounds, four ounces. Nineteen inches long. That's pretty good, considering she came three weeks early."

"I think she knows us," Thor murmured as he caressed the top of the baby's downy head.

The soft, toasty, sweet-smelling little bundle warmed my arms and then my heart. I touched her velvety cheek with one finger. "Such a precious little girl," I whispered to her. "So precious. So adorable."

"Let me hold her," Thor said. Reluctantly, I relinquished my treasure into his arms.

"She's awesome!" he exclaimed. "Rachel would've been so proud of her."

"What happens to this little one?" I asked the nurse. "What happens to babies whose mothers die in childbirth?"

The nurse shrugged. "Social Services takes care of that. We've already called them. Someone's coming tomorrow morning. They'll probably look into whether the father can take her, or maybe another family member. They might put her in foster care for a few days until they decide who's going to take custody of her."

"She'll make someone a wonderful baby," I said. I took her from Thor's arms and cuddled her a few more minutes before handing her back to the nurse.

"Is there anything else I can do for you?" Reverend Lawrence asked as Thor and I exited the nursery.

"I don't think so," I said. "Thank you for your kindness."

But then Thor surprised me by the question he asked. "Reverend Lawrence, would you pray for our friend?"

The chaplain also seemed surprised at the serious request coming from an adolescent boy.

"I certainly will," he said. "Would you like to join me in prayer?"

Thor nodded. The chaplain reached for each of our hands, then uttered a beautiful prayer beseeching God to bless Rachel's soul, and to comfort Thor and me in our time of grief.

We shared a moment of silence, holding hands, heads bowed. Then Thor began to speak in a tremulous voice. "I don't know how these things work, God. But I want you to take care of Rachel. We tried and we couldn't do it, so now it's your turn."

I thought he was finished, but then he added, "And please take care of her baby, too. She doesn't have a mother now, and she needs somebody to look out for her."

"Amen," the chaplain said.

"Amen," I echoed.

The three of us stood there awkwardly before Reverend Lawrence eased the moment by saying, "If you need anything else, you can ask any of the hospital staff to page me." Then we watched him walk down the hallway and disappear into the elevator.

Thor turned his attention back to the nursery window, gazing pensively at Rachel's baby girl. Then he spoke, his voice filled with conviction. "Mom, we can't let anyone else take this baby. Rachel wanted us to have her. Remember the paper she made you sign? You've got to show somebody that paper."

His words stunned me, overwhelming my already fragile state of mind. I sank down on a bench in the hallway, holding my aching head in my hands. "Thor," I said, "I can't raise a baby right now. I'm just getting ready to start a new job. Rachel's parents will want to keep their grandchild. Maybe an aunt or uncle will raise her. We don't have any right to take her away from her family."

"Mom!" Thor's voice sounded indignant. "She's my sister! I'm her family, too!"

She's my sister. I didn't know why I hadn't considered that idea before. I'd always thought in terms of Jake and Rachel's baby, but for whatever reason, my mind hadn't latched onto the fact that this child was my son's sibling.

"What did you do with that paper?" Thor persisted. "You didn't throw it away, did you?"

"No, I didn't throw it away," I said. "But I'm not sure where it is."

"Then let's go home and find it."

"Thor, I can't think straight right now. So much has happened today. Give me a little time to sort it out." I sat back, exhaling deeply. "We should get something to drink. That will give us a little strength. Let's go down to the cafeteria."

I stood up and took a few steps toward the elevator, but stopped in front of the nursery window again. Rachel's baby was sleeping peacefully, her little chest gently rising and falling with the rhythm of her breath. My arms ached to hold her again. I wanted unwrap the blanket and count her little toes. I wanted to feel her tiny fist clutching my finger. I wanted to lay her over my shoulder and caress her back, to feel the warmth of her little head nestled against my neck, to inhale her sweet baby scent.

This is a bad idea, I thought. But I didn't stop myself from signaling the nurse again, and she stepped back out into the hallway. "What time is Social Services coming tomorrow?"

"They said they'd be here sometime between nine and eleven."

"I think I might want to talk to them. Will you tell them? I can be here by nine."

"Yes, I'll tell them," the nurse promised. "What's your name?"

"I'm River Jorgensen. Rachel's friend."

"Well, what do you think, Mom?" Thor asked as we sipped our drinks in the cafeteria.

"About what, Thor?"

"About Rachel's baby."

"Thor, I don't think we stand much of a chance to get her. And I really don't think it's a good idea to take this on."

Thor's face fell.

"But I'm willing to talk with Social Services about it. Just to talk about the possibility."

"Good."

We gazed at each other, and I knew the exhaustion on my son's face mirrored my own condition. "I think we should go home, Thor," I said. "It's been a rough day for us. But I want to see Rachel one more time."

"Me, too," he said.

We headed back to the recovery room on the third floor. As we stood together at Rachel's bedside, I ran my fingers through her long silky hair.

"You have a beautiful baby girl, Rachel," I said. "We got to hold her. As far as I can tell, she looks like you. I hope you can see her from wherever you are. I'm sure you're proud of her."

In the stillness that followed, I could hear Rachel's plaintive voice in my mind. *Leah, if anything happens to me, will you take care of my baby?*

I thought about the day I discovered Rachel's pregnancy, when she pleaded with me to help her raise her child. I'd tried as hard as I could to push that responsibility away from me, but five months later, it had landed on my doorstep again.

Face it, River, I told myself. *It's been your destiny to take care of this baby from the moment she was conceived.*

"I want you to know, Rachel," I said aloud, "that I'll do everything I can to take your baby home with me and raise her. I can't promise, but I'll try."

Thor put his arm around my waist and leaned his head against my shoulder.

Nurse Scott met us as we came out from behind the curtain. "I was able to get hold of Rachel's parents," she said. "They should be here in about forty-five minutes."

"I'd like to speak with them," I said. "My son and I will wait. Will you let me know when they get here?"

I collapsed on a sofa in the waiting room, utterly exhausted. It felt like every cell in my body had begun to tremble.

"Are you okay, Mom?" Thor asked.

"I will be," I said. "I think I'm in shock. Everything that happened today seems so unreal."

"I know."

I closed my eyes and leaned my head against the back of the sofa. It was late afternoon and the waiting room was silent, empty of all occupants except my son and me. But in spite of the outer stillness, my mind was in turmoil, thoughts chasing each other and running in circles.

Then Thor said, "You know what, Mom?"

"What?"

"I think Rachel knew she was going to die."

"What makes you say that?"

He got up and went to stare out the window, then spoke hesitantly, his back to me. "One day when I was nine or ten, Rachel and I were outside in the back yard sitting on the edge of the deck. A bug came crawling along, and Rachel squished it so it wouldn't crawl on her leg. I told her she shouldn't do that, that she shouldn't kill things. She started crying because she thought she'd done something bad. I told her it was okay, that it was just a mistake.

"Then she started talking about people dying. She told me she had a grandpa who lived to be ninety-three, and that when he died, no one got upset because he'd lived a long time. She said that when someone dies young, people take it hard. She said they don't understand that some people are meant to have short lives, and that's just the way it is."

"That's interesting," I said. "Do you think she was talking about herself?"

"Yes," he said. "I think she was letting me know I shouldn't be upset when she died."

He sat down again and folded his arms across his chest, hunching his shoulders, rocking slightly. "But I'm upset anyway, Mom. I can't help it."

Chapter 30

I must have dozed off, because the next thing I knew, Thor was nudging me. "Mom," he whispered, "I think Rachel's parents are here."

I looked up to see Nurse Scott approaching us, followed by a couple who appeared to be in their seventies. I'd often heard it said that spouses in a long-term marriage end up resembling each other, and the man and woman walking toward me were the perfect example of that truism. Both were of medium height and slender build, with olive skin, dark eyes, and black hair now overtaken by gray. The man wore a dark suit and tie, while his partner wore a pair of black slacks, a crisp white blouse, and a pale blue cardigan. I recognized Rachel's pretty features in her grief-stricken face.

"Mr. and Mrs. Rosenbaum," the nurse said, "this is your daughter's friend, River Jorgensen. River, this is Isaac and Esther Rosenbaum."

I stood up and extended my hand, first to Mrs. Rosenbaum and then to her husband. "I'm pleased to meet you, although I wish it were under different circumstances." I gestured to Thor, who'd also risen to his feet. "This is my son Thor."

Mrs. Rosenbaum looked puzzled. "We were expecting to meet someone named Leah."

"That's me," I explained. "Leah is my middle name. That's what Rachel always called me."

Mrs. Rosenbaum smiled, while at the same time tears sprang to her eyes. "Leah was all Rachel talked about when she stayed with us these past two months. Leah and Thor. She thought so much of the two of you."

Tears welled in my own eyes. "I'm so very sorry for your loss," I said. "I can't imagine what a shock it is. Thor and I still can't believe what happened. It doesn't seem possible."

Esther lowered her head, bringing her hand to her mouth. Her thin shoulders heaved as she tried to contain her sobs. Isaac put a protective arm around her.

"Please have a seat," I said, gesturing for them to sit on the sofa.

Thor and I pulled up two chairs, forming a circle around the coffee table.

"Have you seen Rachel yet?" I asked.

They both nodded. Isaac's shoulders were hunched, and his wrinkled face bore an expression of weary resignation. Esther appeared drained, frail, on the verge of collapse. My heart filled with compassion for the elderly couple, and I wondered what they could have possibly done to deserve such vilification by their daughter.

"And the baby? Have you seen the baby?"

"We made a brief stop at the nursery," Isaac said. "We'll pay her another visit before we leave today."

"My son and I spent some time holding her," I said. "She's precious."

A smile flickered across Esther's face. "Yes, she is."

Isaac coughed into his handkerchief, and then struggled to clear his throat. "Please tell us what happened."

I suddenly wondered whether the Rosenbaums thought I'd been negligent in my obligations toward Rachel, whether they blamed me for their daughter's death. I lowered my eyes, biting my lip in an effort to control my emotions, but when I looked up, I saw no judgment on the faces of Rachel's parents. I knew they were not against me, that they were with me, sharing the same loss.

"Rachel called me out of the blue four days ago," I informed them. "It was a total surprise to me. I didn't even know she had my phone number. She wanted to come for a visit. I didn't think it was a good idea. My son and I had just moved here, and we weren't fully settled into our apartment. But Rachel persisted, and I gave in."

Isaac and Esther exchanged puzzled glances. "When Rachel came to stay with us," Esther said, "she told us she'd been living with a friend named Leah. She said she had to leave because Leah was moving, but that she'd be joining Leah in her new home."

Oh my God! I thought. *Rachel had this all planned out. My telling her I couldn't help her raise the baby hadn't daunted her in the least.*

"I honestly had no clue Rachel was planning this," I said. "That was her idea, not mine."

"That sounds like Rachel," Isaac said. "She'd get ideas in her head that no one could talk her out of."

"Given what she'd told us," Esther added, "we weren't surprised when she left our home. We were expecting it."

"Mr. and Mrs. Rosenbaum," I said, "I want you to know that I tried my best to convince Rachel to go back to your home. I told her you were the best people to take care of her. But she refused, and there was no way I could budge her."

"She could be stubborn," Isaac said.

"I told her she should at least call you and tell you where she was. But she just wouldn't do it. I should've called you myself. I'm so sorry I didn't."

Esther looked perplexed. "But we knew where she was. She left us a note. She told us she was leaving for Racine to live with Leah, and that Leah would take care of her and the baby."

That little sneak, I thought. *She knew exactly what she was doing.*

I shook my head. "Believe me, Mrs. Rosenbaum, I knew nothing of those plans. But I tried to do the right thing by Rachel when she got here. She didn't seem to be feeling well, and I was worried. The day after she arrived, I took her to a crisis pregnancy center, and we were making plans for her to move in. I scheduled a doctor's appointment, and he was supposed to see her this afternoon. Yesterday, when she wasn't feeling well, I tried to get her to go to the emergency room. But she refused. I checked on her this morning before I left the house, and she seemed okay. Then while I was gone, my son called to tell me he couldn't wake her up. I had him call the ambulance, and they brought her here."

For the first time that day, the feelings of guilt and remorse that had been lurking in the back of my mind rushed forward, washing over me in a wave of devastation. I felt heavy, immobilized, barely capable of speaking.

"Mr. and Mrs. Rosenbaum," I said. "For the rest of my life, I'll wonder what else I could've done to keep your daughter alive. I feel like

I failed her. I'm so sorry. I'm so terribly sorry." I buried my face in my hands.

Thor scooted his chair close to mine and put his arm around me. "You didn't fail her, Mom," he whispered. "You helped her."

Esther laid her delicate hand on my knee. "Please don't take this on yourself, Leah. We don't blame you. Years ago, my husband and I had to reconcile ourselves to the fact that because of the way she chose to live, some terrible misfortune was bound to happen to our daughter."

"Rachel seemed to have a self-sabotaging streak in her personality," Isaac mused. "Over and over again, she'd refuse to do the things that were clearly in her best interest." He glanced at Esther, and she nodded in agreement.

"We weren't happy when our unmarried pregnant daughter showed up on our doorstep," he continued. "But we tried to respond to the situation the best we could. My wife succeeded in getting Rachel to an obstetrician."

"She went to the doctor twice," Esther chimed in. "But she refused to get the ultrasound that he recommended. I paid for a prescription of prenatal vitamins, and she wouldn't take them because they upset her stomach."

"Every time my wife bought something for the baby, Rachel would get upset," Isaac said. "It got to a point where we truly felt we were stuck in a no-win situation. We wanted to respect our daughter's wishes, but we knew we had to be prepared for the arrival of the baby."

"So when Rachel left us the note saying she was going to live with you," Esther said, "we thought it was the best thing for her to do. We thought perhaps you could provide the guidance she wouldn't accept from us, that she might be more reasonable with you."

I shook my head. "I'm afraid she wasn't. I didn't get much farther with her than you did."

Isaac leaned forward, looking at me intently, kindness in his weary eyes. "I want to make it clear to you, Miss Jorgensen, that we harbor no ill feelings toward you. As a matter of fact, we owe you our gratitude. We're aware of the fact that you provided a stable home for our daughter for six years. That's the longest she's stayed with anyone since she left our home as a teenager."

"She thought the world of you," Esther said. "We truly appreciate all you've done for her. Please don't spend a single minute blaming yourself."

I exhaled deeply, then reached out and took their hands in both of mine. "Thank you for your kindness," I said.

"Thank you," they murmured in unison.

Then Isaac struggled to his feet. "If you'll excuse me, I need to walk around a bit. Could I bring you ladies a cup of coffee?"

Thor jumped up. "I can show you where the cafeteria is."

"My husband is nervous," Esther confided after Isaac and Thor left the waiting room. "He can't sit still at times like this. He needs to pace."

Suddenly, her body sagged, and a sob escaped her throat. I handed her a box of tissues from the coffee table, then joined her on the sofa.

"I was a failure as a mother," she whimpered. "I completely failed my little girl. I tried to do right by her. God knows I tried, but I couldn't seem to provide what that child needed."

She dabbed at her eyes with a tissue. "Rachel came along late in my life. By the time I was thirty-two, I'd given birth to my first five children. My husband and I had planned on that being the extent of our family. But thirteen years later, I found out I was going to have another baby.

"Isaac and I were shocked, but we accepted the fact, as we believed it was God's will for our lives. It was a difficult pregnancy, and my obstetrician thought I was going to lose the baby during the first trimester. But by some miracle, she hung on. She ended up coming six weeks early. She weighed less than three pounds, and she had to stay in the hospital the first month of her life. She was such a fretful baby when we brought her home. She'd cry all night long. My husband and I took turns walking the floor with her. We were exhausted."

She looked at me, her eyes begging for understanding.

"That must've been very hard on you," I said.

She nodded. "Rachel just seemed different than our other children. Her older brothers and sisters were good students, and they all ended up with professional careers. Rachel didn't care much about school. She couldn't stay focused, and we actually felt quite fortunate just to get her through high school.

"We tried to help her select some type of higher education so she'd have a way of supporting herself. But she rejected any idea we came up with. From the time she left high school, she drifted from one thing to another. She'd stay with a friend until she'd wear out her welcome, then she'd come back to our home for awhile. She always seemed angry with us, and I never knew why. She wouldn't stay long, and off she'd go again."

Esther looked down, wringing her hands in her lap. "I've never been able to figure out what went wrong. Maybe we were just too old. Maybe she needed younger parents."

She looked up at me. "I'll always be curious as to why Rachel stayed with you for so long. She must've been very attached to you."

"She was," I said. "I don't know why, but she stuck to me like glue."

"Isaac and I used to worry ourselves sick over Rachel," Esther said. "But after awhile, we realized the choices she made were beyond our control. God knows we tried, but she wouldn't listen to us for a minute."

Her voice trailed off, and she seemed to withdraw into herself. "I failed her terribly," she whispered.

"No, Mrs. Rosenbaum!" I was surprised by the firmness in my voice, the confidence in my words. "Don't let yourself think this way. It's not fair to you, and it's not fair to Rachel. Your daughter was who she was, and it has nothing to do with you. Rachel was exactly who she was meant to be."

Esther stared at me, incredulous. "Do you really believe that?"

"Yes," I said. "I really do."

Isaac and Thor returned to the room, each carrying a cup of coffee.

Isaac's hand shook as he set his cup on the table in front of his wife. "Here you go, dear," he said. Esther flashed him a grateful smile.

He seated himself, sighing wearily. "We have a lot of decisions to make."

"Yes," Esther murmured.

"We need to contact a mortuary and arrange for our daughter's body to be returned to Chicago. We need to plan a funeral. Fortunately, three of our children will be coming to our home this evening. They'll help with these things. I don't think my wife and I could manage all this on our own."

Esther shook her head, tears trickling from her eyes. "And the baby. Our children will help us decide what we'll do with the baby."

Here's where you say something, a voice inside me prompted. *Speak up now. This is your opportunity.*

I took a deep breath, knowing I was about to propose a commitment of a lifetime. "Mr. and Mrs. Rosenbaum, I want you to know that if you don't have any other plans for Rachel's baby girl, I'll be more than happy to take her."

Rachel's parents stared at me, bewildered, clearly caught off guard by my offer.

"As you know," I said, "Rachel was very close to me, and was counting on me to help her raise her child. In fact, she asked me to be her child's godmother, and went so far as to put it in writing. This feels like a commitment I need to honor."

I glanced sideways at Thor. His eyes expressed his gratitude.

Esther continued to stare at me, a befuddled expression on her face. Isaac rubbed his forehead as if deep in thought. "This is all so sudden," he said. "As you can imagine, we're hardly in a frame of mind to give you a response."

A heavy silence filled the room. I could hear every nuance of Isaac's labored breathing, punctuated by Esther's occasional sniffle. I wondered whether I'd offended Rachel's parents, and my anxious heart pounded so wildly, I was almost sure they could see it pulsating in my chest.

"My wife and I need to go home and discuss this with our children," Isaac finally said.

"Please understand," I said. "I don't intend fight you for the baby. I wouldn't dream of that. She's your granddaughter, and she's your responsibility. But if you're willing to let me, I would love to raise Rachel's child. I know that's what she would have wanted."

That's absolutely true, I thought. *As lovely as these kind, gentle people are, Rachel didn't want them to raise her baby. She didn't want her child raised by any of her family members. She was counting on me.*

"This is something we need to take under consideration," Isaac said. "Allow us to go home and think it over."

"Did you know that Social Services is coming tomorrow morning?" I asked.

"Yes," Isaac said. "We're aware of that. We'll be here." He hesitated. "Are you planning to be present?"

"Yes, I'll be here."

"We'll give you our answer then."

"I want you to know," I said, "that I'll respect any decision you make."

Chapter 31

I called my mother that evening. The sound of her comforting voice triggered a cascade of tears that coursed down my cheeks and dripped off my chin, soaking the front of my shirt. She offered consolation in response to my account of the day's alarming events, but expressed little surprise.

"The twists and turns of life happen for reasons we don't readily understand," she told me.

When I confided my uncertainty about taking on the responsibility of Rachel's baby, she said, "You don't need my advice, River. Just follow your heart."

In spite of my mother's reassuring words, I couldn't settle my agitated mind, and I slept very little that night. I tossed and turned until I could no longer stay in bed, and then I got up to pace from one end of my apartment to the other. Thor refused to sleep in the bed occupied by Rachel the last night of her life, and each time I got up, I found him lying wide awake on the living-room recliner.

When morning came, we were both so exhausted and distracted that we barely had the energy to speak to each other. As we fumbled around getting ready for the trip back to the hospital, it occurred to me that I needed to return Rachel's personal belongings to her parents.

When I opened the door to Thor's bedroom, I was greeted by the sight of the rumpled bed, untouched since the paramedics had lifted Rachel out of it less than twenty-four hours ago. Her faded blue jeans lay on the floor, and an inside-out tee shirt was draped over Thor's desk chair. The toe of one flip-flop peeked out from under the bed, while its mate lay upside down next to the door.

My foggy mind registered a sense of déjà vu. For the second time in the span of a few weeks, I was standing in a bedroom vacated by Rachel, overwhelmed with sadness over her departure.

But this time, she was gone for good.

When we arrived at the hospital nursery, I flagged down a nurse. "Is the lady from Social Services here to see the Rosenbaum baby?" I asked, hoping she hadn't already come and gone.

"She's here," the nurse said. "Mrs. Slater is talking with the baby's grandparents."

"Could I speak with her before she leaves?"

"I can see," the nurse said. "They're in the office behind the nurse's station. I'll let them know you're here. You can go to the waiting room down the hallway."

"What do you think they're talking about?" Thor asked as we sat waiting to meet with Mrs. Slater. "Do you think they'll let us have the baby?"

"I really don't know, Thor," I replied. "We shouldn't get our hopes up. This is Mr. and Mrs. Rosenbaum's granddaughter. If they want custody of her, I won't fight them. I couldn't hurt them like that. They've just lost their daughter, and I can't take their grandchild from them. She's part of their family."

"But she's my sister. She's part of my family, too."

"I know that, Thor. But the law isn't going to look at it that way."

Thor slumped back on the sofa, looking frustrated. "Did you bring the paper, Mom?"

"Yes, Thor, I did, just in case we need it." I opened my handbag and showed him the envelope containing Rachel's document.

It wasn't long before the nurse stepped into the room. "Ms. Jorgensen, Mrs. and Mrs. Rosenbaum would like for you to join them. I'll show you where they're meeting."

"Can I come, too?" Thor asked.

"I think it's best if you wait here," I said. "I'm sure it won't be long."

The nursed ushered me into the office where Isaac and Esther Rosenbaum sat at a small conference table, along with two women I'd never met.

"This is Mrs. Slater from Social Services," the nurse said. She gestured toward the woman in a business suit, who was seated at the head of the table with a stack of papers in front of her.

"I'm pleased to meet you, Mrs. Slater," I said, shaking her hand. "I'm River Jorgensen. I'm a friend of Mr. and Mrs. Rosenbaum's daughter."

The other woman extended her hand. "I'm Linda Rosenbaum," she announced haughtily.

I was momentarily taken aback. *The Rosenbaums' daughter? Rachel's older sister? How could this heavy-set, fair-skinned blonde be an offspring of Isaac and Esther?*

"Linda is our daughter-in-law," Isaac explained, as if sensing my confusion. "She's married to our oldest son."

"I drove Mom and Dad here today," Linda informed me, sounding self-righteous. "With what they've been through the past twenty-four hours, they're exhausted. I didn't think it was safe for them to travel alone."

Indeed, both of Rachel's parents looked like they were running on the last reserves of their energy. Esther's thin shoulders were hunched, and dark circles underlined her sad eyes. Isaac's breathing seemed more labored than the day before, and he periodically coughed into his handkerchief. Neither of them looked like they'd slept any more than I had the previous night.

So I was glad they had an escort, but there was something about Linda Rosenbaum's authoritative manner that I didn't trust.

"I brought the belongings Rachel left at my house," I said, holding up the shabby duffel bag. Linda reached for it and placed it on the floor next to her chair.

"I was just talking with Mr. and Mrs. Rosenbaum about the rights of the baby's father," Mrs. Slater informed me after I'd taken a seat at the table. "Apparently, he's nowhere in the picture. Mr. and Mrs. Rosenbaum have told me Rachel gave them no information at all about the father." She looked at me questioningly, as if waiting for me to divulge anything I knew.

Please, please help me! I beseeched the Spirit. *I don't know which way to turn here, because either way seems wrong. I don't want to lie and say I don't know who the father is. But I can't break the promise I made to Rachel.*

I opened my mouth to speak, and was surprised when my words flowed effortlessly. "Rachel wanted to keep the father's identity a secret," I said. "She didn't want him involved. He didn't even know she was pregnant with his child."

That last part is absolutely true, I told myself. *Jake thought she'd lost the baby.*

Linda Rosenbaum exhaled deeply. The relief in her eyes puzzled me. I assumed that, for whatever reason, she was glad the baby's father was out of the way.

Mrs. Slater shot me a curious look. She seemed to be on the verge of asking me another question, but she didn't, and I was glad. "Then it seems appropriate to look for placement within the family," she said. She turned toward Isaac and Esther. "I'm sure you've been discussing that possibility."

"Yes, we have," Isaac responded, speaking slowly and deliberately. "Last night, my wife and I sat down with three of our children to discuss the matter." He glanced at Esther. "Clearly, my wife and I are of an age where it would be foolish to take on the responsibility of raising an infant. The child is our flesh and blood, and we feel deeply for her, but we couldn't provide what she needs. And our remaining children aren't young themselves. They're all in their forties and fifties, with busy lives and careers."

His voice suddenly gave out, and he was overcome by a paroxysm of coughing. While he was catching his breath, his daughter-in-law leaned forward, her eyes glowing with excitement.

"But we do have another option," she said. Everyone at the table turned to look at her.

"My daughter and her husband would make great parents for this baby. They're in their late twenties, with two little boys. They're so excited about the prospect of raising a girl."

An awkward silence fell across the room. Isaac and Esther looked bewildered by Linda's announcement, and I suspected she hadn't discussed her proposition with them.

Linda spoke again, her voice filled with conviction. "My son-in-law has a great career, and he can afford to support another child. My daughter is a stay-at-home mother. They have plenty of room in their home and in their hearts for this baby."

My heart sank. *I tried, Rachel,* I thought. *For your sake, I tried. But there's no hope now. Clearly, this wasn't meant to be.*

Linda continued to chatter about the merits of her daughter and son-in-law as prospective parents. But Isaac shifted in his chair, straightened his posture, and cleared his throat. "However," he said, before he was overtaken by another fit of coughing.

Linda stopped talking and stared at him, apparently surprised by his interruption.

"However," Isaac repeated in a purposeful voice, "we feel we should consider the wishes of our daughter. She had expressed to us her desire to raise this child with the help of her dear friend, Miss Jorgensen. She moved here to Racine with the intention of being close to Miss Jorgensen."

He looked at me. "And you informed us she signed a document."

"Yes," I said, caught off guard by the sudden change in the direction of the conversation. I opened my handbag and handed him the envelope.

Isaac's hands trembled as he opened the envelope and unfolded the paper. Esther leaned toward him, and they read the document together.

"This is a legal document," Isaac said, "signed by a notary. Although it doesn't mean much, it shows us Rachel's intention."

"That certainly is Rachel's handwriting," Esther observed.

"May I see it?" Mrs. Slater requested. Isaac handed her the document, and she perused it silently.

Isaac folded his gnarled hands on the table and looked at me intently. "Miss Jorgensen, my wife and I truly believe it would be Rachel's desire to have you raise her child. So if you're still willing, we'd like to offer you this opportunity."

I could hardly believe what I'd heard him say. I wondered whether my dazed brain was deceiving me, but Isaac was smiling at me and Esther was nodding in agreement. I realized they'd just placed their granddaughter into my safekeeping.

"I'm willing," I said. "I'm absolutely willing."

"I'd like to say that not everyone in the family agrees with this decision," Linda said.

I held my breath, waiting for Mrs. Slater to respond, but she appeared to be lost in thought, oblivious to Linda's protest. Linda shot me a look that made me shiver, a serene smile masking an expression of contempt.

"Ms. Jorgensen," Mrs. Slater finally said, "I believe I can authorize placing the baby in your home after her discharge from the hospital. Then we'll need to work on getting you licensed as a foster parent. There will be a background check and a home study, and you'll need to take a few classes."

"What about adoption?" I asked.

"We'll cross that bridge later," she responded. "It's a definite possibility if the foster placement goes well. But we'll have to go through the legal process of advising the birth father of his rights. We'll run an ad in the paper once a month for three months. If the birth father doesn't come forward within that time, he loses his legal rights to the child. Do you know where Rachel was residing when she got pregnant?"

"Niles, Michigan."

"Then we'll run the ad in the Niles paper."

I think we're safe, I thought. *Jake never reads the paper.*

I leaned back in my chair, overwhelmed with the reality of what I'd just committed to. *Oh my God, how can I do this? I'm getting ready to start a new job. Can I really add this child to my household? Can I manage all these changes at once?*

My mother's smiling face flashed into my mind. *You can do this, River,* I could hear her say. *And you will.*

"We can help financially," Isaac said. "We're in a position where we can do that."

"We have a few things we've already bought for the baby," Esther chimed in. "A bassinette, diapers, blankets. We brought them along in our trunk, just in case you needed them."

"Until the baby is adopted," Mrs. Slater said, "she'll be a ward of the court. That means you'll receive a monthly stipend for her care."

"If you'll excuse us," Linda Rosenbaum said in an icy voice, "I need to get Mom and Dad back to Chicago. We have funeral arrangements to make."

"What happened, Mom?" Thor asked as I walked back into the waiting room.

I smiled broadly. "She's ours!"

My son leaped into the air with a loud whoop, then jumped into my outstretched arms.

The next three days were filled with frenetic activity: signing documents, collecting baby furniture and supplies, arranging day care. On the day of her discharge from the hospital, Thor and I went to the nursery to claim our new family member.

"She sure is a beautiful baby," the nurse said as she placed my daughter into my arms. "But she's a fussy little thing. What did you name her?"

"Molly," I said, gazing fondly at the squirming infant. "She's Molly Rosenbaum for now. Hopefully in a few months, she'll be Molly Jorgensen."

As we rode the elevator to the main floor, Molly's fussing gave way to ear-piercing shrieks. She continued to wail as I carried her out of the hospital to our car, and became even more outraged when I secured her into her new car-seat.

Thor insisted on riding in the back with her. "She shouldn't be alone back here," he said.

Molly's crying continued as I pulled out of the parking lot. Thor leaned forward and spoke into my ear so I could hear him above the din.

"She sure makes a lot of noise for such a little person," he said, chuckling.

"She sure does," I agreed.

"I think she's crying for her mother. She doesn't know we're her family now. But she will."

He leaned back, and in my rearview mirror, I watched him stroke his baby sister's cheek with one finger.

"Sh-h-h," he crooned. "It's okay, it's okay."

Whether it was due to her brother's soothing voice or because of the vibrations of the car rolling along the highway, my baby girl stopped crying, yawned, and fell asleep.

EPILOGUE

I catch my breath as the Washington High School orchestra students file onto the stage. Molly bounces on my lap and points.

"Look, Mommy! There's Thor!"

"Yes, Molly," I say. "There's your brother."

I watch my lanky seventeen-year-old son walk across the stage in his black trousers, white shirt, and black tie. He's six feet, two inches tall now, the same height as his father. His unruly red curls are smoothed down with a hair product, and his freckled face wears a serious expression. He takes his seat, resting his violin on his knees, waiting for the spring orchestra concert to begin.

Shawn tightens his arm around me, squeezing my shoulders. "He has an amazing gift, River," he tells me. "I'm so proud of him."

"So am I, Shawn," I say. "So am I."

It's so easy being with Shawn. This is a real relationship, nothing like my ambiguous association with Jacob Potter. Shawn is Thor's private violin instructor. Shortly after I met him in that capacity, we began dating. We've been together for three years. Jake's monthly support checks nicely supplement my art teacher's salary, and they pay for the luxury of Thor's music lessons. I doubt that Jake would be pleased to know there's a direct connection between the money he sends and me finding a boyfriend.

Shawn reminds me of my dad. He's gentle and reserved, tall, thin, and white-haired, with a neatly groomed beard and wire-framed glasses. He's my kind of guy, for sure. My mother says I've found my soul-mate.

Molly turns to smile coyly at Shawn. Then she scrambles off my lap and onto his, and he cuddles her in the crook of his arm. He's the only father figure she's known in the four and a half years of her life.

Molly looks exquisite in her frilly yellow dress. With her olive skin, delicate features, and silky black hair, she's the image of her biological mother. She's petite, but not as frail as Rachel. She has a hint of Jake's sturdiness in her build, which seems to render her stronger, more capable of handling life than her mother was.

Molly already knows that her birth mother died and that I adopted her. But that doesn't mean much to her four-year-old mind. Someday, she'll want to know more of the truth, and I'll have to tell her. It won't be easy.

Shawn loves Molly as if she was his own, and he plans to adopt her after we get married. Yes, we've been talking about marriage, but for Thor's sake, we're going to wait a few years. Neither Shawn nor I want to introduce any more complications into my son's life. He's been through enough already.

Thor told me there would be a special surprise for me tonight. I scan my program to see if I can discover what he's talking about.

There it is, listed two-thirds of the way down the page: "Rachel's Song," featuring a violin solo by Theodore James Jorgensen. In small letters underneath the listing, it says, "Composed by Rachel Rosenbaum, arranged by Theodore James Jorgensen."

I feel lightheaded. I can hardly believe my son has kept that song with him all these years. I don't know whether I can get through this, whether I can bear to hear that little tune again. I close my eyes, breathing deeply. Molly thinks I'm upset, and she reaches over and hugs me around my neck.

"Mommy's okay, Molly," I say.

I wish Isaac and Esther Rosenbaum could be here to listen to Thor play their daughter's song. They'd planned on coming, but Esther called me last night to tell me Isaac didn't feel well enough to travel.

I've grown close to the Rosenbaums. I promised them I'd never keep their granddaughter away from them, and every couple of months, we make the trip to Chicago to visit them. They're lovely people. They consider Thor to be their grandchild as well as Molly.

Thor has developed an attachment to old Isaac. He spends hours listening with rapt attention as Isaac instructs him in the history and tenets of the Jewish faith. It seems to me that after the confusion and blurry boundaries of his childhood, Thor longs for the structure that the Jewish religion offers. He's become a deeply contemplative young man. No doubt he's moving in the direction of converting to Judaism, which will please Isaac to no end. I can picture a yarmulke perched on Thor's curly hair. It suits him.

My mother still insists that my son was born to be a holy man. She doesn't mind that he's interested in Judaism instead of Shamanism. "The tradition he chooses is irrelevant," she says. "Whatever path he takes, he'll be a light-worker, a way-shower."

My mother isn't coming tonight. My father is very weak now, near the end of his life. My mother won't leave him, but she says she'll be here in spirit.

Thor invited his dad to come, and Jake promised him he'd be here. I haven't seen him yet. I want him to keep his word, for Thor's sake. But it will be easier for me if he doesn't.

Since we've lived here in Racine, Thor has visited his father three or four times a year. Sometimes he takes the train and spends a weekend. Now that can drive, he takes my car over to Jake's house when we're in Indiana visiting my parents.

I haven't gone back to Jake's house since the day we moved. I know that if I'd see my old home, I'd feel conflicted. Jake would tug at my heart again, and I don't want to go through that. My heart is with Shawn now. And if I had to face Jake, it would be difficult to hide the secret I'm keeping.

But Thor seems to manage just fine when he's with his father. He feels duty-bound to honor Rachel's request, and he keeps the secret of Molly's paternity in an impenetrable chamber in his mind.

On second thought, I'm glad the Rosenbaums didn't make it tonight. How would I explain their relationship with my daughter if they came face to face with Jake?

Jake has taken Thor to visit his Mennonite parents. My open-minded son is getting to know his second set of grandparents, and he's eager to learn more about their unusual way of life.

All the members of the orchestra are seated. The director, Mr. Carmichael, walks to the front of the stage and takes a bow. He speaks a few words about the pieces the orchestra will be playing, then turns, raises his baton, and the music begins.

I know this performance by high school students is amateurish, but it sounds perfect to me. My son is immersed in what he's doing, like nothing else in the world exists for him at this moment. He looks like a professional, head and shoulders above the others. I close my eyes, allowing the music to carry me into a state of deep relaxation.

Shawn nudges me. "It's time for Thor's solo," he whispers.

I open my eyes and see my son standing at the front of the stage, his violin tucked under his chin, his bow poised and ready to play. The orchestra begins with background music, and then the sweet strains of Thor's instrument soars above them, playing a familiar tune. The words come to me, and in my mind, I sing along.

Child of love, child of light . . .

It's too much for me. I lean forward, burying my face in my hands. I see the skinny girl in her ragged blue jeans seated cross-legged on the floor with her long dark hair falling in her face, awkwardly strumming my son's guitar, singing out in her sweet, melancholy soprano.

Glowing bright through the dark of the night . . .

My tears begin to flow, my body heaves with sobs. I feel Shawn's gentle hand on my back.

May you shine, brightly shine . . .

Molly can't stand to see me sad. She pushes her way onto my lap and wraps her arms around me, laying her head against my shoulder.

Child divine . . .

I hold Molly close, Rachel's divine child. My divine child.

The orchestra plays variations on the theme, with Thor's solo violin weaving in and out of the arrangement. It's beautiful. It's brilliant, a masterpiece by Thor and Rachel.

The audience claps enthusiastically, and Shawn whispers in my ear, "Your son is incredibly talented."

"I know," I say.

The concert is over. Shawn and Molly and I wait while the students leave the stage. Thor comes to join us, his necktie loosened, instrument case in hand. We hug him, congratulate him, praise him profusely. I tell him how much his surprise meant to me, and my tears flow again.

"Did your father come?" I ask. "I haven't seen him."

"He's right there." Thor points across the room to a couple making their way toward us.

I don't recognize Jake at first. He looks portly, his body thickened, like he's put on fifty pounds. He's cut off his long ponytail, and his snow white hair is now cropped close to his head. My quick calculations tell me Jake is over fifty now. His craggy face looks older than that to me.

A heavy-set, middle-aged woman wearing a frumpy pantsuit walks beside him. Her graying curls frame her broad, smiling face. She clings to Jake's arm as if she's afraid he'll slip away from her.

Shawn glances at me. He understands that I'll need a moment with Thor's father. "I want to congratulate Mr. Carmichael on the performance," he says. He strides up onto the stage to chat with his musical colleague, to discuss my son, their shared protégé.

"Hello, Jake," I say as my former lover approaches.

"Hello, Lee," he responds. "It's good to see you." His dark, penetrating eyes scan my body and then my face. I can tell he likes what he sees. His companion tightens her grip on his arm.

I extend my hand to the woman. "I'm River Jorgensen. Thor's mother."

Her face lights up as she shakes my hand. "I'm Brenda." She glances fondly at Jake. "Jake's girlfriend."

I see Jake wince.

"How nice," I say. "Have the two of you been together for awhile?"

"About a year," Brenda says. "We met at an art fair, of all places. Can you imagine that?"

Of course I can imagine that.

"I make quilts," she continues, "and Jake does woodworking. So we make a good pair. We have our art in common." She giggles, and Jake's face looks utterly pained.

"Did you enjoy the concert?" I ask.

Jake nods, while Brenda gushes, "Oh yes, it was wonderful. We're so proud of Thor."

I'm surprised her comment doesn't threaten me. I can allow this woman to bask in the role of stepmother to my brilliant son.

"We are, too," I say, gesturing toward Shawn on the stage. "A lot of people are proud of Thor." I smile up at my son, who is standing at my side.

Molly tugs on my hand. "I'm tired," she whines. Thor reaches down and scoops her up in his arms.

"Who's the little girl?" Jake asks, looking strangely curious.

Thor looks his father straight in the eye. "This is my sister Molly," he says boldly, emphatically.

I think I'm going to hyperventilate. *Oh my God, Thor, are you going to spill the beans right here and now?"*

Jake looks confused. "Your sister?"

"My mother adopted her," Thor explains.

I breathe a sigh of relief.

Molly continues to fuss. "I'm thirsty."

"The band mothers brought refreshments," I tell Thor. "They're set up in the lobby. Will you take Molly to get something to drink?"

Jake's eyes follow Thor as he carries Molly out of the auditorium. "She's dark-skinned," he observes. "Is she Mexican? Native American?"

I remember the same conversation we had about Rachel ten years ago. I keep my voice perfectly calm. "No, she's Caucasian."

"She's a pretty little thing," he says.

He knows. Somewhere inside himself, he knows. But he doesn't want to know, he won't let himself know that he knows. And it's best that way.

"Do you want coffee, honey?" Brenda asks. "I'll go get us some."

"That's fine," Jake says, irritation in his voice.

Brenda scurries away, and Jake and I stand alone, facing each other. "Why are you with this woman?" I blurt out. "You act like you despise her."

He shrugs. "I'm comfortable."

"I'm sorry," I say. "That was rude of me. She's a very nice person."

Jake shrugs again.

"What did you think of Thor's solo?" I ask. "Did you recognize the song?"

He gives me a blank stare. "What do you mean?"

"Don't you remember? The song Rachel made up for Thor. Remember that day we stood outside Thor's room listening to her sing?"

Something flickers in Jake's eyes, but he shakes his head. "Nope, I don't remember that." I know he's lying to me.

I don't know what else to say to Jake. I don't know this man anymore.

"Well," I say. "It's nice to see you again. I guess I'd better round up the kids and get going . . ."

He interrupts me, and suddenly I see emotion on his face, passion in his eyes. "Lee, do you ever think about coming back home?"

His question stuns me, and I take a few seconds to respond. "Are you kidding me, Jake? You're with someone else. And I'm with someone."

"That can change," he says.

For the moment, I indulge him, playing along with his fantasy. "You'd really want Thor and me to move back in? And Molly? What about Molly? Would you want a little child running around the house again?"

"I wouldn't mind," Jake says. "I wouldn't mind at all."

Brenda walks toward us carrying two cups of coffee. "Here you go, sweetie," she says, handing one to Jake.

A moment later, Thor walks in carrying Molly, who is holding a paper cup filled with fruit punch. I laugh at the pink juice stain on her upper lip.

"Want a drink, Mommy?" she asks. "It tastes good."

Shawn comes down off the stage. "Ready to go?" he asks me.

"I'm ready," I say as I take a step toward him.

Then I turn back to Jake. I have one last thing to say to him. "You gave me a wonderful son, Jake. Thank you. He means the world to me."

Jake stares at the floor, awkwardly shifting his weight from one foot to the other. Then he lifts his head and smiles, his affection for me shining in his eyes.

You gave me a wonderful daughter, too, I think. *I wish I could tell you that, but I can't.* So I just say, "Thanks for everything, Jake."

"No problem, Lee," he says.

He doesn't know what I mean. But then, maybe he does.

Shawn encircles my waist with his arm as he escorts my children and me out of the school building and to our car. For the millionth time, I think about how grateful I am to be with him.

My mother adores Molly. "You were predestined to be Molly's mother," she tells me. "Everything that happens in life is significant, every event has a purpose. It was no accident that Jake introduced you to Rachel, who served as the vehicle to bring your daughter into this incarnation."

She's convinced that both of my children are old souls, having accumulated great stores of wisdom from traversing many lifetimes. She insists that dark-skinned Molly bears an uncanny resemblance to my Native American great-grandmother.

"Whatever, Mom," I tell her. "I'm just glad she's mine."

"All is as it should be," my mother says.

OTHER BOOKS BY LOIS JEAN THOMAS

Me and You—We Are Who? (The Sambodh Society, Inc., 2006)

All the Happiness There Is (The Sambodh Society, Inc., 2006)

Johnny and Kris (The Sambodh Society, Inc., 2014)

Daughters of Seferina (CreateSpace, 2014)

Days of Daze: My Journey Through the World of Traumatic Brain Injury (CreateSpace, 2014)

Made in the USA
Charleston, SC
05 March 2015